I0666727

Dream Catcher Murders
A Buckeye Barrister Mystery

by

David Selcer

This book is fiction. All characters, events, and organizations portrayed in this novel are the product of the author's imagination or are used fictitiously. Any resemblance to actual persons—living or dead—is entirely coincidental.

Copyright 2017 by David Selcer

All rights reserved. No parts of this book may be reproduced or transmitted in any form or by any means, electronic or mechanical, including photocopying, recording or by any information storage and retrieval system, without written permission from the author, except for the inclusion of brief quotations in a review.

For information, email **Cozy Cat Press**, cozycatpress@aol.com or visit our website at: www.cozycatpress.com

COZY CAT
P R E S S

ISBN: 978-1-946063-28-1

Printed in the United States of America

Cover design by Paula Ellenberger
www.paulaellenberger.com

1 2 3 4 5 6 7 8 9 10

To Diane and Dennis Duffy, and to Nancy and Dave Henry

Chapter 1

Sarasota, Florida—paradise! A jewel beside the Gulf of Mexico! More money on deposit in the banks here than in Naples and Tampa combined. One could spend $250 on a meal with ease at any of the town's luxury restaurants. Condos in its gleaming high rises cost upward of two million dollars. Its white powdery beaches consistently voted among the best in the world. Hard to believe the place was once a quiet fishing town. No place for a duffer with empty pockets now.

Lingering over my single-malt Laphroig—lingering, because the scotch cost $14 and that made it worth savoring—I was at Jack Dusty's, a "mid-priced" restaurant, qua bar, at the Ritz-Carlton. Here, an order on the rocks comes with one huge perfectly square ice cube in the snifter, expertly cut to fit the glass, and the bar tender knows you're not a connoisseur because you're not drinking your whiskey straight up with a Perrier on the side. Well, damn it, I just didn't want to pay $8 for water with a few sparkles in it, and you don't just ask for tap water in a place like this.

It's about 3:30 p.m. Wednesday, May 15, 2010. So what's someone like me doing here, you ask? Well, that's a short story that got made long, so indulge me, if you would, for a few minutes.

I'm a lawyer and I'd come to Florida on behalf of Mr. Charles Venable of Columbus, Ohio, a client of mine. In fact, he was my biggest client at the moment. I was to meet with Julius Josephski, a resident of the

Ritz-Carlton, and one of the most prominent real estate developers on Florida's West Coast.

Mr. Venable was a silent partner (an investor if you like) with Mr. Josephski in what was putatively to be the biggest housing and condominium project in the area since Lakewood Ranch. The project was known as, "The Long Bar Harbor Development." Unfortunately, it had died a birthing because of the "Great Recession of 2008."

My job now was to salvage from foreclosure what could be salvaged, by fly-specking all the mortgage documentation for errors and omissions in the default and foreclosure language. In other words, I was going to find ways to hold up the banks in the court room from snatching back their security interests. Florida banks had gotten so voracious during the real estate lending bubble of the early 2000s that in their "Don't leave us out" hysteria, they had become very sloppy with documentation.

The same local lawyers who had messed up the banks' foreclosure documents were now making their money at the other end, siphoning fees off from all the foreclosures. They were now making money setting up foreclosure mills for their bank clients to lead all the unwitting borrowers to the slaughter.

It was an old corporate lawyer's trick called "playing both sides of the game"—not to blame these pin-striped shysters for making a buck the good old American way, that is any way you can. My client, Charles Venable, was now very worried about his investment, so he was looking to me to stop his deal from souring any way I could.

Indeed, half the time, clients like mine found salvation because the documents the banks relied upon for foreclosure couldn't even be found. And, the other half of the time, the pursuing banks created huge foreclosure delays because they went under themselves. Their reserves weren't high enough and they either had to spend all their time finding a "white-knight" partner to merge with and be bailed out. Or, they had to stand by and watch the FDIC padlock their doors. Bank presidents were going to jail, right and left.

It was in this atmosphere that I was to find ways for Mr. Venable to keep the property, securing his partnership's loans. I was charged with finding ways of capitalizing on the incompetence of Florida's lawyers and Florida banks in their document preparation.

That's the short part of the story. The rest is going to take a lot longer to tell. To begin with, suffice it to say, it was good I had that scotch before going up to Mr. Josephski's rooms at the top of the Ritz, because the rest of the story is shocking. He was scheduled to come down to the bar to meet me, but it was now 4 p.m., and our meeting had been set for 3 p.m. I called his room, but there was no answer. So I decided to go on up and knock on his door.

The door to his suite was open a crack when I got there. I knocked, but there was no answer. There was a doorbell. I rang it. Still, no answer. Uninvited but curious, I pushed the door open a tad and entered. Across the room, I could see a panorama of Sarasota Bay through the open sliding glass doors leading to the balcony. The curtains were billowing from the sides of the doors and there was a comfortable breeze in the room.

Emanating from the Bose was something by Brahms. I remembered it as the tune to the Northwestern University Alma Mater, where I went before graduating from The Ohio State University Law School.

"Mr. Josephski?" I called. There was no answer, so I chanced crossing from the front hallway into the living area. There, I saw him, slumped over the keys of a baby grand piano with a knife sticking out of his back among many gouges and stab wounds. "Mr. Josephski?" No breath. No pulse. Just blood all over the keyboard—a mess. Except for that, he looked like a man in his sixties sleeping peacefully.

I reached for the phone, but thankfully before touching it, I remembered. I took out my handkerchief, carefully lifted the receiver and using the handkerchief to hold a pencil I found on the desk, dialed.

"Give me house security please!" I was so nervous I thought I might throw up. My voice was quavering. "Mr. Julius Josephski, please come to his suite immediately . . . yes, the 20th floor . . . yes, it is the penthouse, I guess. . . Please hurry. . . I think there's been a murder. Never mind who I am! I'll be here when you get here. You can ask all you want then."

Within three minutes, the door to the suite crashed wide open loudly. "Hello, Hello? Is anyone here? Who's in here?" It was the hotel detective with a guard who had his gun drawn. The detective was wearing white linen pants, a short sleeve print silk tropical shirt and Armani shoes. His sidekick wore a drab khaki Ritz-Carlton uniform topped off with a faux straw billed cap that said security across the front. "Who's in here?" the detective demanded again. He sounded a little scared, and he looked alert for anything.

"Yes, I'm here. No need for the gun," I responded. I was standing by the body at the piano. I motioned downward slowly with my hand as if to say, put the gun down.

The detective came over and felt for a pulse on the cooling corpse. "And who might you be?" he asked abruptly, with the hint of a German accent, as he took out his cell phone.

"My name is Winston Barchrist III, and I'm a lawyer from . . ."

The detective pointed to a Ludwig Mies van der Rohe copy of a Barcelona chair. "Yah, I went to law school too. Just sit down over there Mr. Barker—until I finish talking with the Sheriff's Office. . ."

"It's Barchrist," I said.

"Whatever," said the detective. "Just stay right there until I tell you different." He was obviously upset by the scene into which he'd just walked. "Hello, Natalie," he said into his phone, "Ralph at the Ritz. Tell Greg to send a cruiser over here with one of your detectives. We've got a 30 here. . . No, no, I don't want to give out any names yet. No, it doesn't mean it's somebody important. Listen, honey, be a sweetie and just do your job without passing out any little crumbs for now to the *Herald Gazette* reporter hanging around your office. He can wait for a departmental release after we do our initial investigation. No, not at the Lido installation . . . I'm calling from our downtown installation . . . The concierge will tell them where I am when they get here."

He turned back to me. "So tell me again. Who are you, and what are you doing here?"

"My name is Winston Barchrist III, and I'm a lawyer from Columbus, Ohio, who represents Charles Venable of Columbus, Mr. Josephski's business partner in one of his deals. I was supposed to have a meeting, and perhaps dinner, with Mr. Josephski this evening. When I came up . . ."

"Well, how did you get in here?"

"The door was open, and after calling to Mr. Josephski a number of times without any response, I just stepped inside, and I found . . ."

"Mr. Barker, is it your habit to just let yourself into the rooms of another person if they don't answer the door?" He asked his question very impatiently.

"No, but I . . ."

"Julius Josephski is one of the most prominent developers in Southwest Florida, to say nothing of the fact that he is a permanent resident of the Ritz-Carlton Hotel, and you're saying you just let yourself in?"

"I was expected, and the door was open."

"Are you saying he left the door open for you; that he just told you on the intercom to come up and the door would be open? Or, did you stop first at the front desk so the clerk could call up and announce you?"

"No but . . ."

"Usually, when one of our residents is having a guest, the guest stops at the front desk to inquire and the clerk calls his name upstairs to the resident."

"Well, that's not what happened here."

He turned to the guard who had re-holstered his gun but was still keeping his hand on it. "Hubert, check all this out with the front desk." Then he turned back to me.

"Mr. Barker, do you have any ID?"

"It's Barchrist . . . and here's my driver's license."

"Are you a guest here at the Ritz?"

Hm, I thought to myself. *I probably couldn't even afford the cost of parking my rental car for one night at this opulent palace.* "No, I'm at the Regency Inn & Suites," I responded.

"I'm sorry, sir, but I've never heard of that one. Where might that be?"

I reached for the slip of paper I had in my pocket with the address of my motel on it. Alert to any possible security risk, Hubert immediately reached for his gun again. So I quickly raised my hands. I had read what a virulent "stand-your-ground" state Florida was. A guy named George Zimmerman had killed an African American kid named Trayvon Martin where it wasn't clear who was standing whose ground, and then he had been acquitted by a Florida jury. I wasn't black, but I was foreign to the state of Florida, a Northerner, and I was extremely overweight. Who knew? Maybe that was enough to get me shot in this little city everyone called a paradise. Returning to the question at hand, I stammered.

"It's on the Tamiami Trail . . . 4200 North Tamiami Trail, I believe."

"The North Trail?" Ralph marveled. "A lawyer dealing with Julius Josephski comes here and stays in that part of Sarasota—out on the North Trail?"

"That's correct," I answered. How was I supposed to know that the North Trail was considered a low class part of the city, attractive to students and to other more base elements like whores and the homeless? To me, it looked like the entire city was arrayed with palm trees, exotically clipped hedges, nearby sun, water and yachts, blue skies, white condos and Mercedes, Maseratis and Porsches.

In fact, my motel was just a stone's throw from the Ringling Museum and the famed Ca'd'Zan, also known as the Ringling Mansion. So how bad could this neighborhood be?

Chapter 2

The name of the house detective at the Ritz was Ralph Kreigelman, and Ralph was a guy who wanted to leave no stone unturned. He was a former Coast Guardsman, and, as it turned out, he'd also gotten a legal degree, but from a match-book law school. That, however, didn't stop him from contemptuously referring to me as "counselor."

When the sheriff's cruiser arrived, Ralph saw fit to invoke the legal doctrine of *res ipsa loquitur*—which means, "the thing speaks for itself."—and since I was the only person found at the scene of the crime, he had the sheriff's deputy arrest me. Ducking my head down like in the movies as I entered the back seat of the cruiser, the deputy had me transported to the police station for interrogation with my hands cuffed behind my back.

After all, Mr. Josephski was dead wasn't he? And I was found at the scene of the crime, wasn't I? I was claiming to be a lawyer working with Josephski, but I was staying on the wrong side of town. Wasn't I? What else was needed to infer that I was the killer? *Res Ipsa Loquitur*—right? Never mind that I had reported the crime.

When we reached the sheriff's office things got worse between Ralph and me. "What was your business with Mr. Josephski?" the linen trousered house detective asked, adjusting his silk shirt.

He just couldn't seem to understand why, if Mr. Josephski was a Florida debtor about to be foreclosed upon, with property in a Florida venue, that Mr. Venable would have me—a Columbus, Ohio, lawyer— looking for loopholes to stop the foreclosure. I realized when they started checking me out in Ohio, the true facts of my situation weren't going to comport very well with my story. Back in Columbus, I was a small-time lawyer who made a living doing simple divorces, car wreck cases and defending small time thugs against occasional criminal charges. One of my specialties was DUI or drunken driving cases. I practiced independently from an office which was located over a Dairy Mart on the edge of the German Village area of town, the rough edge. I didn't seem to have the type of credentials entitling me to do legal work involving a Brahmin real estate developer like Josephski who resided in Sarasota.

What Ralph and my other interrogators would never learn was that I once was a top young securities lawyer in a huge Chicago corporate law firm; that I had had escaped to Columbus to hide from a blot on my reputation caused by a meritless disbarment proceeding where I was acquitted entirely. The disbarment proceeding had resulted from trumped up securities fraud charges made against me by my Chicago firm from investing in its client's new stock offering while trying to keep its own skirts clean. The firm had developed a conflict of interest by investing in a client for whom it had undertaken to write a securities prospectus. When caught, the firm attempted to blame me, as the lowly associate who drafted the prospectus for not discovering and disclosing the conflict of interest in the prospectus.

But the acquittal did not restore my reputation. I couldn't get another job in Chicago. I became despondent, and lost my marriage and my two-year-old little girl. My only gain was 125 pounds from the anxiety. So I had returned penniless and without any self-esteem to start over in my home town, Columbus, where I'd gone to law school.

"What was your business with Mr. Josephski?" Ralph growled over and over, unable to understand that I was working for Charles Venable, not Julius Josephski. I tried to avoid the question by getting a little too cute for my own good and invoking the attorney-client privilege even though Josephski and I had no attorney-client relationship.

"I'm sorry, sir," I replied, "but that information is protected by the attorney client privilege. I can't discuss it with you."

"Well, then," Ralph shot back, "maybe you'll find it easier to discuss it after a night in the lock-up."

The incessant interrogation continued. The Sheriff's men weren't bad, but the Ritz-Carlton detective was. He didn't believe anything I said. To him I was just a pedestrian lawyer from Columbus driving a rented Ford Focus and staying at a motel—a dump so to speak—out on Route 41, claiming to be in town rubbing shoulders with an aristocratic resident of "his" hotel, a highly suspect situation according to his highbrow view of the world. It was becoming obvious that in this town everything was based on your status, and I was from the wrong side of the tracks. The town was divided into four classes: patricians, who had all the money; administrators, who were smarmy politicians or bureaucratic tools of the patricians; plebes, i.e.—retired postmen, army colonels, restaurant servers, other service people, realtors and artists; and undocumented slaves from Mexico who provided lawn care, cleaning services and the like.

Lawyers were supposed to fit somewhere between the patricians and the bureaucrats, depending on how much money it looked like they had. But I fit with the plebes because it was clear I didn't have any money.

Whether or not the Sheriff's people accepted the reasons for my being present at the crime scene, I don't know, but I finally got out of their office because they could find nothing with which to charge me. My fingerprints were nowhere in Josephski's suite. I had touched nothing—except the phone with my hanky.

In fact, there were no fingerprints at all but Josephski's and those of a rising starlet—the 38-year-old lawyer's girlfriend whom he was known to have dated for a year—Alexis Weidenfeld. The knife in his back had been wiped clean. My story revealed no motive for the murder, no evidence of intent, and really, not even any previous knowledge of any facts about Mr. Josephski. There were no witnesses, no confessions and no previous threats.

I managed to maintain the attorney client privilege by explaining that I had gone up to the Josephski suite merely to review certain documents that he and my client had signed, but I insisted I would not reveal what the documents were. I greatly resented, however, that the Sheriff's deputy contacted Mr. Venable, revealing to him that Josephski had been murdered, before I could tell him myself. Then they wouldn't let me speak to him, leaving him to mull over the liability he had as a co-signer on the notes and mortgages that I'd come to Sarasota to review.

I called Venable as soon as I could after leaving the Sheriff. We agreed Josephski's estate was probably a hollow husk after the Great Recession of 2008. Now that he was dead there was a question as to whether the banks would be able to reach residences he owned around the country. Certainly, it would be easier and more convenient for them just to pursue Charles Venable if they could.

"I want you to take as long as you need and stay down there until you find out what's going on," Mr. Venable said. "Spare no expense. I'll pay for everything. Did Julius or his attorneys keep me abreast of problems as they arose with the construction of this project? I want to know. Did he inform me of cost overruns? Did he properly monitor construction of the projects? Were his attorneys investors? Did they have conflicts of interest? We put 60 million into this project. Where did the money go? From this day forward, you now have two jobs, Winston. Find deficiencies in the documentation being relied on by the banks to claw these properties back from investors like me. And second, find out what liability Josephski's estate might have to me, that is, if he has any estate left after this all shakes out. The answer to the second question may lie in figuring out who killed him. Any leads on that yet?"

"So far—no. In fact, only two people are currently associated in the minds of the police in any way with his murder because both were found at the place where he lived—me, and someone named Alexis Weidenfeld, who was apparently his girlfriend."

"Well, the girlfriend may be a lead," Venable suggested.

Chapter 3

The first thought that came to my mind after hanging up from Mr. Venable was Trudy. Maybe she could help me.

Trudy Fischel is a computer geek, actually an accomplished computer hacker from New York with an investigator's license, whom I sometimes employ in my cases back in Ohio. In her mid-forties, she had long bleached blond hair and nice legs, although she's beginning to look a lot like the women who advertise on Cheaters.com. She can break into any computer, and with that skill she's been invaluable to me on the paltry handful of big cases I've had since coming to Columbus.

Never mind the ethics of computer hacking. It was rumored that before obtaining her investigator's license, Trudy had started her career by breaking into a Chase Bank cash machine in Brooklyn, then running to Ohio with the proceeds. I don't know if she ever got caught. I just knew she could be very useful. Maybe she could hook me up with somebody similar here in Sarasota. I was certainly going to need the help. So I called her.

"Yes, as a matter of fact, I've got just the person for you," she said, "but you're not going to be able to contact her by phone. You'll have to go see her, and when you do, Winston, be prepared for something I don't think you've done before—ever. Her name is Stella Starbard, but she goes by 'Kit-Kat,' and she knows everyone in Sarasota. If she doesn't actually know someone, she'll know everything you need to know about them. In fact, I may even be able to give you an address, her business address that is. Yes, here it is. I still have it, 5642 W. Tamiami Trail." When she gave me the address, I realized it was very near where I was staying.

Kit-Kat's place of business was a doublewide rebuilt trailer on Route 41 north of town in Manatee County. It was squeezed between Route 41 (the "Trail") and Runway 4 of the Sarasota-Bradenton International Airport (SRQ). Although not one of the more vaunted tax-paying businesses that the Airport administrator had bragged that he had attracted to the airport's out lots and apron parcels, it was, nonetheless, one of the more profitable. This business paid no taxes.

A neon sign hung in the window proclaiming "Always Open." An American Airlines MD-80 strained into the sky from behind the trailer, its engines roaring, as I approached. Across busy Route 41 a McDonald's was serving its customers from a drive-thru window. This stretch of Route 41 was seven lanes wide, including its center turning lane, and it was in the no-man's land between Sarasota and the town of Bradenton.

When I knocked, a very thin Romanesque-looking lady who reminded me a little of a sexy Olive Oyl, Popeye's wife, came to the door. She wore green hospital scrubs and heavy rimmed glasses. Incense burned inside the doorway. "Massage with a Happy Ending—Always," proclaimed a sign on the wall over the reception desk behind her.

"Are you Kit-Kat?"

"Yes, what can I do for you?"

"Trudy Fischel from Ohio told me I should come out here and see you. Do you remember Trudy?"

"Oh yes, I remember her, although it's been a number of years now. How could I forget? We met in New York. How is she?"

"Oh, she's really well. How did you meet?"

"We were both staying at the same place."

"Really? Where?"

"Rikers Island—so what can I do for you? We have Swedish, deep tissue, aromatherapy, hot stone, shiatsu, Thai, reflexology, perhaps a sports massage?" Then she looked at me more closely. "No, on second thought, perhaps not a sports massage."

She was staring at the huge purple-veined flabby white legs poking out of my Bermudas, like the Michelin Man on a Florida vacation, and at my over-stuffed sandals.

"Well, a massage is not really what I had in mind."

"No matter," she replied. "We can do anything you like. I can have your case handled by a Swede, a German, a Thai, a Chinese, someone French maybe, or perhaps you'd prefer just an old fashioned healthy American cheerleader type. We can even perform a form of acupuncture called dry-needling if you wish." She looked me up and down again. "If we can find big enough needles to fit your size."

"My goodness—you have all those people back there in the rooms in this little place?"

"No, no, we have girls on call." Then she laughed. "Oh for heaven's sake, that doesn't sound right, does it? What I mean is I can have any one you like here within ten minutes to take care of you, just by using my little cell phone here."

"Well, I don't know. Perhaps I've made a mistake. This isn't exactly what I had in mind when I talked to Trudy about you. Actually, I was looking for somebody adept with computers."

"Oh, I see, well that would be me too. I have my own blog, and I get about 25,000 hits a week. Perhaps she didn't tell you, but at night I become a different person. Oh my gosh! That doesn't sound right either, does it? Well, anyway, at night I go around trying out various restaurants in the area, 'secretly shopping them,' if you will, and then I discuss them in my blog from the standpoint of cuisine, service, atmosphere, cleanliness, price, etc. It's a very popular blog, and I make beaucoup money from all the advertisers on it.

"Is that why you're here? Do you want me to review your restaurant? I warn you. I can do you a lot of good, or a lot of bad. I make my money off the advertising from blogging, not fees from restaurateurs looking for good write-ups. Most people don't approach me on this because they don't know how to find me. It keeps me from getting sued. You know . . . but obviously, somehow Trudy knew. In fact, most people don't even know I'm a woman. I write the blog under the name 'Damon Runyon-Century 21,' but my real name's neither Damon Runyon nor Kit-Kat."

"I know. It's Stella Starbard."

"My gosh, Trudy should know better than to give out my real name."

"Trudy said you might be able to help me because you know everybody in Sarasota, or about everyone of any means, but it doesn't sound from all this like you're the person who can help me."

"Well, why don't you try me? Tell me what you want, or who you want to know about, and let's see if I can be of any service."

"I'm looking for somebody named Alexis Weidenfeld."

"Lexi? I know her personally. What do you need from Lexi Weidenfeld?"

"What can you tell me about her?"

"Well, Lexi, or Alexis as you call her, is quite a woman. She's one of the classiest up and coming lawyers in Sarasota—serves on all sorts of boards, legal, charitable and otherwise. She established her own law office where she does real property closings, all sorts of real estate law and title work. She even has her own title insurance company now, I think, and she's always out there speaking at various forums. She's received lots of awards from her alma mater and she's among the top people to look out for in the Tampa Bay area according to the *Tampa Tribune*'s "Who's Who" section. Very well known. And, to boot, at 38-years-old, she's richer than all heck. Her family has lots of money, but hers comes mostly from her own endeavors, real estate investments, of course. She's also very high in Sarasota social circles, what with her dating the big developer, Julius Josephski."

"Did you know Mr. Josephski just died?"

"No, no—my gosh. I knew Julie pretty well, mostly through Lexi. What happened?"

"He was murdered."

"No! Who would do such a thing?"

"Well, right now, the police have only two persons of interest in mind: Alexis Weidenfeld and me. Alexis, because her fingerprints were all over Mr. Josephski's living quarters, and me, because I was there when the body was discovered. I want to find out everything I can about Miss Weidenfeld, and about Josephski as well for that matter, so I can deflect the suspicions of the police away from me.

"And toward Lexi? I can assure you, if her fingerprints are in his apartment it's because she was often his guest there."

"By the way, my name is Winston Barchrist III. I'm a lawyer, and I've come here to Sarasota on some business that my client in Ohio had with Mr. Josephski, only to walk into his apartment and find him dead. I can't think of anything more inconvenient that could have happened. I, really we, needed his help on a business deal, and still do, but now he's dead and I can't leave because the police told me not to leave town until they say it's okay."

"Look, Mr. Barker . . .

"Barchrist."

"Barchrist. That sounds exactly like the kind of situation I don't want to get in the middle of. Lexi is not just somebody I know. I consider her a good acquaintance of mine. In fact, I know a side of her that most people don't. We're both members of Sun Ghost Psychic Trackers together.

"What's that?"

"It's a paranormal club that tracks ghosts and spirits along the entire west coast of Florida in the smaller somewhat deserted towns most people have forgotten about."

"You're kidding! I thought you said this lady was a leader in the legal field . . . and now you're telling me she's a ghost buster—someone who attends séances?"

"Mr. Barchrist, you don't help your cause with me much by making comments like that . . . I think we should end our meeting." She turned away from the door and began closing it, but I stuck my foot on the threshold.

"Please Kit-Kat," I said, "I'm sorry for the comment about séances. I need your help, and I don't think I've had the chance to make myself clear. I don't just want it *gratis.* I want to pay you for it, to employ you for a period of time. Please, check me out. Call up Trudy Fischel. Ask her anything you want about me."

"Now you're helping your cause with me, Mr. Barchrist. Maybe I'll just do that. Why don't you come by next Friday. Maybe we'll have something to talk about then. Maybe we won't."

Chapter 4

Back at the Regency Inn & Suites, with nothing to do for the rest of the day, I Googled Alexis Weidenfeld and looked for her under "images." Wow, this lady was really something, even "hot" as some would say—a brunette with semi-long straight hair, cut somewhat scraggily at the ends, and straight bangs over her eyebrows, hanging halfway into her green olive-shaped eyes. She had satin white skin and dimples at the corners of her red mouth, with an impish smile making her look part vampire and part angel—hardly a match for the dead developer I had found slumped over the piano at the Ritz. Julius Josephski was a little partially bald stringy man somewhere in his sixties, whose angular facial features and heavy black glasses frames made him look like a dead weasel, not like bait for an angel-vamp.

Lunch time rolled around, and never one to miss it, I went downstairs and inquired of the guy at the front desk where to eat, since my hotel had no restaurant. He suggested a place called Moore's Stone Crab at the northern end of Longboat Key. When I went back to my room to pick up my car keys there was a very strange message call waiting on the room phone.

"Winston Barchrist? This is Johnson Horseman with The Florida Wildlife Federation in Sarasota. Please call me back for a meeting and a time to meet with me, this week, out at Linger Lodge, east of Bradenton. I'm at 739-5170."

Who was Johnson Horseman? Was it a wrong number? No. He'd addressed me by my name in the message, so somehow he knew me. I Googled him. The first thing that popped up was a Wikipedia article:

"Johnson Horseman a/k/a Horse VI, was born in 1943 in Micanpy, Florida. He is a descendant of John Horse, a mixed blood Seminole (half Black) Indian who led certain Seminole Indian settlements until the early eighteen-hundreds, when they were removed to the north from their lands. It is said that the confrontations over the removal of the Indians were known as the Seminole Wars of the eighteen-hundreds.

"Horseman built himself a substantial career as a wild-life advocate, fighting various Florida developers. In 1990, Mr. Horseman established the Wildlife Federation of Sarasota, which has since grown into a multi-million-dollar tax free entity for the preservation of wildlife throughout the state of Florida. Mr. Horseman, the current CEO Emeritus of the Florida Wildlife Association, lives today in Arcadia, Florida, and maintains his offices in his home."

Well, whoever, or whatever Johnson Horseman was, my stomach told me with a growl that he was going to have to wait because I was getting really hungry. I would Google this Linger Lodge he mentioned later.

Moore's Stone Crab Restaurant was much further away than I had intended to go. Apparently, the restaurant had been in the same place for more than 70 years, located on a small inlet off the Intercoastal with a really fine view down the channel to Sarasota Bay. Boaters could dock outside the restaurant and walk up the landing for a good meal of stone crabs brought in daily, or fresh fish, served either on the porch or inside. Everything from 19-foot Grady Whites to 40-foot yachts docked at Moore's for lunch.

The dining room had just been remodeled and the menu revamped to claw back some of the customers lost to the much newer place next door that featured peacocks walking around in the open and scallops wrapped in bacon.

Being alone, I grabbed a seat at the bar. "You're not from around here. I can tell," said a beefy man smiling broadly. He was sitting next to me at the bar and he looked like a friendly hedgehog with a crew cut.

"How can you tell?" I asked.

"The hat," he answered. I was wearing my special Ohio State University "National Champions" cap commemorating the Ohio State Buckeyes defeat of the Oregon Ducks to win the national college football championship in 2014. "It's ironic," the hedgehog continued, "in 2012 we, the Florida Gators, that is, defeated Ohio State for the national championship with Urban Meyer as our coach up there at Florida State in Gainesville. He retires from FSU and two years later, he goes to Columbus and wins the damn thing again coaching Ohio State. Either he's a great coach, or he's running a big money laundering racket." He leaned over. "Jackson Rainspring," he said, offering me his hand. "Most people just call me Jack."

"Or he could be what they call a double dipper," I opined. A much smaller, very bald man fidgeting in his seat to the right of the hedgehog stirred. "Oh, and this is my partner, Irving Caputo. We live together," said the hedge-hog. The small bald man had an intelligent but concerned look on his face. He smiled with tight lips in a very controlled fashion and offered me his hand somewhat limply. "Nice to meet you," he said. "So what brings you here?"

"I have some business involving a place called Long Bar Harbor," I replied.

"Ah," said Irving, with a strange knowing look, "good ole Long Bar Harbor."

"You know of it?"

"Oh yes," he answered, "every realtor in town knows Long Bar Harbor. Before I became a realtor, I was on the staff of the Manatee County Engineering and Development Division, and I got to know Long Bar Harbor very well. A lot of developers have been after it for years, but until recently, none of them had been willing to pay for the access roads that real estate needs. They've all wanted Manatee County to foot the bill."

"Well, right now I don't know a thing about it. I don't even know where it is."

"Ha," laughed the hedgehog. "Well you're practically sitting on it. He pointed out the window and across the water. "You see that land over there? Well, that's an island called Jewfish Key. Just beyond it is the channel to the little fishing village of Cortez on one side and the southern part of Anna Maria Island known as Bridge Street and Holmes Beach on the other side. On the other side of that channel is the mainland where Long Bar Harbor juts out. Right now, it consists of 700 acres of strawberries cultivated by the Florida Fruit Farm Company along the last undeveloped unprotected shoreline area in Manatee County. But the developers want to turn it into hundreds of housing units, a deep water marina and a 300-room hotel, with an attached commercial development, retail and conference center."

"To do that, they plan to tear out 225 feet of mangroves, dredge a boat basin and shear 15,000 feet of the mangroves down to a uniform hedge six feet high so the bay can be seen from the housing development," Irv added. "All that's a no, no here," he continued. "It's really controversial. It'll kill off all the wildlife in the area. The birds will have no place to nest or hide from predators. The fishing will go dry. You can imagine how vituperative the environmentalists are in their opposition to this, to say nothing of the small vacation operators over in Holmes Beach and around Cortez Village. Their livelihoods are at stake. Long Bar Harbor's draw to wildlife is their bread and butter." The Florida Wildlife Association went ballistic over the project. "And who are the developers?" I asked. "I was under the impression there was only one developer, Julius Josephski." I felt it best not to reveal at that point that I knew Josephski was dead.

"Oh no," said Irv. "There are actually three—three of the biggest, richest boys in town—Julius Josephski, the hotel builder; Jesus Agronez, a home builder, and a guy named Edwin DeVertollo, the well-known shopping mall builder, who has a corporation called Cravenstall Ltd. Word is that one of the reasons the development has stalled is these guys are all at each other's throats. Josephski hates DeVertollo. DeVertollo hates Josephski, and Agronez is just sitting back hoping they'll kill each other—financially, that is, so he can come in and take over the whole thing."

As I listened, all of this was new to me—all except the name, "Florida Wildlife Association." I'd heard of it before, in the phone message Johnson Horseman had left me. Other than the legal documentation involved in the Venable/Josephski deal, however, I really didn't know a thing about Long Bar Harbor. Perhaps I'd stumbled my way across one of the things that had stalled the project. *Hmm, rich developers and screaming environmentalists—not very conducive to progress in a business deal,* I thought, *and of course, Josephski must have known all about this, but how much of it had he revealed to my client?* Oh yes, and what about those access roads the county had not been willing to build?

"Well, did the county ever put in those access roads that were needed to make the project go?" I asked Irv, whom I was now slowly beginning to consider as a possible expert witness concerning engineering matters if Mr. Venable ever had to sue.

"No, not the county," Irv replied. "The developers wound up footing the bill for the roads themselves. It's too bad, because after they were put in, the whole project stalled due to the poor economy. Word is there are mucho foreclosures brewing now."

Hmm. Maybe that's where Mr. Venable's 60 million went, I thought to myself. It seemed like I was really getting a good start on one of the projects he'd given me, just by talking to these two guys. Of course, everything would have to be checked out. The waitress came by behind me and interrupted.

"What'll it be, honey?"

"Stone crabs, of course," I answered.

"Large or small plate?" she asked.

"Large, of course, and with all large-sized claws."

"That'll cost you over $75.00 bucks," Jack objected. "And you won't be able to finish them." Obviously, he had neither examined my girth. Nor did he know how much a man my size could eat at one sitting.

"Large," I insisted.

"Hot or cold?" she asked, her eyes lighting up at the thought of the size of her tip.

"Cold," Jack advised.

"Cold it is then," I said. "And bring me a bowl of chowder and some French fries too."

"Oh, ma'god," Jack said looking at Irv.

Irv shot him a cold glance. "Jack, stop it," he commanded. "You know you're known to be a pretty good eater too." Then, disgusted with Jack, he turned to me and asked, "So how long you in town for?"

"That's a good question. It looks like I'm going to be here for quite a while. I don't know, maybe three weeks, a month, maybe longer. It looks like I'm going to need a better place to stay though. Right now I'm at the Regency Inn on 41 at $125 a night, which is kind of expensive, and I'm told I'm not on the right side of town, or in the right place. What I really need is some place that'll rent me an efficiency by the month."

"I've got just the place for you," Irv volunteered, handing me his card. It had a palm tree logo on it and it said "Rebekah Bay Realty." "Call me tomorrow and I'll show you."

"Well, I don't have any snazzy cards like that," Jack mocked, "but what are you driving—a rental car? I'll bet I can do better for you."

"A Ford Focus. It's pretty tough for a man my size to get in and out of."

"Oh yeah, we can top that easily. How'd you like a Lincoln Continental or a Chrysler 300 at 60% of the price?"

It turns out that Jack, was literally a "Jack of all trades," making a living by buying and selling used cars, fixing people's roofs, watching their homes for them when they were away, moving furniture, walking dogs, mowing lawns and helping out with redecorating projects. He had also moved more than a few older disabled people from their homes into assisted living facilities and the like. And, he was president of the neighborhood association where he and Irv lived. Time would later show that he could be trusted with just about anything, including another person's security and safety when necessary.

"Well, write down your number on the back of this card. I'll certainly call both of you tomorrow. Seems like I've been really lucky to meet you." *And, neither of the two of you look like you'd ever think of ripping anybody off,* I thought to myself.

Chapter 5

After talking with Irv and Jack, I decided it was a "must" that I accept Johnson Horseman's invitation to meet. After all, his organization seemed to have played a large role in stalling the progress of the Long Bar Harbor development. But I needed to know as much about the man as possible before sitting down with him. That meant inquiring about him with Kit-Kat, even though I knew she would probably become the "town crier" about my inquiries, especially if the police asked her anything.

"Oh yes," Kit-Kat reported, "I know John Horseman, although not many people in this town really know him that well. He's a strange man, not too well known by anyone here, but I know him pretty well. Can you guess why?"

Kit-Kat and I were sitting at place called Crager's, on the north Tamiami Trail, well recommended for its breakfasts. There was a line of customers out the front door waiting to be seated. "What do you mean strange? He's a well-known wildlife enthusiast, isn't he?" I replied.

"Well, yes—that's in his public life. But if you look at the police blotter over a period of time you'll find a smattering of misdemeanor arrests, and even a felony or two attached to his name. Reason I know is he's one of my clients, and the girls have come in after being with him, reporting that he's crazy, violent and abusive to them. He's even required some of them to go with him on these sort of 'missions' where he pins signs on trees with Indian daggers warning people against destroying wildlife or vegetation, then shoots into the sky with his rifle until they come out to read the postings.

Thing is, you won't find any convictions on the record because he's a bona fide member of one of the Seminole tribes around here, and they always take jurisdiction over any criminal matters involving him. It's kind of like diplomatic immunity. He lives on a ranch where he pretty much keeps to himself, out close to Arcadia."

"Well, do you think he's dangerous, Kit-Kat?"

"I don't know."

Linger Lodge turned out to be a little known historical landmark. It was located along the picturesque Braden River, that flows from near the untouched Myakka River State Park into the Manatee River above Bradenton. The lodge and grounds consisted of little more than an old clapboard restaurant with a deck over an alligator infested stream surrounded by verdant trees and a trailer park. It's owned and operated by a Florida state representative, known for his real estate speculation, who goes to work every morning at the Legislature in Tallahassee.

Linger Lodge's restaurant specialties included frogs legs, alligator and catfish. The walls of the lodge and its tables were covered with some of the finest forms of taxidermy known to man, representative of every species of snake that has crawled across the South Florida peninsula in the last 100 years.

Of particular interest were the county sheriffs' insignia shoulder patches going back at least 50 years that are kept in glass cases from all the counties in the state. One wall was covered with a fish tank full of piranhas, and another with license plates from the 50 states. The lighting in the restaurant was dim, emanating from naked bulbs hanging from wires.

Johnson Horseman looked very much at home sitting across from me on the Linger Lodge deck. His graying, dried up hair stretched over his scalp, ending in a foot-long pony tail. He wore a colorful short-sleeve Tommy Bahama Florida shirt, open from the neck down, over a black T-shirt, carefully tucked into his Orvis safari pants. His naked forearms bristled with tattoos of Indian insignia and they seemed far too robust for an 85- year-old man.

"Om glad ya could meet me heeyah today," he announced in a heavy unexpected southern accent that startled me. "I cain't always get meetin's so fast with people that know who Ah am. Ah assume that by now y'all do know who ah am?"

"I think I know who you are, Mr. Horseman, but maybe not completely. Could you fill the blanks in for me?"

"Well," he replied, "let us juss say Om the spirit around these heeyah parts that keeps the sawgrass attached to the sands, the mangroves in the water and the fish a swimmin' in the swamps. I keep the birds flyin' in the air, the coral on the reefs and the manatees matin' in the coves. This heeyah land, well it's eternal, and Ah aim to keep it that way."

"That makes you sound like a god, Mr. Horseman, not like a man."

"Well, it is sacred what Ah been doin' all my life— fulfillin' a sacred trust left to mah people to keep the land around heeyah from becomin' a sewer operated by white mankind and his developers. So ya see, I ain't no god, but I also ain't the kind of man y'all is used to."

"Yes, I know, Mr. Horseman. I know you established the predecessor to the Florida Wildlife Association, that your ancestors were Seminoles, and, that you're an eminent conservationist. What I didn't understand was how ardent you were about it. Now I know."

"Oh O'm odent, as you say—as odent as they come."

"But tell me, Mr. Horseman. Do you still live in Micanopy where your people are from?"

"Naw, that's just a tale people tell. Micanopy was mah great, great—five times great-grand pappy's name. He was an Indian chief. A'we family lived fah generations in the area. The White man renamed it Micanopy, after my grand pappy. A course the White man didn't get theyah until way afta mah grand pappy died. Ah left theyah when I was a boy."

A long silence persisted before what came next. I looked down the river at two Sand Hill cranes wading near the bank with the sun reflecting off their deep red head caps. Horseman busied himself with his food— fried alligator chunks. Suddenly, he looked up, grasping my arm gently.

"Well, sa," he said, "all this prattle's been nice, but now Ah want to get to the crux of wha Ah asked to talk with you."

"Yes, please tell me why."

"Mistuh Barchrist, do yah know what a dream catcha is?"

A blank stare on my face must have betrayed my puzzlement, because he just continued on without a response from me. "A dream catcha's a ring, made from a willow twig with a net of string owah hemp stretchin' across its inteeria. Beaded feathas and colaful bits of stone hang from the bottom of the ring. It's a special talisman used by the Miccosukee Indians to manipulate the spirit world around them. The Miccosukee was part of the Seminole nation, ya see. In auwah lore, dreams travel on the night air. Some are good dreams and some are nightmares. The dream catcha catches the nightmares in its netting and causes them to ooze down the beaded feathas at the bottom so slowly that they get caught by the rising sun and burn up. That way they can do no harm to the people sleeping, owah to the environment around them. The good dreams flow right on through the netting in the hoop to enrich the atmosphere and invigorate those who sleep."

All of this is a charming superstition, I thought to myself, *but why's he relating it to me?* He must have sensed my confusion because he went on to explain. "Ya see, Ah been a human dream catcha fowah years when it comes to protectin' Long Bar Harbor—keepin the hah-rises away, blocking the breakup of the land into condos, and the buildin' of shoppin' malls and unnatural harbors. Ah've made it so all the fish can continue to spawn around Long Bar Harbor, the dolphins in the bay can continue to eat, the mangroves can stay in the water and the manatee can continue to mate. They's somethin' beautiful about Florida's natural foliage that all the developahs seem to want to spoil for the sake of the almighty dollah. Ah try to make sure theyeh' nightmares burn up befowah they kin ruin auwah dreams."

So that's what this is all about—Long Bar Harbor— I thought. *And, why with all the symbolism? What was he really saying? Maybe Kit-Kat was right. There was something a little scary about this man.* So, I decided to try to bring the discussion out of the realm of Indian lore and more into the realm of concrete fact.

"Well, your group, and a lot of other conservationists have done a marvelous job of saving Long Bar Harbor," I offered.

"Have we?" he asked, looking at me with what seemed like an intense glare.

"Well, it seems to me the fight is pretty much over now. Isn't it?"

"Is it?" he said looking almost straight through me now. "True, the developahs, and all the government suppautas for change out theyeh have stopped theyeh campaigns to change that little part of the world—Hell, Julius Josephski's even dead now and all, but is the campaign to change Long Bar Harbor really ovah?"

I was starting to feel very uncomfortable in this man's presence.

"Well, with the biggest developer now dead, I think that's pretty good insurance it will keep the banks and future development away now for a long time," I offered.

"Maybe so—maybe not," Horseman rejoined. "I guess that's wha theyah's still dream catchas hangin' from so many of the branches out on the Long Bar," he said.

I was also beginning to get annoyed by all the ominous symbolism and superstition Horseman seemed to be relying on to convey his point to me. And besides, I still didn't know what his point was. "Well, all the nightmares are pretty much over aren't they," I suggested. "Who do you think put the dream catchers up on Long Bar Harbor anyway?" I asked.

"I know who did," he retorted.

"Who?"

"I did," he answered. Then he gave me a threatening look, got up and left.

"Thanks foa the lunch," he said over his shoulder.

I hadn't offered to pay for lunch, but apparently the bill was being left to me. Why had this man even asked to have lunch with me?

Did he know why I had come to Sarasota? Did he know I represented Charles Venable who had sent me here to try to save Julius Josephski's real estate interests in Long Bar Harbor from the banks? He hadn't even mentioned Charles Venable. Did Horseman know Venable existed? If so, how? Now that Josephski was dead, did he expect Venable would somehow try to carry on Josephski's interest in Long Bar Harbor? It was all a mystery.

Chapter 6

The next day, I decided to call Jack Rainspring and Irv Caputo back, but before I got around to dialing either man, my cell rang. It was Rosanne Harmon who, right off the bat, began asking me questions in her cheerful voice.

"Hi, honey, how's it going?"

Rosanne is my accountant. I guess you could also call us "an item." We sometimes work on cases together, too. She has an eleven-year-old daughter, Gayna, who calls me "Pizza Man," probably because I'm so heavy and round and eat a lot of pizza. I'm not Jewish, but I met Rosanne at Rabbi Billy Goldman's Sunday study class. I went to his class one Sunday when he was doing an outreach program; took one look at Rosanne and kept going back every week. So now Rosanne's my girlfriend, and I guess you could say Billy's become my rabbi. Everybody should have one.

"Great, everything's going great, honey," I told her. "Yesterday I had myself a mess of stone crab at this wonderful restaurant on the water, and the day before that I had myself a drink at the premier hotel in Sarasota. The sun shines every day and it's like paradise here."

"Okay, Winston, what's wrong? I can tell by your voice that something's wrong—going on about stone crabs and drinks, when you're down there on the biggest legal project you've ever had. What is it? What's wrong?"

"Which do you want first, the good news or the bad?"

"The bad."

"Well, Mr. Josephski's dead—murdered—and I'm a suspect, and the police told me I can't leave Sarasota until they say I can. . ."

"Oh, my god, Winston, what happened? What are you going to do?"

"But here's the good news. Mr. Venable doubled the size of my project down here when he heard all this, which means double the fees, and he's paying all the expenses while I'm here. I'm going to lease a Lincoln Towne Car, and . . ."

"Hold it, Winston. That's all bad news. I know you're excited your fees will be doubled, but you're not going to get home until who knows when. That's all bad news, not good news. Spring vacation's almost ready to start, and Gayna is counting on you to rent that cabin with us at Salt Fork State Park for a week. Now she'll be disappointed, and how can I even explain it to her without lying? 'Winston can't come because the police require his presence in Sarasota'? That's not really the case is it? Because you could always ask them to let you leave in order to honor your commitments in Ohio. I know you didn't murder Mr. Josephski. You know you didn't do it either. And they know it too. They have to either charge you or let you go. You know criminal law. It's really the extra money you're going to make, isn't it? You want to stay in order to make all that extra money."

I loved Rosanne, but sometimes she could be a bitch. Once I had promised her a vacation but it wound up that I had to go to Belgium on a case. So I ended up taking her with me, as a sort of vacation. Except for the fact that she complained a lot about it, it was okay.

"Well, you didn't let me finish, Rosanne. I wanted to invite you and Gayna down here to be with me during Spring Vacation. Do you think she'd like that? I can use the extra money I'm making to pay for it."

Easy come, easy go, I thought to myself. "Well, what do you think? Siesta Beach, the Ringling Estate, St. Armand's Circle, maybe a dinner theater—how hard would that be for the two of you to take?"

"Winston, did you just think all that up now, or were you really planning to ask us to come down there?"

"Oh, no, I've been planning it ever since Mr. Venable doubled my fee." *One of the perquisites that comes along with having a girlfriend is the right to tell white lies,* I thought .

"Well, I'll talk to Gayna about it and call you back." Her voice was decidedly more excited when she hung up than when she said hello. Damn! I jotted down 'two-bedroom apartment—not efficiency" as soon as I hung up. Then I added the words "price—and not near North Trail." It's not that I didn't want them to come. It's just that I felt I could get further along in my investigation more quickly if I didn't have to go to the beach every day. But as I hung up, I was happy. At least I had solved the potential problem with Rosanne and Gayna that was mounting because of my prolonged absence from Columbus.

I dialed the number on Irv's Caputo's card. I knew Rosanne would come and bring Gayna, and I wanted to tell Irv what I needed now in the way of accommodations. But before anyone from his real estate office could answer, there was a knock on my door. The rooms at the Regency Motel and Suites were connected by an outside walkway. I was on the second floor, and anybody could approach my room from the outside just by walking up the stairs. When I opened the door, at first all I could see was the greening water in the pool below, next to the parking lot. Then a head with two round brown eyes in it, wearing a white cloth hat with a very wind-blown broad visor surrounding it, poked around the corner.

"Helloooo," Kit-Kat smiled. She looked really different, wearing the hat, a set of white knee length jumpers, deck shoes and a blue and white striped jersey. At first, I didn't recognize her. Outside the wind was gusting, and it blew her hat off. Then I knew who she was.

"Kit-Kat," I said, "come in."

"Well, I don't know if that would really be appropriate in a place like this," she said.

"How did you find me?"

"You told me where you were staying," she replied.

"No, I didn't. I distinctly remember that I didn't."

"Well, then let's just say that a little birdie told me."

"I'm afraid that just won't do as an answer. Right now, I'm highly sensitive to everything. You know, being a murder suspect and all, and I feel like things—everything—is just getting away from me—out of my hands, so to speak." As I was talking to Kit-Kat I was still thinking about how Rosanne had manipulated me into inviting her and Gayna down to be with me. "So I'd really like to know how you found me. Right now, I feel very out of control of things."

"Ah, control is but an illusion, my dear," Kit-Kat replied. "You don't have any belief in psychic things at all, do you? There's nothing paranormal to you, is there?"

"Oh come now, Kit-Kat. You're not saying you found me by putting your hands around some crystal ball or something, and some spirit came and told you where to find me."

"My dear, all I can say is that when I opened the door to my place of business on the Tamiami Trail and first laid eyes on you, there was a shining orb of light just over your left shoulder. When I remembered that, I considered your proposition about hiring me, that is, and I decided that there are certain higher powers affecting you right now. I want to work for you, but I can't—not unless you're able to open your mind and accept that paranormal things might exist And of course, assuming the compensation will be acceptable to me. So I've come here to invite you to go on the next outing of the Sun Ghost Psychic Trackers this weekend in Micanopy to see if we can't pry your mind open a little."

"Oh, no Kit-Kat—I'm afraid I won't be able to do that. I've got too many other pressing concerns." My mind skipped to a vision of me picking Rosanne and Gayna up at the airport.

"Micanopy spelled 'M I C A N O PY,' but pronounced 'Mick-an-oh-pee,' with the accent on the "o," is one of Florida's great little ghost towns—right up there with Arcadia, Everglades City, Cedar Key and Punta Rassa. You'll love it. The town is so old, there's not even a sewer system. Everything runs on septic tanks, so if you use the bathroom at a restaurant, they ask you to leave a dollar to help keep up their septic system."

"Well, all that's very nice, Kit-Kat, but I'm afraid I can't go."

"Oh, and did I tell you, Lexi Weidenfeld is signed up for this trip? Does that by any chance change your mind?"

"Completely. What do I wear on a trip like this, and where do we meet?"

"Jeans, not Bermudas, and I'll let you know where we're going to meet as a group as soon as I know. But

Winston, you've got to take this seriously. You can have fun, but no wisecracks about all the paranormal paraphernalia, or about our procedures. You'll need to do exactly what you're told to do."

"Geez, she's not taking very long to mourn her lost boyfriend, is she?"

"Who?"

"Alexis Weidenfeld—taking a trip like this after Josephski's death indicates she's not exactly grief stricken."

"Oh, yeah—well, Lexi told me they'd just broken up about a week before—not exactly a friendly parting either. She left him."

"Still . . ."

"Winston, I see it's going to take you a while to get used to Sarasota. This is a town of 'cougars,' and Lexi Weidenfeld is a cougar. A cougar feasts on her prey for as long as the flavor holds out, and then she goes on to her next kill. You'll get used to it."

"Are you a cougar, Kit-Kat?"

"Me? Ha! I'm what they call a 'local.' Besides, I live in Bradenton, not Sarasota. Some folks call it Bradentucky. "

"Well, what's the difference? The two towns are right next to each other. It's practically all one city."

"Yeah, but Bradenton's 'blue collar,' a real hillbilly town and Sarasota is a 'white shoe' town. Cougars are white shoe women who wear diamond tennis bracelets and live on the Keys. Or, they're single professionals who've dumped not only their husbands, but sometimes their kids too. They spend their time prowling high dollar charity events in Sarasota. As realtors, they show multi-million dollar condos to single guys from up north, and then eat out with them at restaurants like Euphoria Hay on Longboat Key or going to Polo at

Lakewood Ranch. They go through men like you and I go through the Sunday paper.

"Locals live on the mainland. They spend their time working as secretaries, servers and small business sales people and they usually work two jobs. They go home at night to be single parents raising their kids, and on weekends, they spend their time shopping at Publix and Target.

"So listen, Winston, I gotta go now, but I'll be in touch about our little outing to Micanopy. Oh, and listen, in addition to wearing jeans, bring a flashlight, a hat and a whistle."

"Why the whistle?"

"You'll see."

Then she turned around, opened the door and disappeared like a mirage. I looked down into the parking lot for her. She was driving one of those Smart Cars that looks like a four-wheel motor scooter, or a tennis shoe on wheels. Hers was black and yellow like a bumble bee. It's hard to believe those things are built by Mercedes-Benz.

Chapter 7

It was a day later before I finally got around to calling Irv Caputo to take him up on his offer to find me new lodgings. There was no answer after five calls but finally Jackson Rainspring said, "hello." I asked him if Irv was there or at work, and which was the better place to call for him. What Jack said next, was shocking. Irv had been arrested and was in the Manatee County lockup. Jack was beside himself.

The police had just walked into Irv's office at Rebekah Bay Realtors and placed him under arrest. The whole thing must have been very embarrassing for him.

"What's he charged with?" I asked.

"Theft in office. I'd like to lay my hands on the bastard who pressed charges against him. You said you were a lawyer. Maybe you can tell us what to do Mr. Barchrist."

"Well, yes, but I don't have a license to practice in Florida. I can advise you of this, however. Don't lay your hands on any bastards or you'll wind up in jail with Irv. Has anybody posted bond for him?"

"I don't think so."

"Then that's the first thing we've got to do. Who charged him with theft in office, the county?"

"I don't know. There was something about engineering fees he collected when he worked for the county—but I didn't get all of it. I'm very much afraid for him. You just don't know what the other prisoners will do with a man like Irv when he shows up in jail. He can be a pretty meek and compliant guy. He doesn't like any sort of violence, and the problem is he's pretty well known as a public figure from his former campaign for County Commissioner."

"From the campaign—what campaign?"

As it turned out, Irving Caputo had run for County Commissioner after being put out of his job with the county by the great recession. He was not the candidate of the big developers in the county. In fact, he spoke out many times about the unlimited urban sprawl they were visiting on the Sarasota/Bradenton area. The big developers and big business hated him. But he was the darling of the environmentalists and all of the little municipalities around Sarasota Bay, and he got to be quite well known.

To the shock of the people who run Sarasota and Bradenton, he almost won, losing by less than a hundred votes, even though prior to the campaign he was a virtual unknown. The people really liked him, but big business hated him, and there was a great fear that he'd run again in the next election and win.

"I bet it was one of those political bastards who are in league with the developers," Jack opined. "They're not above pressing false charges against Irv, just to keep him off the next ballot. Put a few bucks in their pockets and they'll do anything. Don't you think it was pretty interesting how nobody offered him his old county job back when things picked up after the recession?"

"I really couldn't tell you with what little I know about Sarasota or Bradenton politics. But I'm beginning to learn, I guess."

"Well, anyway, we've got to get you set up in an efficiency, don't we," Jack continued. "Irv gave me the address of the place he had in mind for you. It's got two bedrooms but you will get it for the price of an efficiency. I've got the keys, and I've also got a car lined up for you. You wanna see them? We can go today."

"Sounds great, Jack, but first let's get bond posted for our friend Irv."

We called a bondsman at "Sunny Days Again Bail Bonds" and I posted a $500 bond with my credit card, figuring I'd write it off as an expense on my Venable expense account. After all, these guys were giving me information I needed to do my job on Mr. Venable's behalf. Theft in office is a felony, so bail was $5,000, and the bond 10% of that. Irv's arraignment was to be in a week.

The Manatee County lockup was at the northern end of Route 41, just before you come to the edge of Tampa Bay. Irv was sitting on one of the benches waiting for us in a courtyard surrounded by palm trees at the entrance to the building. It was a large modernistic structure with a sweeping roof and cantilevered overhangs showing great architectural flair. Like all of the governmental new-builds in the area, it was overbuilt and under-financed. It was completed with useless pre-build expert studies and unnecessary architectural fees, using money which was needed much more by schools and social service agencies.

"Well, jail was an enervating experience," Irv said as he got into the car. "Breakfast in the clink consists of an under-boiled egg, one strip of smoke-dried jerky and three premium saltines with a cup of warm Sanka. I wonder who their dietician is. Everybody in my cell kept calling me Pops. When they found out I was a realtor, they all wanted to know where my vacant listings were, probably so when they get out, they could go rip the copper off the air conditioning units."

"Well, one thing's for sure," Jack said, pointing, "You were certainly safe from an attack against our country in there. There were close to 25 police cruisers parked in a lot across the street that looked like they'd never been used, along with two Bradley IFVs (Infantry Fighting Vehicles) and one AAV (Assault Amphibian Vehicle).

"Yeah," said Irv. "Our county taxes at work."

"Irv, who do you suppose was behind putting you in Jail? Do you have any enemies? And why do you think it happened now? What's going on?"

"I don't know," Irv said pensively. We drove on. "Oh, well," he continued, "Jack told me while we were picking up my things at the inmate possessions window that you called today to find out about the place we picked out for you. Do you want to see it?"

"If you're up to it, why not?" I said.

The apartment Irv and Jack showed me was perfect. It was actually the vacant servant's quarters of a large Spanish style house on Westmoreland Avenue in Bradenton, complete with orange tiled roof, balcony windows, wrought iron railings, and a big wooden door leading to a pool on a veranda between the house and the garage. Gayna and Rosanne could use the pool at their convenience. The place was on a street that bordered Sarasota Bay at its widest part, and was full of wildlife and good fishing if there ever was any time for it. Three blocks to the east, Route 41 coursed by. About a quarter mile north on Route 41 from where the Spanish style house sat on Westmoreland, there was a marina with boat rentals, a boater's motel and the "Bearded Clam," a tiki bar that looked like a lot of fun. In the parking lot to the boater's motel, Jack showed me a black rental 2004 Lincoln Towne Car he had obtained for me.

They'd done it, Jack and Irv. Without my even asking, they'd turned my Sarasota captivity into a suitable vacation for Rosanne and Gayna, and made it possible for me to get some work done, too. I really felt I owed these guys. The only way I could pay them back was to help Irv out of his current legal jam, but not having a license to practice law in Florida was a big hurdle. I would have to hire a criminal lawyer for him, and then kind of act as that lawyer's investigator.

The guy I hired would not only have to know his craft as a criminal lawyer, but he'd also have to know the ins and outs of politics in the Sarasota/Bradenton area. When I asked Irv and Jack who'd be good for these purposes they both said there was only one answer: Stanley Schwartzencaup. "He's the dean of all fraud lawyers in the area, whether you're defending or suing for fraud," said Irv.

"And, he knows every municipal and county official in the area," Jack added. "Hell, they've all been to him for one thing or another."

"But he gets $500 an hour," Jack interposed. "We can't afford him."

"Asks," I said.

"What? What do you mean?"

"He '*asks*' $500 an hour. That doesn't mean he '*gets*' it," I explained. "I've never met a lawyer who won't negotiate his fees, especially for the right client."

"What makes you think I'm the right client," Irv asked.

"I don't know. We'll just have to see. Who are the local politicians he's close to right now?"

"I don't know—really nobody," Irv responded. "Everybody likes him but I don't think he's on anybody's payroll right now. City and county politicos steer clear of him in public for fear of being associated with a fraud defense lawyer because they all want their skirts to look clean to the public."

"So Schwartzencaup needs you. You're going to run for Commissioner again, aren't you? Everybody who's trying to climb up any sort of a ladder needs a County Commissioner in their pocket."

"Yeah, especially down here," Jack added.

Chapter 8

Jack and Irv dropped me off at the Regency Inn & Suites, my hotel. As I went in, I notified the people at the front desk that I'd be leaving at the end of the week. I then went upstairs and called the bank that had financed most of the Josephski/Venable deals to make an appointment for the next week with them. With Josephski now dead, the police were in no mood to allow me to go through the copies of the mortgages and notes pertaining to these deals that Josephski had kept at his suite at the Ritz. I also made an appointment to visit Stanley Schwartzencaup with Irv, at which time I would offer my services as an investigator for him on Irv's case. It was my guess that Gayna would okay the idea of spring vacation in Sarasota, so I had a lot to do before she and Rosanne arrived at the beginning of next week.

I also knew I had to notify the police I was moving. If I didn't, and they wanted to talk to me again, it would only increase their suspicions about me if they couldn't reach me at the Regency Motel and Suites. From what I'd seen of the cops in the south so far, that would result in their putting out an APB on me, or some other type of overreaction.

So, the next day I called the Sheriff's office. As it turned out, they were thinking of me as I was thinking of them. It was enough to make me consider believing in mental telepathy. They put me straight through to Deputy Anton LaFarge, the officer with whom I'd been dealing on the evening of my detention—or arrest—or whatever it was, after I'd found Josephski's body. LaFarge said they wanted to see me again as soon as possible.

"What's it about?" I asked. "What do you want to see me about?"

"Just a few more questions, that's all Mr. Barchrist. Can you come in right away?"

"Do I have a choice?"

"No, not really."

"Is there any real hurry. I've got some other things planned for today."

"Yes, I'm afraid there is Mr. Barchrist. You've been quite a busy fellow since we last talked—out to Kit-Kat's Massage on Route 41, posting bond for someone at the Manatee County lockup, setting up appointments at local banks, and entertaining Johnson Horseman at Linger Lodge. We'd like to talk to you about a few things."

Deputy LaFarge's comments smelled of wire-taps, computer tracking of my credit card, following me, and possibly interviewing people about my actions. "You've been shadowing me," I protested.

"Yep, shadowing's a great little procedure invented by Allen Pinkerton in the 19th Century. You know—he was the ace of all 'private eyes.' In fact, that was the logo for his detective agency, a big eye in the center of a diamond. He provided security to Abraham Lincoln at one time, you know. We've found shadowing works pretty well for picking up information, especially when we don't have anything to start out with."

"Well, I resent it that I'm being followed around. If you've got anything to charge me with, then you should do it. Otherwise, you should leave me alone, or at least, let me go back to Ohio."

"Hold on there, Yankee. No need to get your panties in a bunch. We may just be helping you more than we're hurting you. You never know. We're just doing our job. Now can you come on in here for a few more questions?"

"All right, I'll be in as soon as I can, after I pick up a car I've rented."

"That would be a 2006 black Lincoln Towne Car, right?"

"Jeez, you've really been on me, haven't you?"

"Power of the computer. It's the biggest crime solving tool in today's world."

It looked like the police were going to occupy most of my afternoon, whether I liked it or not. When I got to the station, the deputy handed me the current day's edition of the *Sarasota Gazette*. "Have you seen this?" he asked.

The front page story was about Julius Josephski's squeeze, Alexis Weidenfeld. The story claimed she had defrauded some banks in connection with personal real estate loans she'd taken out on multiple properties simultaneously. She was claiming each was to be her primary residence in order to get favorable interest rates. Weidenfeld complained that was a lie, and that she had planned to live in these properties. But when the Great Recession heated up, she blithely defaulted on the loans. The paper didn't use the term "blithely," but it was implied—requiring that the properties be sold at short sales which helped ruin the banks holding the mortgages.

The *Herald Gazette* had learned of the matter when somebody anonymously dumped a package of mortgage document copies and a typed explanation at its door. The story added that Weidenfeld had warned the *Herald Gazette* that the story was false and should not be printed, and that she was planning to sue the newspaper for $25 million for libel and defamation if it did print the story. Weidenfeld claimed the false mortgage fraud allegations and supporting public documents were provided anonymously to the newspaper as part of a "vendetta" against her. She had offered a reward for information leading to the person who had spread the allegations to the newspaper. She gave out no details, however, concerning the claimed vendetta, preferring to defend herself through social media. According to the *Gazette*, neither the police nor the bar association were investigating the matter. Weidenfeld was a past president of the Young Lawyers Division of the Bar Association.

"Well what do you make of all that?" Deputy LaFarge asked.

"I don't know. What should I make of it? I don't know Alexis Weidenfeld. I've never even met her."

"You know, Mr. Barchrist, it's very strange. We went over Julius Josephski's place with a fine tooth comb, and there was not a fingerprint to be had except those of Josephski himself and those of Alexis Weidenfeld. We couldn't find one fingerprint of yours. Either you never touched anything the entire time you were up there, or you were careful to wipe all your prints away."

"Sir, I'm afraid I don't like the tone of that. Anyway, what's it got to do with this newspaper article you've just shown me?"

"Well there is one fact there we're sure is wrong. That's the business about the police not investigating Ms. Weidenfeld. We are. We just say we aren't in order to protect her name. But we are. What do you know about the vendetta, Ms Weidenfeld claims somebody has against her? What do you know about that?"

"Nothing—I told you I don't even know Alexis Weidenfeld."

"That's not what I asked, Mr. Barchrist. My question actually is do you know who has a vendetta against her?

The article references a vendetta. Word is, she and Julius Josephski had a pretty tough break-up recently. Some people are saying he wouldn't have been above outing her in the paper, or making up something false about her, to get back at her. Affairs of the heart and all that—you know."

"No, I don't know. What do you think all this has to do with me?"

"Well, she did offer a $5,000 reward for information leading to the person who spread these lies about her. Frankly, we are wondering if you were the one who collected that reward, and maybe something a little more for helping her take *her* revenge once she found out who'd spread the lies about her."

"That's ridiculous. I told you, I don't even know the lady, and besides, how do you know what the paper wrote about her was a lie?"

"Well, wasn't Mr. Josephski your client?"

"No, he was not. Are you telling me I should find myself a lawyer?"

"We don't advise anyone on that subject, Mr. Barchrist."

"Well, are you charging me with anything?"

"No, not at the moment."

"Then I hope you won't mind if I just leave."

Chapter 9

It was true I didn't know Alexis Weidenfeld, but I was soon to meet her. On the forthcoming Friday she was going to stop being Sarasota's mini-condo mogul. The legal starlet of the Florida West Coast and Julius Josephski's ex-squeeze, at least for a while, would become Alexis Weidenfeld, explorer on the outing with Kit-Kat's paranormal club that I'd been invited to join. After reading the *Herald Tribune*'s article about her, any qualms I had about going on the paranormal outing disappeared. I would go in order to meet Alexis Weidenfeld.

The Sun Ghost Psychic Trackers were scheduled to meet in the parking lot at the Ringling Museum, from which they would embark for the little town of Micanopy. The lot was filled with the parked vehicles of Asolo theater goers who were attending the repertory's production of *The Matchmaker*, leaving little room for others to park, except in the back, close to where New College abutted the Ringling Estate. As I sat in my rented car waiting and observing, a huge brown and white Thor Motor Coach RV rolled into the lot and parked in the back. Kit-Kat had told me to watch for this van and to follow it to where the other club members would be parked. I still wasn't certain I was going to join the entourage of psychics and paranormal explorers who were assembling, but I followed the van. Then Kit-Kat pulled in, driving her bumble bee. She caught sight of me almost immediately.

"Hellooo, Winston! Glad you could make it—even more glad you brought this big heavy Lincoln with you. It'll be very helpful in transporting some of our members, including me, I hope. I'm sure it'll hold the road if there are any quakes."

I was astonished. "Quakes? You mean like earthquakes?"

"Well, it's only happened once so far to our group. We were up at Britton Hill, the highest point in Florida. It's on the border with Alabama—345 feet above sea level."

"I didn't know they had earthquakes in Florida."

"They don't—not usually. But we were up there exploring an ancient Indian cave, and suddenly it happened—just as we caught an indistinct vision through one of our video recorders of Miccosukee warriors dancing around a camp fire. The Miccosukee have been extinct for almost 200 years, but we could tell it was them because it looked like they were wearing thick grass boots, which is a Miccosukee characteristic."

"Are you kidding me?"

Kit-Kat slowly nodded her head no. "Remember, Winston, an open mind—keep an open mind to the possibility that the paranormal exists." She took me over to the RV, parked at the end of the lot and knocked on the door. A man in his early 60s answered. "Winston, meet Dr. Ben Temple. You might say he's our leader. Oh, and this is his girlfriend Cherry." A thin dark-haired Italian-looking woman in her mid-30s looked up from her perch behind the RV's steering wheel and smiled. "Ben, this is the new member I emailed you about," Kit-Kat continued.

"Glad to have you with us," the doctor said. "Had much experience at this, have you?"

"No, not really—actually none at all. This is my first time."

"Well, that's okay," he said, "as long as you're not a skeptic."

"Well, to tell you the truth . . ."

"Don't worry," he interrupted, "as long as you believe there's evil incarnate in the world, and that Jesus Christ is your savior, you won't be a jinx to our endeavors today, and you'll be all right."

I didn't answer. Instead, a picture of my friend, Rabbi Goldman, flashed into my mind for a second. "Religions are nothing more than differing presentations of the same propositions we all believe when it comes to push or shove," he used to say. "If you're a Christian, when you die you go to Heaven if you believe in Jesus. If you're a Lubavitcher Jew, and you die having failed to observe all 613 of the commandments in the Torah during your life, you're reincarnated until you succeed in fulfilling them all. Then your soul becomes one with God. What really is the difference? Hindus get reincarnated as animals, or into higher classes, depending on how they've behaved while alive, and if you're a devout Buddhist, well, you were never really here anyway."

So I guessed I could put up with Dr. Temple's standard. I looked past him into the RV. It was filled with equipment used by ghost hunters: Thermo-imagers, static charge e-field imagers, full-spectrum camcorders, laser lights, infra-red spectrum lights, thermal cameras, individual first-aid kits, spectral imaging devices, motion sensors, an EVP recorder, radiation monitors and flashlights with pulsar switches and remote auxiliary batteries. There was also a large desk computer.

Dr. Temple explained that each ghost hunter would be fitted out with a Blue-tooth microphone through which he or she could record what was being observed. The transmissions all came back by wireless to the computer. If any images were sighted, they too could be transmitted via wireless to the computer if the person who thought they saw them was equipped with video equipment.

Suddenly, from outside the RV came what sounded like the rush of a powerful engine, and then the squeal of brakes straining to stop a vehicle. Through the window, I could see a black Porsche Targa with a white interior coming to a strained stop. A woman wearing dark sunglasses with hair as black as the Targa stepped out. Even with the sunglasses, I could tell she was beautiful.

"That's Lexi Weidenfeld," Kit-Kat said, peering out the window with me.

I don't think I'd ever seen a woman like Lexi before. Perfectly tanned, she was wearing a short khaki safari skirt with soft tan boots that rose to mid-calf level, and a light green Columbia brand outdoors shirt with long flopping lapels. It had the sleeves cut out to reveal just enough of her rounded bare shoulders. Her figure was curvy and enticing, though obviously well worked out to produce a slim look to a slightly overweight woman. Her face was at once angular and hard, but at the same time soft and inviting when she smiled. "C'mon," said Kit-Kat. "I'll introduce you."

We climbed out of the RV and approached Lexi from behind. She was leaning over the trunk of her Targa, straining her ample derriere and swearing under her breath as she struggled to lift out a piece of cumbersome equipment. When Kit-Kat tapped her shoulder from behind, she snapped around with the fury of a big cat ready to strike. But when she saw it was Kit-Kat, she quickly flashed her a winning smile.

"Oh, you scared me. For some reason I'm very touchy these days. Sorry Kit." And with that, she threw her arms around Kit-Kat's shoulders and hugged her.

"Lexi, I want to introduce you to Winston Barchrist. He's a lawyer. He's here, was here, doing some business, with Julius, dare I say, before . . ."

"Yes, Mr. Barchrist. Julie mentioned you to me. It's terrible, just terrible what happened."

I couldn't tell whether this greeting was sincere or not. Maybe she had heard of me, but I couldn't imagine why. Julius Josephski would have had absolutely no reason to mention me, or my coming to Sarasota to see him, to his girlfriend, or should I say, his former girlfriend. But all this speculation somehow melted away when she took my hand into her warm brown hands to greet me in a very sort of feminine way. It was more classy than feminine, although very feminine, too. For some reason, the woman seemed very sexy to me. I felt like a huge manatee who'd just had his fleshy flipper gathered up by a beautiful mermaid. I hoped I wasn't blushing.

"It's a pleasure, Ms. . . ."

"Weidenfeld," she interrupted, "Alexis Weidenfeld. Julius and I used to be an 'item' you might say." A frown crept onto her face. "But we'd gone our separate ways before the recent event that overtook him." She turned back to her Targa and the piece of machinery she was taking out of it. "In fact," she continued over her shoulder, "Micanopy, where we're going today, used to be one of our favorite places to go antiquing together."

"Oh, really," I asked, self-consciously trying to keep the conversation going with this awesome woman. "Was he into the paranormal too?"

"Oh no. In fact, he used to laugh at me about that." She frowned again. "Truth be known, I always thought he was a bit of an asshole when it came to this little hobby of mine. But I don't suppose we should speak ill of the dead, should we?"

Her attitude showed an unexpected hardness toward him. Here she was preparing, just a few days after his death, to run off for recreational purposes to a place they'd often shared, and she was referring to him as an asshole. It was hardly the response one would expect from a former lover, even if their relationship had broken up.

"Well, I had no time to get to know him before he died," I responded. "I'd be grateful if maybe you could tell me a little about him while we're on this trip together, Ms. Weidenfeld."

"Lexi," she corrected, looking up and smiling impishly from the trunk of her car. "Sure, I'll tell you about anything you want to hear about him, if you'll help me get this damn tripod out of my car. Why don't we ride up to Micanopy together and we can talk?"

"Fine," I agreed. "Your car or mine?"

"Oh, mine, of course," Lexi answered with the air of someone who always liked to be in control.

I peered down into her Targa trying to judge whether I would fit in it and reconsidered, deciding it would be a bad idea for me to try fitting into that thing. "No, I insist," I said. "There's no reason to expose an $85,000 car like yours to the open road when my humble Lincoln Towne car will do just as well."

"$130,000."

"Beg-pardon—what?"

"The Targa cost over $130,000," she said unabashedly with a twinkle in her eye. "But okay, we can go in yours if you insist. Is anyone else riding with you?"

"Just little ole me, so far," Kit-Kat blurted out.

"Fine," said Lexi. "I hate traveling with a large group. So tell me, Mr. Barchrist..."

"Winston," I insisted.

"Do you still have business here now that Julius is deceased?"

"Yes, the only difference is, now I'm going to have to go to the bank to look at his mortgage loan documents. The police have impounded everything and they won't let me back into his suite."

"Oh, that would be the New Band Bank, I presume."

"That's correct," I answered.

Chapter 10

We headed up Interstate 75 toward Gainesville in a caravan with Dr. Temple's van in the lead, then me, then two cars following me. Altogether there were 15 of us. Many of the ghost hunters rode in the RV. Lexi sat in the passenger's seat of my Lincoln with her glorious knees and half her thighs protruding from her khaki skirt. Kit-Kat sat in the back. My trunk was filled with equipment belonging to the two women.

We started out riding in silence. Then Alexis broke the ice.

"So, Mr. Barchrist, I suppose . . ."

"Please. My friends call me Winston." For some reason I felt warmth in this woman's presence.

"I suppose, Winston, you've had a chance to read all about me on the front page of the *Herald Gazette* by now. None of it's true, you know."

I remained silent. From the back seat, Kit-Kat piped up. "Lexi, the article mentioned you thought somebody had a vendetta against you, but you didn't say. Who has a vendetta against you? You should definitely sue them for all of those lies, as well as the newspaper."

"I would if I could prove it." Alexis' face was now beginning to turn red, but I couldn't tell if it was from rage or from embarrassment. Her body quaked and she seemed uncomfortable in her seat.

"Are you alright?" I asked.

"Yes," she replied, almost in tears.

Clueless as to Lexi's discomfort, Kit-Kat pursued the question. "Well, who do you think it was?"

Through her tears, Lexi said, "I think it was probably Julius. He was so upset the day after I broke up with him. He called me, begging me to come back, and when I said I wouldn't, he said, 'I'll ruin you'." She began sobbing. "Then he came to my condo and stood outside yelling and shaking his fists in the air."

"Well, could he have ruined you, I mean?" Kit-Kat asked. "Are you saying you're actually guilty of what the newspaper says you did to the banks, and Julie knew about it?"

"I'm not saying he knew about it, but I am saying he counseled me to do it—to cross out the words in the mortgages that said, 'will live on the premises as her primary residence' and insert the words *'intends* to live on the premises as her primary residence' instead. It was so I could get the most favorable interest rate. I did it because if the bank thinks you're just speculating, the interest charges go way up. But if there's an intention to make the place your primary home, it gives you the residential rate, not the commercial rate. He told me he'd done it many times in his earlier days, and once he'd even won a lawsuit over the question. He just went into court and testified that when he signed the note and mortgage as modified, he had truly intended to make the property his primary residence, but something came up to prevent it. So he got to keep the lower interest rate."

"Well, but, you were intending to make the real estate you were financing your primary residence when you did that, weren't you?" Kit-Kat insisted.

Alexis didn't answer.

"Let me ask you this, Lexi. Was Julius Josephski a lawyer?" I inquired. "Was he a member of the Florida Bar?"

"No."

"But you are, aren't you?" *At the moment—I was thinking of myself and my troubles with the Illinois Bar.* "So, you should have known better. People have been disbarred for less."

Again, there was no answer. "Oh well," I said, "why don't we just drop this subject for the time being and have a good time? Later, if we can get some alone time, maybe I can add a little information that may shed some light on your situation, Lexi. I've had some troubles with a bar association in my time."

But Kit-Kat just wanted to keep drilling away. "Oh, really! What have you got to add, Winston?"

"Later, Kit-Kat—just later—okay?" It was obvious that Alexis Weidenfeld was wracked with pain over the whole thing. But I couldn't tell whether this was out of concern for her own scalp or because of the death of her ex-boyfriend. She stood to lose a lot, not only her personal reputation, but as the only truly viable suspect in the murder of Julius Josephski. If the police ever stopped protecting her and truly dug into the case, she could lose big time criminally if she was charged either with criminal fraud or murder.

As we approached Gainesville, we drove across what seemed like a huge prairie, and at its edge, we came to an exit that said Micanopy. "No entrance to the south," the sign added. Dr. Temple, who was leading us at the wheel of his RV, turned on his right turn signal and pulled onto the exit ramp. Alexis stopped crying and Kit-Kat became downright excited. "If we're lucky, Mr. Winston Barchrist, you're in for something you never before thought could happen," she promised.

"Oh, and what is that?"

"I can't tell you because I truly don't know. You'll just have to wait and see. But I feel for certain that today someone from the nether world will appear, and maybe say something to us."

We came down off the ramp into a different world. There was a gas station/general store with one pump. There was a dilapidated barn with a huge flag of Dixie painted on its side, and a forlorn playground with broken swings and a single metal merry-go-round. The ramp led onto Florida State Route 441. You could go left or right, but there was also a wooden sign across the road sharpened like a picket at one end harboring straight ahead that said Micanopy. That road was shaded by live oaks supporting a garland of Spanish moss waiving in the breeze and bordered on each side by a five-foot high, black iron fence laced with purple wisteria. The road led to a cemetery with a huge gate. Dr. Temple stopped at the gate, and waited for all of us to catch up with him.

Then he stepped out of the van and began explaining to the group that Micanopy was the first distinct United States town of non-Spanish origin in the Florida Territory ceded by Spain in 1820. It was founded by Moses Elias Levy, a wealthy Jewish trader and philanthropist who was involved in trade with the West Indies. Levy was also a utopian and an ante-bellum reformer. The town was named after the Indian chief, Micanopy, to appease him and to acknowledge his original authority over the land. Two wars with the Seminole Indians were fought here between 1837 and 1843 before the Seminoles were removed to Indian lands to the north and west. Notable people from the Micanopy area were author Marjorie Kinnan Rawlings, who wrote *The Yearling* and *Cross Creek,* zoologist Archie Carr, conservationist Marjorie Harris Carr, and the actor River Phoenix. The film *Doc Hollywood* starring Michael J. Fox was filmed here. After his history lesson, he concluded with the fact that the town is home to 600 people.

"Why have we chosen to come to Micanopy?" he continued. "Well, before the town, as we know it today, was founded there were Indian settlements here. The Spanish explorer De Soto came across one of them in 1539. They lasted all the way up until the Indians were removed in the 1800s when a mixed blood black Seminole leader named John Horse was leading them. It is said that John Horse haunts the house that Moses Elias Levy lived in, because that's where John Horse's hut was pitched. We've come to find John Horse."

"Did you know that there are still ancestors of this John Horse living in the area?" Kit-Kat whispered. "This guy I told you about, John Horseman, who favors my business establishment is said to be the great, great, great grandson of John Horse. I actually know him," she said.

As he concluded his remarks, Dr. Temple turned to get back into the RV, then stopped as if he remembered something else. "Oh, and one last thing," he said. "If anyone needs to use the facilities in town, remember these people have nothing but a septic system here—no sewer system. So if you use the facilities, please leave them a dollar to help them pay for the periodic pump outs they have to get—or just use the toilet in the van."

"So what do you think of all this, Mr. Winston Barchrist?" Kit-Kat asked excitedly.

"Hmm, well what do you think of it?" I asked, turning to Lexi

"I don't know, but I gotta pee," she announced, and she walked into the cemetery away from the rest of us and squatted over one of the graves. "I just hope that wasn't the grave of Moses Elias Levy," she said when she returned. "I wouldn't want to be peeing on the grave of a lantzman."

"Especially not if we're going to be snooping around his house looking for a black Seminole Indian," Kit-Kat added.

With that, we got back in the car and followed Dr. Temple into the town. I don't think I'd ever seen a town like Micanopy before. It was historically old, not historically quaint. There were three two-story brick buildings in the business district housing antique stores and used book sellers. Across the main drag, there were also some restaurants that served people on the porch or inside, and there was a dairy and a grocery. Every house in town, even the Victorian type mansions, were made of wood and built off the ground on blocks with crawl spaces underneath. Everything was overgrown with succulent plants and vines. There were five pecan trees in the middle of town in a sort of grassy area that was supposed to pass for a park, and there were a few dogs running free. It looked like the forest surrounding the little city had barely allowed it enough room to exist.

"Well, what do we do now?" I asked.

"We go get ourselves a late lunch and then we wait for it to get dark," said a voice behind us. It was Cherry, Dr. Temple's girlfriend. She came up to Alexis and greeted her. "Hey Lexi—nice article in the paper yesterday—any of that crap true? You know what attorneys say. Any publicity, even bad publicity, is better than no publicity at all."

Lexi looked daggers at her. It was pretty obvious these two women did not like each other very much. "You can't believe everything you read," she said. Then she laughed. "I guess I haven't had to worry too much about publicity in the past, and I think it's been what most would consider to be pretty good publicity for me."

But Cherry wasn't having any of that. "I saw you pee in the cemetery back there—too cheap to help these poor folks out with their septic system, eh?"

"C'mon Cherry," Kit-Kat piped up. "Give us a break. Everybody deserves a break once in a while. It's a nice day for ghost hunting. Let's not gum it up with any negative energy."

The four of us then had lunch on the porch of one of the restaurants across from the pecan trees. Cherry explained she was a school teacher suffering under the administration of the Manatee County school system. She also doubled in the afternoons as the receptionist in Dr. Temple's office. She had become a ghost hunter after her third husband died of melanoma but kept visiting her at night while she was sleeping, telling her how to spend his money and asking for sex.

"Yep," she said, "the sex was great with Burt, so great that he kept coming back, I guess. It scared me." Nothing else was very good though, she explained, at least not until she met Ben Temple who showed her through the world of the paranormal. "Ben's view on things really gives me a sense of security," she added, "and now paranormal sex is great. Ben showed me that Burt was coming back because I'd left certain things undone."

"Thanks for sharing," scoffed Lexi.

Chapter 11

At nightfall, our little caravan proceeded to the former home of Moses Elias Levy, a large wooden American Gothic style structure which was on the National Historic Register and was framed by two huge pink magnolia trees. The house had a dark screened veranda wrapping around three sides, a second floor with gables and decorative cookie-cutter lath extending from the eaves. Dormers in the roof evidenced a third floor, and a large turret extended up another flight at one corner of the house, formed a tower. There were five brick chimneys. The roof was made of serrated clapboard—and, yes—it looked haunted.

The first piece of machinery to come out of the van was a gas-operated generator. Lines from it were quietly run to large lights on stands that were placed strategically throughout the house on all floors. Gradually, all the equipment everyone had lugged along on the trip began appearing on the front lawn. It was very quiet and the people who were setting up were being certain to keep it that way.

"That generator," Kit-Kat whispered, "will only be used in case of emergency. Otherwise, the noise from it would scare away anything that's in there. But if things get out of hand, Doc or Cherry will flip it on and the whole place will suddenly be illuminated by those lights they're taking in. It's the only way of taking back control from any power that might be circulating in the house. In other words, it's protection for our people."

As I looked around the lawn, I noticed people removing their shoes and socks and replacing them with rubber sandals. "It's so they won't be grounded," explained Kit-Kat. "You don't want to be a conductor of electricity when you're messing around with this stuff." People were also connecting to Bluetooth audio units and placing flashlight harnesses on their heads that were connected to auxiliary batteries worn on their belts. Because I had none of this equipment with me, Dr. Temple suggested that I man the computer in the van and that I also act as a relay for messages between the trackers. Actually, it was an important job. I was to capture any videos taken by the trackers and place them into separate files along with any sound that was relayed with the video.

There was a strict procedure to be followed. Doc had an architectural drawing of the house he had obtained from the historical society. He assigned each tracker a room in the house. The first thing they were to do was go to that room and video everything in it completely from right to left and send their pictures back to me on the computer. Next, sonic equipment would be taken into the house and placed room by room, and a video tracker was to re-video the room. Doc would then compare the video with the earlier video of the room to see if anything had been moved or was out of place. While that was going on, the rest of the trackers were free to roam the dark house performing whatever tests they chose to perform, or just exploring. Anyone who ran up against trouble—a fall, a door closed and locked behind, or shattered glass—anything at all—was to blow his or her whistle until a fellow tracker arrived.

If there were any possible indicators of paranormal activity, such as sounds, door squeaks, voices, lights, drafts, unusual wetness, inexplicable movement, or fog, they were to be reported back to me and recorded, if possible. The first incident occurred shortly after the trackers were released individually to enter the house. Cherry, who was carrying video equipment, reported from the second floor hallway that something was bumping her from behind. Suddenly, a door squeaked open and a dim light shown through it. Alexis saw the light but did not encounter the bumping. Carefully, she entered the door, followed by Kit-Kat.

Nothing! "There was nothing inside," reported Kit-Kat over her Bluetooth, and she left, as did Cherry. Alexis remained behind taking photographs of the room to later determine through comparison with our initial photos whether anything was out of place. Suddenly, there was a scream. Lexi departed the room hurriedly, running down the hallway. She was so flustered that she stumbled down the stairs. Cherry returned to the room, and though she could see nothing unusual, turned on her video equipment and did a panoramic view, starting with the left wall, across a huge bed and past a fireplace to a dresser on the right wall. Then she turned her camera lens back to the fireplace and lingered there, turning on her pulsar flashlight.

There was something there but she couldn't tell what. It didn't look like any sort of an Indian, but more like an old three-branch tree with the middle branch thrashing and waiving. The other two branches were reaching upward with small spheres the size of tennis balls at each of their tips. It was just standing there next to the fireplace dimly shining in the pulsating light. Cherry called back to Doc immediately, suggesting he bring up the static charge e-field imager for a better look. Just then, Lexi appeared at the door to the RV, still flustered and disoriented. She was crying, and there was a bloody gash down her left cheek.

"It was him!" she shrieked.

"What?" said Doc. "It was who?"

"Julie—Julius Josephski." Now she was whimpering and shaking. "He was standing there with his arms raised and his fists clenched, yelling, like when we broke up."

"Julius Josephski and Alexis were an item for almost a year," I presumptuously explained to Dr. Temple. How irrelevant my comment must have seemed to him. Doc was a Sarasota resident to whom both Josephski and Weidenfeld were well known, whereas I was just a new guy in town. Of course, he knew they had been an item.

"Let me see you," Doc said to Lexi. "Is that blood on your cheek?"

"I fell down the steps when I saw him," she answered. "He's in there, up on the second floor."

"But why would Julius Josephski be on the second floor in the bedroom of the home of Moses Elias Levy in Micanopy, Florida?" Doc asked

"Because he's following me," blurted Alexis in a frustrated voice. "We used to come here a lot on Sunday drives to go antiquing, and when I broke up with him he was very angry. He shook his fists, just like he did up there in the house and yelled that he'd ruin me."

"But Julius Josephski's dead, Lexi, how could he be here?"

"Isn't he though," Lexi replied wryly, "and he always used to taunt me about believing in the paranormal."

"So you think you saw his ghost up there waiving his fists at you like on the day you broke up with him?" I asked.

"The day after," she corrected impatiently, "and I don't *think* it, I know it."

"Well, there's only one way to find out," Doc said. "You come with me, Mr. Barchrist. I think things will be all right in here if you leave your post here for a while. I'm going to need your help in the house. Besides, Lexi can stay here and handle the computer."

We gathered up a thermo-imager, a static charge e-field imager, a motion sensor and some infra-red spectrum lights, and made our way into the house quietly and up the stairs. It wasn't easy carrying all the bulky instruments. Cherry was waiting for us at the bedroom door. "It's gone," she whispered. "I've been standing in this doorway since I caught it with my pulsar light, and I haven't seen, felt, heard, smelled or touched anything, but it's not there anymore, so I think it's gone."

"Any other way out of this room?" Doc asked.

"No."

"Have you seen any auras at the windows?"

"No."

"Then it can't be gone. Whatever it is, it's still in here, I think."

"What about the fireplace?" I asked.

"Maybe, you've got a point there, Barchrist, if this thing is a Santa Claus ghost or something like that. But usually their actions have the same properties as our actions. Oh they can walk through walls and all that, but otherwise, they choose to move about just as we would, through doors and windows or upstairs and the like. You won't find too many humans entering or exiting through chimneys."

I could hardly believe I was actually listening to this guy, as if he was some kind of expert instead of some kind of kook. How would he know how ghosts preferred to move about? And, even the question of how he would know this assumed there actually were ghosts, something upon which in truth I was agnostic. I began to believe that after all, maybe I shouldn't be involved because my doubt would just jinx their entire endeavor. But then, again, there was Alexis with her bloody cheek. It was hard to believe spirits didn't exist when a creature like her had actually professed to seeing one.

"Well, let's get set up," directed Doc. "We'll put the thermo-imager in the doorway and the motion sensor in the middle of the room. Then I can run the static charge e-field imager slowly around the periphery of the room, and you try to catch anything you can with the infrared spectrum lights."

Everything was set up and we turned on the equipment and watched for five minutes, but there was nothing. We repeated the whole process with Cherry shining her pulsar light through the infrared spectrum light as it went around the room. Still nothing. Doc flipped off the equipment. "Okay, here's what we're going to try now," he said. "Cherry, get on the Bluetooth and tell Lexi to get up here, but tell her to wait just outside the door until I give her the go-ahead to enter the room."

When Lexi was outside the door, the doctor turned on all of the equipment again, and we all left the room. As we passed Lexi, Doc quietly told her to step into the room and just wait there with all of the equipment running. After a minute or so, we heard whimpering from Lexi coming from inside the room. Doc motioned to Cherry to step into the room behind Lexi and to start videoing. After a minute or so, Cherry backed out of the room and said, "I got it!" Then Lexi fainted.

Doc and I struggled to pick her up and take her downstairs, leaving all our equipment except Cherry's video camera in the room. Cherry and Kit-Kat followed. When we reached the van, Lexi came to, and sat there drinking some Perrier that Kit-Kat had brought up from my car. We turned on Cherry's video and replayed it.

There it was. Doc tinkered with the controls, fine tuning the picture into perfect view. Kit-Kat watched it, clasping her hands together with approval. I watched in disbelief. Cherry congratulated herself. Alexis Weidenfeld turned gray.

In front of the bedroom fireplace was a brightly lit fuzzy image of what could have been taken for a stubby tree with three branches, but actually looked more like a man with a weasel-like face with two raised arms shaking his fists above his head. Cherry had turned the camera's audio on, but the only noise that could be heard was the sound of Lexi's whimpering before she collapsed.

"Who is it?" Cherry inquired.

"That is...."—she cleared her throat—"that is Julius Josephski," Alexis answered in almost a whisper.

"I say we invite all the others in here to have a look, and then we get out of here," Dr. Temple proclaimed triumphantly. "We've had a good day."

Alexis coughed, got up and left the RV muttering. "A good day—that's what you say," she sighed. Kit-Kat and I later found her sitting in the back seat of my car sulking. "Let's get out of here," she said. "I've had enough of this place. Get me back to Sarasota—too many bad memories here."

"Lexi, tell me truthfully," Kit-Kat began. "Do you really believe that was the ghost of Julius Josephski you saw in the house?"

"It was," Alexis brooded. "I know it was, Julie. The way he had his arms raised, and his fists—it was just like the day he came to my house angry because we were breaking up."

"Are you scared, Lexi?" I asked.

"Very, very scared"

"Well. Why do you suppose he would come back to you as spirit medium?" Kit-Kat asked.

"I don't know," Lexi answered. "We always used to come to Micanopy together. Maybe that's it." Then she fell silent. Hardly a word was spoken by anyone until we reached her place on Longboat Key. When we arrived, she prevailed on us to stay the night with her. She didn't want to be left alone to recover from the shock of the day's events.

Chapter 12

My God! It was the ghost of Johnson Horseman's ancestor we were looking at when we were in Micanopy—I thought to myself—*John Horse, the Black Seminole! Could we have found him?* I was in the midst of waking up from a dream, a dream about dream catchers.

Hard as it was to believe, I was in Lexi Weidenfeld's guest bedroom at Tangerine Bay on Longboat Key. I got up to look around. Kit-Kat was in the other guest room. Then I remembered how overwrought Lexi had been by her expedition to Micanopy. We stayed the night as she had asked us to help alleviate her fears that the ghost of Julius Josephski might show up again to haunt her. Now ask me if I really thought there was a ghost of Julius Josephski. Hogwash! Not for a minute! But Lexi was a hard woman to turn down, especially when it involved an overnight stay with her at a place like hers.

Talk about opulence! Lexi's place was the paradigm of opulence—sliding glass doors opening on to Sarasota Bay; mahogany walls in her home office; foot after foot of marble in her entryway, Persian granite on her kitchen counters, Egyptian cotton sheets with a 300 thread count. Alexis Weidenfeld knew how to live, and she wasn't shy about showing it.

As I continued reconnoitering the place, I came across a French Provincial style mahogany desk at the end of a mammoth room, almost the size of a small dance hall. The middle drawer was partially open, and I was never one to be above snooping. So I did.

Inside were two wills with pour-over trusts, one signed by Alexis Weidenfeld and the other by Julius Josephski. Each trust gave the deceased's total estate to the other for the time that person remained alive with whatever remained at the bequeath's death to their heirs outright.

My god! He'd left everything to her in trust for as long as she lived! Beneath these testamentary documents was an unsigned affidavit, prepared for the signature of Irving Caputo. It stated Edwin DeVertollo had exerted pressure on him causing the Manatee County Engineering Department to hold up its approval of the Long Bar Harbor project until such time as DeVertollo said it was okay to go ahead. The affidavit's second paragraph explained how DeVertollo exerted this pressure by blackmailing Caputo. If Caputo didn't follow DeVertollo's instructions, DeVertollo would expose him as a gay person to the Manatee County administration and seek his dismissal. Apparently, the Gay Rights Movement had not reached far enough into the South yet to affect local government mores, and there were no ordinances on the books of the county protecting gays. At the bottom of the unsigned affidavit, it was noted that its drafter was none other than Alexis Weidenfeld. My stomach jumped. Quickly, I put the papers back in the drawer.

"It's a piece from the 17th Century," a low voice from across the huge room announced suddenly.

"What?" I replied, turning around quickly while quietly pushing the open drawer closed with my hip.

Lexi was standing there across the room, dressed in a trim black business suit with her brief case. I couldn't help noticing her stiletto heels and how professional she looked.

"I said that French Provincial piece you're admiring is from the 17ᵗʰ Century. It's worth a fortune," she bragged.

"Oh, yes," I answered. "It's truly beautiful."

The contents of the desk, particularly Josephski's will, might even be priceless to Lexi, I thought to myself. *And what was going on here? Did Edwin DeVertollo know that Lexi Weidenfeld was working on doing him in with this draft affidavit about his dealings with Irving Caputo? Were Josephski and Weidenfeld working together on this before they broke up? Did this piece of paper somehow have something to do with the crime in office charges that had been leveled against Irv?*

"Winston, I want to thank you and Kit-Kat for staying here with me last night," Lexi continued in her low alto tone. "Obviously, after our trip to Micanopy, I was quite upset and in need of some company. For that, I apologize. By now, I should know how to handle the paranormal better than I did yesterday. As I stand here, I'm not even sure I saw the same thing as all the others did in the little event we witnessed up there. It may be that I'm still more sensitive than I know about the loss of Julius."

"No need for any apologies here, Lexi. Actually, I've enjoyed meeting you, and it's been a real pleasure to see your house and be in it."

"Fine. That's good." And with that, she said, "I'm afraid I'm going to have to run now. I have two closings today at my office, and I'm late. Just drink some coffee in the kitchen, make yourself some breakfast, and stay as long as you like." Then, she turned and left the room.

Lexi was the kind of woman you didn't stop thinking about immediately after she left a room. This was especially true now after seeing what I'd seen in her desk drawer. Eventually, however, my mind leapt to the other things I wanted to do that day—one of them was actually to seek an appointment with Edwin DeVertollo as part of my investigation in my soon-to-be new job of helping Stanley Schwartzencaup prepare the defense of Irv's case. Maybe I was jumping the gun on this a little bit, since I hadn't even talked to Mr. Schwartzenkaup yet about the role I wanted to play in that case. But the draft affidavit I'd seen in Lexi's desk drawer put a whole new slant on the matter from my point of view.

Originally, I was under the impression that DeVertollo, or someone from his organization, had caused the charges of theft in office to be instituted against Irv. But now I was beginning to wonder. Had DeVertollo really pressured Irv Caputo to prevent the Manatee Engineering Department from issuing permits for the Long Bar Harbor project, as the affidavit in Lexi's desk drawer alleged? If so, what was Lexi's interest in exposing DeVertollo's actions? By virtue of their reciprocal wills and trusts, Alexis Weidenfeld actually did have an inchoate interest in the land at Long Bar Harbor owned by Josephski's business. If that land wasn't developed in a timely fashion, Josephski's business would lose its value and she would lose a valuable inheritance.

But what would that have had to do with DeVertollo's causing theft in office charges to be filed against Irving Caputo at this particular Harbor in time? Apparently, according to the affidavit, the permits DeVertollo was trying to stop the Manatee County Engineering Department from issuing had never been issued. So why would anyone from DeVertollo's organization now have trumped up theft in office charges filed against Irv Caputo?

Did the charges have anything at all to do with that permit, or was somebody just trying to get back at Irv for running for County Commissioner and coming so close to winning? After all, Irv was known to have been on the side of the environmentalists, and against the interests of all the big developers in the area who were overdeveloping Sarasota and Manatee counties. Hopefully, some of these questions could be answered if I talked with DeVertollo.

Chapter 13

Etched into the cement header above the main entranceway to a high rise at the corner of State and Main Streets was, "The Edwin DeVertollo Building—2003." The lobby opened into an 18-floor high atrium with balconies around the sides and trees and plants growing up from the center. At the far end, over a mahogany doorway, set off by glass sidelight windows was a foyer over which appeared, in gold leaf letters, the name "Cravenstall, Ltd." It was the opulent lair of Edwin DeVertello.

"My name is Winston Barchrist III," I whispered to the receptionist. "I work for Stanley Schwartzencaup—the attorney." (At that point I was lying. I didn't work for Stanley yet.) "Oh yes," said the attractive receptionist. "We know Mr. Schwartzencaup well here."

"I was wondering if I could make an appointment to see Mr. DeVertollo in the near future. It shouldn't take more than a half hour or so." The receptionist looked down at a calendar book on her desk, following along various columns and pages. Gradually a look of distress overtook her face.

"One moment please." She made a call, presumably to DeVertollo's assistant, who seemed to take forever answering her, and then she looked up. "Mr. DeVertollo is leaving the country tomorrow for two weeks in Italy, after which he will be going to Costa Rica on business, and then to the Caymans. He really won't be able to see you for almost a month. But he wonders if you have time to talk to him now."

"Now? Right now? Well, yes, that would be fine, if he can spare the time."

Edwin DeVertollo looked like a Sicilian godfather. Rough tanned leathery skin with craggy eyes, deeply set under a full shock of hair that was still mostly black. He moved around his office on a cane and spoke in a raspy voice with a Brooklyn accent. Not a man to mince words, he came right to the point, revealing why he'd granted me an audience on such short notice.

"So I heard you was an attorney from Ohio or somewhere, who'd come to town and was working with Julie Josephski. But now you say you're working for Stanley Schwartzencaup. What's up with that?"

Obviously, this man had tentacles reaching as far as the sheriff's office and the staff of the Ritz Carlton. Maybe even as far as the management of the New Band Bank, where Julius Josephski was heavily in debt, or he wouldn't have known about my connection with him. That's what power can do for you in a small town. Be that as it may, I decided to answer him with equal candor.

"I'm not here about Julius Josephski. I'm here about Irv Caputo."

"Too bad about what happened to Julie. Isn't it?"

"Yeah, too bad about what happened to Irving Caputo, too. Isn't it?" I said it just like that to see whether DeVertollo actually had any knowledge that Irv had been jailed and charged with fraud in office.

"Personally, I think that craven Weidenfeld bitch did it," he mused, still stuck on the subject of Josephski's untimely death.

"Did what?" I asked. "Set up Caputo for theft in office charges?"

"Huh? Oh, I was talking about Julie's murder. Irv Caputo? Well, at least he's got the right attorney anyways, doesn't he? Stanley Schartzencaup. Political criminal allegations can sometimes be messy. But where do you come to Stanley Schwartzencaup? You're from Ohio or Iowa, or something, aren't you? And you were here to talk with Julie Josephski?"

"Obviously, you know everything that's going on in your town, Mr. DeVertollo. I can see that."

"But Irv's from the next town up the coast—Bradenton. So I wonder. Can we just quit the shadow boxing and get down to why you're here, Mr. Barchrist? I don't understand your connection with Irv."

"But you do know Irv."

"Yeah, so what?"

"Well, to make a long story short, Mr. Josephski told my client in Ohio you had said things were moving too slowly on the Long Bar Harbor project because . . .

"And who might your Ohio client be . . . ?"

"My client is Charles Venable—Mr. Josephski's partner in an investment partnership called Long Bar Harbor Hotel and Yacht Club, Ltd. which was formed for the purpose of anchoring the Long Bar Harbor development with a hotel, a yacht club and a golf course."

"Ah, yes—the resort, so to speak on the Long Bar—go on." A disgusted look creased his face, and I thought I saw him roll his eyes.

"Well anyway, you had apparently told Julius Josephski the reason things were moving so slowly with the Long Bar Harbor project was because huge environmental problems were holding things up. Irv Caputo, who I met serendipitously for the first time here in Sarasota one day at lunch, worked for the Manatee County Engineer's Office at the time. And he just happened to be at the center of all those problems when he worked there, or so he said. He and I became friends. Then, lo and behold, here he is, arrested about two years after leaving the County Engineer's Office, for a previous alleged theft in office during his tour of duty at Manatee County. He believes he was framed because he will be running for Manatee County Commissioner in the next election, and he asked me to help him get to the bottom of the matter. But I don't have a Florida license to practice law, so I told him I'd help whatever Florida lawyer he hired with his investigation of the situation. Hence my connection with Stanley Schwartzencaup." (Again, I was bending the truth. I didn't really have that connection yet.)

"Yeah, okay, yeah—but why'd you come here?"

"Basically, to see what you may know about Irv's situation. He says all the big developers in the area are against him, and wouldn't find it convenient to have him as a commissioner. In other words, we are looking for the reason why these charges were instigated against him."

DeVertollo stood up abruptly. "Oh, now wait a minute here," he said, emphasizing each of his words with a poke of his cane on the hard wood floor. "You don't think I had anything to do with it, do you? Mr. Barchrist, I'm too busy for the intramural games that go on between the politicians in this town." His eyes were on fire now. "And I . . ."

". . . I can honestly say we don't think you had anything to do with getting Irv Caputo charged with theft in office," I said, sincerely, looking him straight in the eye. But at the same time, wondering what role he may have actually played in the environmental controversy that plagued the Long Bar Harbor project at the county level. If those problems still existed, DeVertollo would be against Irv Caputo in the upcoming election for County Commissioner because Irv was pro-environment.

"No, sir, I certainly would not attempt to interfere with Mr. Caputo's right to run for office over a thing like that. Why, that would be downright illegal, and my ethics are certainly better than that. If I got an environmental problem in one of my developments, I'll stand up and face it like a man—negotiate and abate— you know what I mean? I don't need to engage in, shall we say, scrotal manipulation, with any politician or county staff member to further my own causes."

"Did you know Irv Caputo when he was a member of the county engineering staff?"

He looked at his watch. "Mr. Barchrist, all I can say is you're barking up the wrong tree here—ya know what I mean?" Then he opened his center desk drawer and pulled out four printed baseball passes and signed them. "Here," he said, handing them to me. "While you're in town, why don't you be my guest in our box over at Ed Smith Field. You like the Orioles? Sarasota's pinning its hopes on them this year, with the new stadium we've built and all that. Or maybe you like Pittsburgh better. These two passes here are for my box at McKechnie Field in Bradenton to see the Pirates play. Go ahead. Take your pick. Enjoy yourself."

I didn't know what he was talking about, and it must have showed.

"Baseball, man," he rasped, "baseball—it's spring training. Don't you know you're in the spring training capital of the world? Go. Enjoy. Enjoy." Then he rang for his personal assistant who came in and showed me to the door.

On my way out of the building, I looked up at the atrium, and caught sight of a gaggle of people gathered around a very modernistic glass door on the third floor. They were snapping pictures and they looked like reporters. When the crowd parted for a moment, I could make out the stenciling on the glass door—Alexis Weidenfeld, LPA, Attorney at Law. Then, Lexi suddenly emerged. She saw me standing in the lobby I'm sure, but strangely, immediately turned her back on me. This woman seemed to change from one minute to the next. On the one hand she had made me comfortable in her home. On the other hand, she was now acting like I didn't exist.

In any event, my day was not over. My move from the Regency Inn & Suites to the apartment on Westmoreland had yet to be accomplished, so I spent the rest of the day doing that. In the evening, I made plans for the little vacation I thought I was going to take with Rosanne and Gayna. I bought tickets for a performance of *Man in the Glass Box* at the Golden Apple Dinner theatre. I thought the girls would enjoy that, and for another evening I got tickets to the Sailor's Circus. I skipped the performance scheduled at the Opera House because I didn't think I could stand that, but I hung on to the baseball passes DeVertollo had given me. Baseball might be a nice diversion for Gayna, and if Rosanne got bored, there was always the possibility of a tour through the Ringling Estate. By Saturday, I was all set and waiting for them to arrive, ready to pick them up.

Chapter 14

Moving from the Regency Inn and Suites, with its one king bed and bath, into my new place on Westmoreland was like moving across town to the other side of the tracks for me. It was a giant step upward. No longer did I feel like an itinerate business traveler out of his element, unappreciated, and just waiting until I could get home. I had stocked the cupboards in the kitchen with canned goods, filled the refrigerator with frozen pizzas, and opened all the curtains to let the morning sun into the place. As I passed through my new living room, with its plush mission-style furniture and its southwest dry sand and desert color scheme, I knew Rosanne would see this apartment as a "lucky find" in vacation rentals, especially with the pool being just off the kitchen. To me, there was nothing like pleasing Rosanne. I had a feeling of pride as I walked out to my newly-rented Lincoln, proceeded to the airport, and waited to collect her and Gayna.

It was still early in the morning. The mist was rising from the tarmac. As I waited inside the brand new terminal I was quite pleased I had managed to turn lemons into lemonade by substituting a Florida vacation for the wrecked promise I'd made to spend time with the girls at a lake in Ohio over spring vacation. It seemed my needs were always interfering with their plans to spend time with me, and they were always disappointed. Finally, I had made good on one of my promises to them.

Many people said this "international airport," midway between Tampa and Fort Myers, which had their own airports, was a totally unnecessary political boondoggle supported solely by rent from the off-runway businesses developers had thrown up on the surrounding real estate. To say that ten flights landed here a day was probably an overestimation. Those same people would tell you the airport was much better in the days when your plane simply pulled up to a long out-of-doors conveyor belt protected by an open-to-the-air shed roof, there was no air conditioning, and airport ground crews just rolled a portable gangway out to the aircraft's passenger door.

Now, locals picking up their relatives are obliged to wait at the head of the airport's long, very modern air-conditioned concourse by a huge floor to ceiling aquarium teeming with various tropical specimens. The tank is located just across from a balcony containing an assortment of diverse restaurants, and under the balcony is a roaring waterfall. All quite nice but unnecessary. Passengers disembark onto covered jetways carefully guided up to aircraft portals, and from there they walk up the long concourse to greet their relatives waiting at the gargantuan aquarium. Everyone then just goes down an escalator to the marble baggage claim area.

I confess I was excited waiting. I watched closely for Rosanne and Gayna to make their way up the concourse. Gayna was first, wearing a short yellow sundress, blue tennis shoes and a matching blue visor in her hair. She was carrying a tennis racquet in one hand, an iPod in the other, and had a tiny earphone in her ear. On closer scrutiny, I could see that she wasn't actually walking up the concourse. She was dancing.

Rosanne was behind her burdened with her huge leather purse over one shoulder, a slightly smaller Macy's bag in her other hand, and pulling two roller suitcases. Rosanne was not dancing. Rather, she was looking quite put out because of her struggle with all the things she was carrying and dragging with no help from Gayna. I could tell Rosanne was not in a Florida vacation mode yet. She looked great, but she was dressed like she was going to her office today instead of coming to Florida.

When we got into the car, Rosanne expressed her happiness to see me, but it was clear she was reserving judgment on the supposed little vacation I had cooked up for us. "Well, what's on the agenda?" she asked. "Let me guess. In addition to going to the beach when we can, you've got some work you need me to do to help you out with whatever it is you're working on down here," she said sarcastically.

"Well, as a matter of fact . . ."

I never got to finish my answer because Gayna was so excited, she wouldn't stop jabbering. "Are we gonna see any alligators while we're here? How far from the ocean are we right now? Is our place on the ocean? Wow, look at all these palm trees! What kind are they?"

"Those are Royal Palms," I told her.

"Neat!"

"What are those?"

"Palmettos," I said, "the only palm tree that is native to Florida."

"Really? Neat! So tell me, Pizza Man, what kind of case are you working on down here?"

"It's a bankruptcy case that's turned into a murder case."

"Really? Wow! That's so cool. Are you in any kind of danger?"

"I doubt it. I really don't think so."

"All right," Rosanne interjected. "Winston—both of you—that's enough. Gayna, I don't think we have to get into Winston's work with him. And, Winston, that goes for you too. She's only 14-years-old. She doesn't need to hear about these things."

"About to be 15," Gayna objected.

When we reached my new place on Westmoreland, Rosanne's demeanor began to change. I could feel the skepticism leaving her. She sat on the bed. She went from room to room marveling at the decorating. She opened all the drawers in the kitchen, and when she went outside and saw the pool, she returned with a huge smile on her face. "How did you find this place?" she asked.

"It's a long story. Do you like it?"

"Like it! I love it."

"Good. What do you say we go out and get something to eat now? I know an interesting place just up the road called The Bearded Clam."

The Bearded Clam is an outdoor tiki bar. It's adjacent to the water at a marina behind a building that was once an upscale Holiday Inn Resort. It was complete with an Olympic-sized pool, hot tubs and a large sauna complex. Today, the inn has been rebuilt into small condos offering accommodations to sailors who've docked their boats at the marina and don't want to live on shipboard while docked. Huge sailing yachts are tied up there, not just sloops, but also two-masted yawls and ketches. Filled at all hours of the day, the Bearded Clam rocks at all hours, with bikini-clad 50-year-olds, and somewhat aged but strapping sea-salts, sporting tattoos, grizzly Jimmy Buffet straw hats and tank-tops. The air is filled with the music of a local band.

Gayna's eyes became bigger than saucers when she saw the scene. She plowed straight through the crowd to the gates separating the harbor berths from the tiki bar area and ran out on the dock all the way to the end.

Her mother called after her but she didn't come back. I satisfied myself with trying to locate a place for us to sit in the pool area because the tiki bar itself was too crowded. Next to the pool was a picnic table I felt would fill the bill.

The sun was at its noon strength now and there was another mile-high Sarasota blue sky surrounding it. Life was good. It has never ceased to amaze me, however, how quickly my fortunes can change. On the picnic table was a copy of the morning's *Sarasota Herald Gazette*. As I removed it, I glanced at the front page. Shocked by the headline, I sat down to read it. My stomach began to turn.

—SECOND SARASOTA DEVELOPER FOUND STABBED—

According to the article, Edwin DeVertollo was found murdered in his car in the parking lot behind his office on Friday evening, which was the day I'd visited him.

> "Slumped over the wheel of his Maserati, Edwin DeVertollo was found with a knife in his back. He was one of the key developers in the controversial Long Bar Harbor project on the border between Sarasota and Bradenton. His death comes only days after the murder of Julius Josephski, another of the prime movers in the development.

The article made me queasy. I felt I was going to throw up. I ran for the bathroom, where that's exactly what I did. On my way out, there was Gayna staring at me. "Gawd, Pizza Man, did you know they've got a little floating chapel out there at the end of the pier that you can take out on the bay and get married in?"

"No, Gayna, I didn't know that."

"It's absolutely amazing."

"Maybe so, Gayna, but now I'm afraid we're going to have to leave. Where's your mother?"

Chapter 15

Back at my place, the phone was ringing when we walked in. It was a very upset Jack Rainspring. "You see this morning's paper yet?" he asked. "Edwin DeVertollo's dead, murdered."

"I saw. But why are you so upset? Why are you calling me about it?" I was as nonplussed by the news as Jack was, and for some reason I found his calling to repeat it exasperating.

"Funny coincidence, don't you think? DeVertollo was found stabbed in the back, just like Josephski , and there were no clues—no fingerprints, no nothing, just like with Josephski. DeVertollo was found slumped over. He was in his car, with the engine running around 4:30 p.m. Yesterday. There was a knife between his shoulders, like someone was trying to gut him from behind."

"Okay, okay, but why are you calling to tell me all this?" The call was making me nervous. "Surely you don't think I had anything to do with it, do you?" I was sensitive about my position in what now seemed like The Great Sarasota Developer's Massacre. "How do you know all these details anyway?" I asked. "I didn't see them in the newspaper."

"Lexi Weidenfeld. Oh, by the way, Irv's gone."

"What do you mean Irv's gone?"

"Flown the coop! He packed up his electric toothbrush, all his aftershaves and many of his clothes, took his Oldsmobile and left."

"Left for where?"

"I don't know Winston. That's why I'm calling you. I don't know where he is and I thought you might know."

"Well how would I know? All I know is that he can't just take off like this. I posted a bond for him. You don't think he's jumped bail, do you? Why would he do a thing like that—over a charge like theft in office?"

"Because Lexi Weidenfeld told him to."

"What? Jack, Jack—wait a minute. Let's just start all over from the very beginning. What's Lexi Weidenfeld got to do with this? I didn't even know Irv knew Lexi Weidenfeld, or she him. How does she fit into this?" Actually, I did know Lexi probably knew Irv. I'd found it out when I was snooping around Lexi's house and reading the draft affidavit in her desk drawer that she'd prepared for him to sign.

"Yes, Irv and Lexi know each other. First of all, do you know who she is? She's a real estate attorney who often works with Irv at closings and such."

"Yes, I've met her, and she's quite a bit more than just a real estate attorney. But I didn't know she and Irv worked with each other."

"She's also Mr. Josephski's girlfriend—"

"—Was Josephski's girlfriend—"

"Well, of course, I know he's dead now."

"But did you know they broke up before he was killed?"

"No, but to answer your question as to how she fits in, let me tell you what happened, Winston. I get home last night and Irv was nowhere to be found. So I checked the message machine while waiting for him, and there's this long message from Lexi for Irv. She tells him DeVertollo's been killed and all the details about the crime scene I've already given you. Then she tells Irv that about an hour before DeVertollo was found dead, she saw you come out of DeVertollo's office. Lexi's and DeVertollo's offices are in the same building. His office is on the main floor and her office is three floors above his, but there's this huge open atrium and from her office door she can look down and see everything that goes on down on the main floor. That's how she saw you."

"Yah, I know about that atrium. I was there yesterday, and, in fact, I saw her up above me standing outside her office."

"She told Irv in her phone message she told the police you were there, which she found to be very strange because she knew you were working with Julius Josephski or something like that. She also said she knew you and Irv were working together on his theft in office defense.

"She goes on to tell Irv that somebody witnessed *him* hanging around DeVertollo's car in the parking lot about 25 minutes after she saw you come out of DeVertollo's office. She said the guy fit Irv's description to a T, and she was calling to give him a 'heads up' that the police were probably on their way out to see him."

"Wait a minute! Wait just a damn minute, Jack. How could she have known that?"

"Because she was out there in the parking lot talking to the police when they showed up. They told her they had identified the guy as Irv and were going to go get him."

"It seems like she was trying to tie Irv and me together, implicating us so to speak. How could she have known that Irv knew me or I knew him. I never told her."

"I don't know, Winston. Maybe Irv told her. They were more than just business associates. They were kind of friends. Irv, being the way he is, makes friends with a lot of women in town. They don't consider him a threat and they like to gossip with him."

"What's all that supposed to mean, 'being the way he is'?"

"C'mon, Winston, think! You know what I mean." Irv Caputo is the kind of guy good looking ladies are pals with. They're like girlfriends and Irv is one of the girls. Lexi Weidenfeld supported him in his first run for County Commissioner. It's not unlikely he would have told her about the recent criminal charges against him or that you would be helping Schwartzenkaupf with his case."

"Well, I'm going to have to think a little while about all this, Jack." I hung up flummoxed by the call. I checked other phone messages. There was one from the Sheriff's office. They wanted to see me again. Well, of course, they wanted to see me again in light of all these new developments! No doubt Lexi had told the police she'd seen me come out of DeVertollo's office. Never mind though, they could have easily learned that simply by inquiring of DeVertollo's receptionist for the names of people who had been in and out that day to see him. But why would Lexi want to implicate me?

"Honey, are you all right?" Rosanne asked. "You're white as a sheet and you look peaked. Maybe you ought to lie down. Gayna and I will be outside here at the pool if you need me. She just wants to pack everything she can into this vacation. She loves it, you know. And so do I—so far."

So far, I thought to myself. *Well, we'll see just how much you love it in a few days if they lock me up in the county jail. That's really going to be the test of what you love.* I toyed with the thought of telling her ahead of time what might happen to me, but instead I fell asleep.

When I woke up, it was dark. Light was coming only from a small green shaded desk lamp. Rosanne and Gayna had gone to bed. There was evidence on the table that they had ordered a pizza before doing so. I felt around in the dark for my watch—9:00 p.m. I was wide awake now and voraciously hungry. Fortunately, the pizza was a large, and more than half of it was left—sausage, mushrooms, pepperoni and scallions, with banana-peppers—just the way I liked it. Rosanne was such an angel. She had ordered it this way, just as I like it, even though she and Gayna didn't. She probably assumed I'd wake up and want to eat. The little piles of sausage, scallions and banana-peppers on the box that had been picked off were evidence of her intent. What a lucky man I am.

I knew the police would want to talk to me about DeVertollo's murder. It sounded like Lexi had implicated me. But, there was nothing I could do about it except soldier on. I had come to Sarasota to do a job, and I was going to do it unless and until someone stopped me. But what if someone did try to stop me?"

That thought suggested maybe I should involve Rosanne so she could carry on where I might have to leave off. I decided then and there to include her in my investigation on Mr. Venable's behalf. She might not like the idea, but she had been involved in some of my previous cases and had been very helpful. First thing in the morning, I called the New Band Bank to confirm the meeting I'd previously set up with them. The meeting was set for 1 p.m. that day. I told them I'd be bringing Rosanne.

Chapter 16

Rosanne and I arrived at the New Band Bank of Sarasota at 1 p.m. sharp. I introduced myself as the attorney for Charles Venable. Rosanne introduced herself as his accountant. Rhett Kessler, executive vice president of the New Band Bank of Sarasota, greeted us. He was a very young looking 70-years-old. Tall and fit, he still had most of his hair and a very boyish face. He had started out in the banking business by repossessing vehicles, and risen from that lowly position to a level where his approval was now required on every loan the bank made. During his career, he had hopped among five different banks in the Venice-Sarasota-Bradenton area, each time collecting stock options and various other movable perquisites. He was known by just about everybody in the banking business and all the prominent entrepreneurs in town.

Only recently had he also become known by the bevy of FDIC investigators who had descended on him after the failure of Anchors Away Bank, his previous employer. Just before going under, it had merged with the New Band Bank of Sarasota in order to save its depositors' assets from the effects of the Great Recession. The Feds were now obligated by law to inspect every aspect of that transaction, and the recent sinking of Anchors Away, to make certain no officers or directors had pocketed any money on the side from these events. The reason New Band Bank was keeping Kessler on its payroll was to collect all the toxic loans

Anchors Away had made in its heyday before springing leaks in its reserves.

Kessler had a corner office at New Band very near the vault, which gave him a perfect vantage point from which to ogle the backsides of all the young female tellers as they stood at their stations. He became annoyed when he learned that Rosanne and I were paying him a visit in order to flyspeck his documents. And, that we were looking for mistakes that could hold up or stop foreclosure proceedings on the property out at Long Bar Harbor in which Mr. Venable held an interest as a limited investor. Nevertheless, he did not allow our presence to interrupt his habit of gawking out his door at the female bank tellers. Rosanne was appalled. I was amused.

"Excuse me for just a minute, will you?" he said. Looking through the open door to his office, I could see him outside in the main banking area making a call. His head was bobbing up and down nervously as he talked. Then he came back into his office, all "hale and hearty" again.

"I doubt you'll find anything interesting in those loan documents," he said, craning his neck to glance out his open door every so often. A particularly pretty woman came in to get his signature on a bank draft. As she leaned closely over his shoulder smiling at him from behind, she asked, "Going to church this Sunday, Rhett?"

I thought I saw her eyes flash when she said it.

When she left, Kessler winked at me. "That's Theresa," he said. "We sometimes go to church together."

"Oh, really," I replied. "How nice. What denomination are you?"

"We go to St. Mattress," he answered, laughing lasciviously. "It's the only place we can relax on

Sundays. Hah, ha, hah." He winked again. "Theresa says it makes her feel real spiritual." Rosanne looked appalled once again.

Then Kessler escorted us over to a small table in the corner of his office where there was a stack of copies of notes and mortgages. These presumably were the notes and mortgages Messrs. Josephski and Venable had executed with the Anchors Away Bank before its troubles began, and had been prepared for our inspection. "I personally approved these loans," he said, "and never in a million years thought there'd be any problems with them when I did. Mr. Josephski was one of the biggest developers on the west coast of Florida."

I began picking up the documents and shuffling through them, but what I was reading didn't make any sense. The mortgages were for single family homes and condos on Siesta and Longboat keys.

"Oh, wait a minute," Kessler said, grabbing the top few documents out of my hands and sorting them out. "These instruments were signed in other transactions involving different people. Here just look at the documents on the table, and I'll take these other documents back. Gosh, I hope I haven't violated any federal privacy law or some kind of stupid Sunshine Law or something by showing you somebody else's papers."

Most of the paperwork we actually reviewed looked pretty standard, except I noticed the indemnity clauses, where Josephski was to indemnify my client against breaches caused by Josephski's actions alone, were not initialed by Josephski. There also was no language accelerating the entire amount of the loans upon a breach. That was significant. As a result, if a default occurred, it could be said the papers allowed the borrowers to keep the loans without foreclosure if the defaults were remedied. Neither the notes nor the mortgage papers spoke to the question of how much time the borrowers had to remedy the situation. This was a bad hole in the bank's defenses. Another deficiency was there was no clause stating the partners had to remedy environmental issues to the county's satisfaction before making draws on the loans. Nor, was any time period stated for remedying such issues. The major prohibition on the use of funds was that they had to be employed in the construction of "real estate," not for other uses such as impact fees or site improvements. This was a hook the bank would probably be hanging its hat on in court, along with the fact that the borrowers had defaulted on their payments, although the period they were in default had not gotten extremely long yet.

"What is the bank's position on these papers, Mr. Kessler?" Rosanne asked. "By that I mean, where is there a default that cannot be cured under these papers?"

"Oh, it's very simple," Kessler answered, as he continued to eye the women outside his door. "The mortgagees were behind in their payments, and they used funds drawn down on these loans for prohibited purposes, such as building streets and roads on the site instead of erecting buildings and the like."

"And what evidence do you have proving that the draws were used for streets and roads, instead of the intended purposes?" Rosanne pursued.

"Huh?" Kessler asked. He was clearly distracted by the bevy of beautiful butts outside his door, and not paying very much attention to us at all.

She asked him again. "How are you going to prove they used the bank's money for roads instead of for other matters?"

He brushed off her question dismissively. "Oh, that's quite clear and simple, I think. As we sit here today, there's not a building, foundation or any excavation on the property—only roads."

"But how do you know the money was not used for environmental studies, surveys, architectural fees, or even as the initial down stroke with a building contractor?"

"Really, ma'am, you're getting out of my area of expertise when you raise issues like that. I think I should refer you to our litigators to answer those questions. Outside of negotiating these loans, overseeing document preparation and closing the loans, I had very little to do with them, so I know very little about what happened on these projects. I didn't even personally draw up the loan documents. They came from our legal department."

"You didn't have to approve the documents even though you were the negotiator?" I asked.

"No. That's correct. I didn't. Anchors Away Bank was very anxious to make these loans to Josephski, and very proud of the deal, before it started to go under, that is. We were in competition with other banks, and yes, we were in a hurry. After the negotiations I didn't remain that close to the transaction. All I really know is that great environmental problems arose with this deal after the documents were executed, but just about everyone knows that I guess."

"What can you tell me about the environmental problems?" I asked.

"Well. The Florida Wildlife Federation led the attack. It was joined by the Manatee County Audubon Society and The Save the Manatee Club. The Florida chapter of the Sierra Club also played a big role, as did the Tampa Bay Conservancy. Then EcoLaw, a not-for-profit environmental law firm, got involved. Tree huggers, all of them, but let me tell you, really vituperative tree huggers!

"Everything the developers wanted to do was wrong as far as these groups were concerned. They claimed dredging to build the harbor would kill off valuable sea grass in which seatrout spawned. Tearing out mangroves would ruin the nesting grounds for various kinds of birds—I don't know what they're called, and they also claimed that the fishing for snook, redfish and mackerel would be ruined. They argued it would destroy one of the last refuges for the manatees in Sarasota Bay before they reached the relatively open stretches of Tampa Bay, and that the dolphins would be spooked by putting another harbor in the area.

"But all this was nothing compared to what happened when the politicians got involved and the developers began fighting among themselves. Actually, there were three developers—Julius Josephski, a home builder named Jesus Agronez, and the well-known shopping mall builder, Edwin DeVertello. Your guy, Venable was just the largest outside silent investor of Josephski's as I recall. I don't know if he had anything to do with any of the other developers.

"Anyway, as the story goes, DeVertello became upset about Josephski's plan to develop a plat larger than he was planning to develop for retail and office buildings. DeVertello had planned the hotel and marina with associated shops, and he was afraid Josephski's project would detract from his. So he made an alliance with Agronez to stall the entire development until Josephski felt he either had to give in to DeVertollo by making his retail/office plan smaller, or go belly up. To achieve his goal, DeVertollo supposedly called in chits he had with three of the county commissioners in Manatee County. He got them to temporarily refuse to approve his harbor project, which was the key to the whole deal, until the Manatee County Engineering Division okayed dredging of the harbor. It was all a ruse, you see, to allow DeVertollo to control the whole project, and Josephski's role in it. By manipulating the government, DeVertollo made it look like governmental regulators were holding up the harbor from going forward, when he was actually in control of everything. He hoped the delay would either break Josephski down or destroy him financially. The Division, at the prodding of the Commissioners, refused to approve the harbor on environmental grounds, which made those guys the darlings of all the environmentalists who were whining about the deal. DeVertollo's plan actually did hold Josephski up long enough to ruin him. Now, here you sit, looking for a way to get Josephski out of his obligations to the bank.

"Did Josephski know DeVertollo was behind the whole delay of the project, and that he had called in his chits with the County Commissioners?" I asked.

"Oh sure. Everybody knew about it," Kessler said. But nobody could prove it. Josephski came to me not long ago, wanting to bring his loans current using money he'd borrowed elsewhere. The *Herald Gazette* got wind of it and published a big front page piece on it because it had nothing else to write about—"LONG BAR HARBOR TO MOVE FORWARD AS PLANNED" That caused the whining environmentalists to get their panties in a bunch over the project again. But as you well know, Josephski died before he paid us. Therefore, we are now looking to his co-investors (partners, if you will) for the money, and the whole project still remains stalled. And, that's about as far as my knowledge goes on what's happened to this project."

Kessler's version of what was happening out at Long Bar Harbor couldn't be proven of course. But it was close enough to what Irv Caputo had related to me that a picture was beginning to form in my mind as to what had happened. It also supplied the first evidence I had come across of a possible motive for doing away with Josephski. Apparently, DeVertollo hated him enough to try to kill him, financially speaking, that is.

As it turned out, Josephski had never bothered to update my client about his squabble with DeVertollo. He reported only environmental problems the project was encountering were holding it up. As for putting in access roads, my client had been led to believe the money he was putting into Shops at Long Bar Harbor was all going toward construction of the buildings. Mr. Venable was only an investor in a partnership with Josephski called Shops at Long Bar Harbor Ltd., not a partner in the Long Bar Harbor project itself. Shops at Long Bar Ltd. was one of three partners in LBP on the Bay, which was the lead partnership formed to develop Long Bar Harbor.

When I told Mr. Venable about the battle between Josephski and DeVertollo, he was taken totally by surprise. "Winston," he said, "you've done me well on two fronts—blocking of these foreclosures because of the omissions you've found in the paperwork and the collection of evidence for my suit against the Josephski estate. Stay down there and keep up the good work."

"Right, that's what I'm going to try to do Mr. Venable. I've rented a small apartment because . . ."

"That's just fine, my boy. Go ahead and make yourself comfortable. It's probably cheaper in the long run than a hotel. Don't worry. I'll cover it. Just keep doing what you're doing."

It felt great to have the approval of my client, especially the part about making myself comfortable. What could be more comfortable than having Rosanne down for a few days? Yes, Gayna would be there too, taking the steam out of what otherwise could have been a little romantic diversion in paradise, but it would still be a nice time for Rosanne and me. Painfully gained experience told me the best thing to do was a little pre-planning: restaurants, cultural events, plays, perhaps a visit to Selby Gardens or to the Ringling Museum. Sarasota was supposed to be a very cultural place, I'd heard. They even had an opera house. None of this, however, assuaged Rosanne. She considered her new involvement in Mr. Venable's matter as the real reason I had brought Gayna and her to Florida. Suddenly, she was thinking that my ultimate goal in bringing them to Sarasota was not to have some vacation time for the three of us, but rather to have her work on my case for Mr. Venable with me. What had started out as a very warm reunion between the two of us now began to take on the attributes of an icy winter in an Alaskan cabin.

The best tactic I could think of to counter this was to stay away for a day or so. Although I was in no hurry to do it, I decided I would leave our little enclave on Westmoreland the following day. I would then show up at the police station in answer to the message that was on my machine when I'd returned from the Bearded Clam the evening I'd learned about DeVertollo's death.

Chapter 17

The next morning it was raining—no, storming. The street was filling up like a creek and the palm trees were leaning low behind the wind. Disappointed, Gayna looked out into the yard, watching the heavy drops make little craters in the sandy lawn, longing for the beach. She didn't seem to hear me when I told her that in Sarasota, one minute you could almost be having a hurricane, and in the next, the sun could be shining in a mile-high blue sky.

The girls decided to go to Mote Marine without me, and I made it quite clear I was going to the police station. Then we'd see about the weather and the beach, *assuming they let me out of the police station.* Mote Marine's an interesting place, especially for someone who doesn't live in the area. It's actually a scientific nautical research station for the northern part of the Gulf of Mexico. Supposedly there are 99 dolphins residing in Sarasota Bay. All of them have been tagged by the people at Mote Marine, and all of them have names. They swim up beside your boat and follow you on the water, lazily arching their backs against the waterline as they swim.

When I arrived, to my chagrin Ralph Kriegelman was there again. I don't know why, but I didn't expect to see him.

"What?" I asked. "Did Edwin DeVertollo live at the Ritz too?"

"Interesting, Mr. Barchrist, that you would bring up Edwin DeVertollo. Why?"

Why indeed, I thought to myself. That's what I get for trying to be a wise guy. I had just assumed they wanted to talk to me about DeVertollo. Maybe they didn't. Suddenly, I got the same feeling a contestant on a game show must get when he hears the buzzer go off because he's given the wrong answer and just lost $20,000. I remembered the proverb my old law school professor used to try to inculcate in me. "To assume, Winston, is to make an ASS out of YOU and Me." Time to just shut up.

Kriegelman led off the interrogation. "Just to let you know, you're not the only suspect in this case. We went out to the New Band Bank to check out the mortgage activities Alexis Weidenfeld has been involved in. And, lo and behold, when we went to look at some of the mortgages she'd signed, not only did her prints appear on them, but yours did too. It kind of connects the two of you, and we just wanted to ask you about that."

"Well, well, I—I don't know what to say to you about that." I heard myself stuttering but I didn't know why I was. I guess it was just out of complete surprise. H*mph*, I thought. *The police in this opulent little paradise of a town bend over backward to protect its rich patricians, but when it comes to work-a-day plebes like me or my friend Irv, a "nobody" who shows promise of winning a powerful county commissioner's position, they crash into his office and arrest him on vague political charges framed by some political retainer of the rich and powerful. As for people like me, they're not above coming up with outrageous stories like my fingerprints being on Lexi Weidenfeld's bank documents. It's Chicago-type politics, but with the sheen of southern manners rubbed over it. Here in Dixie, where everyone is supposed to be polite, the schnooks still get the hooks, while the fat cats wield the big bats.* Weidenfeld was a fat cat who mattered.

Josephski was also a fat cat, but he didn't matter anymore because he was dead. Irv Caputo and I were just schnooks. How could my fingerprints have gotten on mortgage documents Alexis Weidenfeld signed?

Sheriff's Deputy Anton LaFarge walked in holding a file and sat down at his desk very matter-of-factly. For a long time he said nothing, apparently just reading through the papers in the folder. Finally, he began.

"Mr. Barchrist, I see you've got some guests," he said. "Who are they?"

I don't know why I felt this was an embarrassing interference with my privacy, but I did. Maybe it was because Rosanne and I weren't married. Maybe it was because Gayna was a very nice looking healthy pre-teen. Or maybe it was because I was a jerk, but I quickly decided this was not the time to be flippant.

"Rosanne Harmon is my friend, and Gayna is her daughter. I had promised to take them on a little spring vacation in Ohio, but we had to change our plans because of your office's request that I stay in Sarasota. So they have come down here to be with me."

"And we noticed you've moved," continued the deputy.

"Yes, a friend found the place I'm now in for me. I believe I called in and reported my move to you."

"And who would that friend be?"

"Mr. Irv Caputo."

"Aha!" Kriegelman chortled.

"Sh, sh," ordered LaFarge, looking at Ralph.

"And just to refresh our notes, can you explain to me what it was that brought you to Sarasota in the first place?"

"Yes. I'm an attorney. My client in Ohio sent me here to discuss some business with Julius Josephski. But when I got here, I found Mr. Josephski dead—

murdered, I believe—in his rooms at the Ritz Hotel. Since I was the one who found the body, your office asked me to remain in town until certain matters concerning the death could be cleared up."

"What type of business did you come here to discuss with Mr. Josephski?"

"It was legal business, protected by the attorney-client privilege, so I can't say."

"Mr. Barchrist, we've done a little of our own research into this attorney-client argument of yours. Didn't that privilege die with your client."

"I couldn't say as I stand here. I'd have to do some research on that myself. But you need to understand that it was not Mr. Josephski who was my client. My client is Charles Venable of Columbus, Ohio. He's the one entitled to the protection of the attorney client privilege."

"How do you know Mr. Caputo?"

"I met him here one day when I was having lunch—out at Moore's Restaurant, I believe."

"You did not know him before?"

"No, I met him for the first time while I was in town."

And did you know a man named Edwin DeVertollo?"

"I met him three days ago."

"At his office?"

"Yes."

"Why were you at Mr. DeVertollo's office?"

"Mr. Caputo wound up being arrested for theft or fraud in public office, or something like that, from the time he worked for Manatee County's engineering office. He asked me to help him with the charges against him because he knew I was a lawyer, but I couldn't because I have no license to practice law in Florida. So I was going to contact a Sarasota lawyer named Schwartzenkaup, and help him with the leg work on Mr. Caputo's case, which led me to Mr. DeVertollo's office."

This was a little bit of a stretch, but I felt comfortable saying it. It was actually pre-case investigative work I was doing in order to fill Schwartzenkaup in on the facts before he was actually hired.

"Was Mr. Caputo at Mr. DeVertollo's office with you?"

"No."

"Did you know Mr. Caputo was in or around Mr. DeVertollo's building on the day you visited with Edwin DeVertollo?"

"No."

"Did you know Mr. Josephski and Mr. DeVertollo were partners in a project called Long Bar Harbor?"

"I did."

"Well, this just gets better and better, doesn't it?" Kriegelman interrupted, unable to contain himself any longer. "Here, we've got a man claiming to be a lawyer experienced enough to deal with Julius Josephski over business matters, when actually our investigation shows he's just an ambulance chaser from Columbus, Ohio. He comes into town, and Mr. Josephski winds up dead with this man at the scene. Then he serendipitously meets a man named Irving Caputo, whom he claims he did not know before coming here, and Caputo just happens to have ties to both Josephski and DeVertollo. As everyone knows from the papers, Mr. DeVertollo did his best to ruin Mr. Caputo a few years ago when he ran for county commissioner in Manatee County. And when someone from Mr. DeVertollo's organization files charges against Mr. Caputo for theft in office, Mr. Barchrist here winds up at DeVertollo's office, claiming to be helping Mr. Caputo out with his legal defense, even though Mr. Barchrist has no license to practice law in Florida. An hour later, DeVertollo winds up dead in his car, and Mr. Barchrist says he didn't even know that Caputo was there that day.

"I firmly believe Barchrist came to Sarasota to put Josephski and DeVertollo out of business any way he could," Kriegelman said. "And that includes murder if necessary, and that he conspired with Irving Caputo to do so. He visits Mr. Josephski at the Ritz, and Mr. Josephski winds up dead. He goes into Mr. DeVertollo's office three days ago to make sure he's there, and he comes out and tells Mr. Caputo that DeVertollo's in, so Caputo can wait around for DeVertollo in the parking lot!"

"Ralph, just be quiet," demanded Deputy LaFarge. Then he turned to me and asked....

"I'm not an ambulance chaser, and I resent that," I responded.

"You say you didn't know Mr. Caputo was at Mr. DeVertollo's office on the day you were there? Is that correct?"

"Yes, it's correct! And I'll tell you something else I just learned from Kriegelman. That it was somebody from DeVertollo's organization who filed the criminal charges against Irv Caputo. I didn't know that either. That's what I went to Edwin DeVertollo's office to find out."

"Well," continued LaFarge, "just for the record, what have you got to say about the theory Mr. Kriegelman just expounded? It seems to make sense, doesn't it?"

"No, Deputy LaFarge," I replied. "It does not make sense. In fact, it's pure circumstantial rubbish. If I came to Sarasota to put Mr. Josephski and Mr. DeVertollo out of business, who was I working for, and why would that person want these men out of business?

Apparently, according to Kriegelman here, Mr. Caputo had a motive for wanting Mr. DeVertollo dead, but why? There's nothing proving he even knew Mr. Josephski, or that he ever had any dealings with him. As to the question of whether I happened to meet Irving Caputo just by chance, there's a witness to the fact that that is exactly what happened."

"And who might that be?" asked LaFarge.

"A man named Jack Rainspring," I answered. "And, now, may I leave?"

"Yes, you can go, but we're going to have to continue to keep in touch," said LaFarge. "We're going to want to talk with Mr. Rainspring, also."

"Wait a minute. Wait one minute here," piped up Kriegelman. "Surely, you've got enough to hold this man right now!"

"No, Ralph, I'm afraid we don't," said LaFarge. "There's not enough to support an arrest, and we can't just hold him on suspicion. A decent lawyer would have him out of here within hours."

"I think he's right, Ralphie," I chimed in. "Even an ambulance chaser would know that, and I'm no ambulance chaser, buddy."

As I stood up to leave, Kriegelman quickly moved his chair back with a loud scraping noise. Looking back over my shoulder, I caught LaFarge with his hand on his mouth, stifling a laugh.

Chapter 18

Just as I had predicted to Gayna in the morning, as I stepped out of police headquarters the storm was over and the sun was shining. My thoughts turned to Rosanne. Maybe it was time to attempt to make up with her. Maybe it was time to call her and discuss going to the beach after Mote Marine. But before that, I decided to celebrate the successful outcome of my meeting at the police station with a little lunch. After all, I was still a free man. They had not required me to stay in their lockup over the DeVertollo tragedy, and like all my times of victorious accomplishment, I had become ravenously hungry.

Just down the street was the Main Bar Sandwich Shop, a little lunch place that had been on Main Street for decades. It was one of those places that has its walls covered with black and white photographs of notables who've eaten there over the years—in this case, mostly circus performers.

I stepped inside and slid into one of the booths for four that line its walls along a long walkway leading from the front to the back of the narrow lunch room. With my huge girth, I filled one entire side of the booth. I ordered a bowl of barley soup, two Reuben sandwiches, a large order of fries, a sweetened iced tea and a mint chocolate chip sundae—two scoops—for desert. As I was sitting there contentedly eating my lunch and thinking about Johnson Horseman, for some reason, my cell rang.

It was Jack Rainspring. "You heard anything from Irv?" he asked. "I've made a few calls looking for him, but without any luck."

"No, I haven't heard from Irv. Who've you called?"

"Oh, his office, Lexi Weidenfeld and Schwartzencaup's office. Nobody knows where he is. I even called his mother in Indiana. There's neither hide nor hair of him anywhere. The police were here, but there was nothing I could tell them."

"I was just at the police station myself. They didn't say much about Irv, but they really got their panties in a bunch when I told them I knew him, especially the detective from the Ritz Hotel."

"You mean Ralphie Kreigelman?" Jack laughed.

"Yah, you know him?"

"The only thing that makes Ralph Kreigelman dangerous is his own stupidity," Jack opined. "Listen, if you hear from Irv, let me know right away, will you?"

"I will for sure, Jack. Hey, before you hang up, do you know anything about a guy named Johnson Horseman? He fancies himself as a descendant of some important Seminole Indian from southwest Florida." A long silence followed my question.

"Jack?"

"Yah, listen to me Winston. Johnson Horseman is a guy you want to stay away from."

"What do you mean?"

"Maybe I can tell you more when I see you. For now, just heed my warning. Keep clear of Johnson Horseman." He hung up.

Suddenly it occurred to me to call Stanley Schwartzenkaupf. I planned to introduce myself, tell him about the charges against Irv Caputo, and about the information I'd picked up at the sheriff's office. I'd also tell him how Ralph Kreigelman had managed to blab about how someone in DeVertollo's organization had manufactured the theft in office charge against Irv. I also planned to tell him that I'd tried to get this information from DeVertollo himself when I was at his office but I hadn't gotten to first base with him.

But Schwartzenkaup had a surprise for me when I got through to him. "Mr. Barchrist, I feel it would be in everybody's best interest if you and I didn't go any further with this."

"But Irv was hoping to hire you, and I could assist you as an investigator since I am a lawyer. I just don't have a license to practice law in Florida."

"No," he said, "I don't think that would be a good idea at all."

"But Mr. Schwartzenkaup," I said. "Why do you feel that way?"

"Let's just say I do. In fact, I think it would be a good idea to terminate this call right now."

"Okay then. If that's what you want. I'll let Irv know," and I hung up. I did not let on that I had no idea where Irv was. Nor did I let Schwartzenkaup know I knew somebody in DeVertollo's organization had filed the theft in office charges against Irv. Frankly, it was pretty shocking that Stanley Schwartzenkaup had fired me before he'd even hired me, and he had done so with no explanation. Had someone from DeVertollo's organization gotten to him after I left DeVertollo's office, or was there something even more menacing at work here?

Given Schwartzenkaup's attitude, I had nothing left to do for the day but follow through on my plan to make up with Rosanne. While I was still at the Main Bar Sandwich Shop, I called her at Mote Marine on her cell to see if she and Gayna wanted to go to the beach. They were just finishing the manatee show when Rosanne answered. She was still being testy.

"Marinda called," she announced with ice in her voice.

"Marinda? Why did she call you?"

"Because you haven't been answering your cell," she spat back at me.

Marinda is my secretary, assistant and all-purpose person, who takes care of things for me in my Columbus office. I hired her to do typing years ago when she was working for Molly Maids cleaning the office, and she's turned out to be a real savior on the typing. I have no compunctions about leaving her in charge to answer the phone and take messages when I'm out of the office. She really knows how to keep my business private from others, but she's a little dense on anything else that calls for using good judgment. "What did she say when she called?" I asked.

"That somebody named Johnson Horseman has been trying to get hold of you. She says he's called three times wanting to talk to you again or maybe 'have another meeting.' She said she didn't know what it was all about but it sounded important, so she thought she ought to call you."

"Okay, thanks—I can take care of that from here."

"Who's Johnson Horseman?"

"He's a naturalist from Sarasota, a conservationist. He's with some wildlife organization—you know, a tree hugger or someone like that. I'll tell you more about him when I see you. In the meantime, are you outside where you can see the weather? It's great now. We should go to the beach. I can pick you and Gayna up there in about an hour. That will give me time to get back to the apartment to get our suits."

My suggestion met with a long silence. Then grudgingly, Rosanne said okay, but she made it clear that she was only doing this for Gayna. "We'll be waiting for you at the main entrance."

Man! When that woman got angry at you, it wasn't easy to break the ice but apparently I'd done it. She wasn't going to let her exasperation with my involving her in my work ruin a nice vacation in Sarasota for her daughter.

Remembering Jack Rainspring's warning to me about Horseman, I decided I needed to know more information about the man before answering his calls. That meant firing up Trudy Fischel, my personal computer geek back in Ohio, to get information for me once again. Putting me on to Kit-Kat when I called her once before turned out to be a base hit. Maybe we could convert that into a double if she was able to dredge up more information about Johnson Horseman than I already knew.

I called her but there was no answer. This often happened with Trudy because she was sleeping. She spent her days asleep, and her nights awake until all hours working on various projects for which people paid her, sometimes big bucks, for breaking into corporate or government computers and such. I should have known. The best time to get hold of her was not during the day, but around 4:00 a.m.

So there truly was nothing left for me to do today but go to the beach and wait until early in the morning to call her. But first I had to go home to get everybody's bathing suits. I backed out of my diagonal parking space on Main Street and drove west to the Tamiami Trail, turned right and pulled up to the light at Gulf of Mexico Drive. Behind me there was a white Toyota Avalon with smoked windows, making it impossible to see the driver. *Back in Ohio*, I thought to myself, *that was against the law. Drivers were not permitted to drive around hidden from the police by this type of sun-protecting glass.* When the light changed, I headed north on the Trail out toward Westmoreland and our apartment.

I decided that after I picked up the girls at Mote Marine, we would go to the beach at Lido Key, which is the closest beach to downtown Sarasota. As I left Westmoreland, I drove south and picked up the Trail again south of our place at a little intersection where Westmoreland joined the Trail diagonally, stopping to search in my left rear view mirror for oncoming traffic on the Trail.

There I caught it. Was it my imagination or what? As I looked in the rear view mirror, I thought I glimpsed the same white Toyota Avalon with smoked windows I'd seen behind me when I left the Main Bar Sandwich Shop downtown. I drove south toward town on the Trail and turned right when I reached Gulf of Mexico Drive, went across the Ringling causeway bridge and down into St. Armand's Circle. A quarter of the way around the circle, I turned right, onto Gulf of Mexico Drive again, and proceeded across the bridge over New Pass, at which time I realized I had gone too far. The turn-off to Mote Marine, where I was picking up the girls was before New Pass, not after it. I pulled into the driveway apron at Longboat Club Road to turn around and head back in the other direction. As I was headed back to the bridge at New Pass, I was surprised to see the same white Toyota with smoked windows that had been behind me on the mainland, turning out of Longboat Club Road and heading south behind me again. Or was it the same Toyota? After a while, all these white cars looked the same, and in Florida, every third car had heavily tinted windows. In any event, as soon as I passed back over the bridge at New Pass, I caught sight of the turn-off to Mote Marine on my left, and I turned down the road.

I did not come to the conclusion that the white Toyota Avalon was actually following me until I passed it going out Mote Marine Drive, after I had Rosanne and Gayna in my car. I was headed back down the road from Mote Marine to Gulf of Mexico Drive when I saw it coming down the road the other way. I quickly drove back into St Armand's Circle and parked on a side street from where I could see the main road going back into the Circle. Sure enough, within minutes the white Toyota had turned around and was headed back into the Circle after me.

"Winston, what are we doing?" Rosanne sounded exasperated.

"I think we're being followed for some reason, Rosanne, and I'm trying to throw them off our trail."

"Followed by whom?" Rosanne demanded.

"I don't know."

"Cool," Gayna piped up from the back seat.

"Well, what are we going to do?" Rosanne asked.

"We're going to go to the beach," I said. "I think we can get over there by using some of these back streets. Keep your eyes peeled for a white Toyota Avalon with heavily tinted windows, and if you see it, let me know right away."

"Cool," said Gayna again.

"Yeah, that's real cool," said Rosanne. "When are we going to have a vacation without any of your usual intrigue, Winston?"

"No big deal, Rosanne. If we can make it to the beach without them spotting us on the way, we'll have the whole afternoon to ourselves there, among the beachgoers. They'll never spot us."

"Cool," said Gayna. "I heard that one whole section of this Lido Beach is a nude beach."

"Well you can just forget about ever seeing that, miss," Rosanne advised.

Nobody spotted the white Toyota on our drive through the back streets over to the beach. Fortunately, the rest of the day passed without incident. Slowly, things even calmed down enough between Rosanne and me that she even consented to letting me take the two of them to dinner at the Columbia on St. Armand's Circle.

Chapter 19

The next morning, I made a point of getting up before 4 a.m., so I could make a connection with Trudy, who was probably just getting ready to go to sleep. When she answered her phone, I described the meeting I'd had two weeks ago with Johnson Horseman out at Linger Lodge, and asked her to see what she could find on him—newspaper articles, tax returns, Florida Wildlife Federation records, other living relatives and such. I also told her about the Wikipedia article I'd found about him.

"You call Kit-Kat like I suggested?" she asked.

"I did."

"I know you did, because she called me to check you out. She wanted to be sure you could be trusted because you seemed like such a skeptic to her. Heard she took you on a little paranormal gig down there. She was really into that stuff when I knew her in New York. Nobody believed her. In fact, she did some time for supposedly ripping off a widow living in the Gracie Mansion area of Carl Shurrz Park by performing séances to contact her deceased husband to the tune of $10,000 per connection. Used a hologram or something like that. Thing about it was, there were other reliable sources who also claimed to have seen the husband after his death, but nobody ever really communicated with him."

"Well," I said, "I, for one, have a decent level of confidence in Kit-Kat when it comes to her paranormal activities. In fact, that little 'paranormal gig' she took me on, as you call it, actually may have resulted in making a connection with someone from the nether world. We had gone out to this little ghost town called Micanopy looking for a Seminole Indian named John Horse, who I now know was supposedly the great, great, great grandfather of Johnson Horseman, and instead we supposedly made a connection with a recently deceased man named Julius Josephski, the man I came down here to meet with. He was murdered while I was here."

"Winston, my dear, are you sure you haven't just gotten your hands on some bad Seminole peyote to use while you're down there? I wouldn't put it past Kit-Kat to . . ."

"No, actually, Kit-Kat has been very helpful to me in a lot of ways. . ."

"...by playing one of her frisky little tricks on you."

"No, it's not that, Trudy. I'd ask Kit-Kat for help here, but I'd like to find out is if he's one of those illusionists—you know, a paranormal trickster who plies his trade with mirrors, sleight of hand, holograms and such. Kit-Kat won't accept that idea for a minute because she's so into the paranormal."

"Why are you trying to check him out?"

"Because I've been tipped off by Kit-Kat and another person I consider to be a friend that I should stay as far away from him as possible. But they won't tell me why."

"Okay, Winston, but this is going to cost you. You know it's election season right now, with the primaries and all, and I've got Republicans, Democrats and super-pacs of every ilk breathing down my neck for information. They're all looking for dirt on the other party's candidate."

"Don't worry. I can pay. That is, Mr. Venable will pay. This could be important to his interests down here.

I have reason to believe the environmentalists in the area played a role in the financial demise of the man my client sent me down here to meet."

"Whatever, Winston, just don't be looking for any breaks on the bill this time."

"Trudy, you know you can trust me—trust me to pay your bill that is, not trust me to not turn you in for breaking the computer privacy laws."

"Very cute, Winston. Just remember the reverse of Ruth in the Bible, 'Where I go you go.'"

Just as Trudy and I hung up, the birds started singing. It was still dark out, but it was that hesitant gray darkness just before the dawn. I opened the front door and walked out into the driveway that led around back to the coach house where we were staying. Suddenly, I heard the newspaper slap on the driveway as the deliveryman drove by on Westmoreland. I began walking toward the paper intending to retrieve it and to put it on the front stoop of the main house, and then I saw it. The white Toyota Avalon with the dark tinted windows was parked across the street. I couldn't see if anyone was in the car. I thought very carefully what to do. I did not want to let this opportunity to discover who was driving the car pass. I heard the words I would say, almost as if I was rehearsing them. I would open the door and say, "Is there something I can do for you? I know you're following me. What is it you want?"

Slowly I began moving toward the car, crossing the street, still in my bathrobe, pajamas and slippers. A warm breeze was blowing off the bay, across the street and into my face as I walked. Through the side window I could barely make out a shape or shadow inside the car. It wasn't moving. I strained my eyes to see if the shape held a weapon. Still it didn't move.

"Hello? Hello. Hey in there. Hello?" I called from outside the door. Nothing! No movement, no voice returning my call. Nothing. It seemed like something inside was pressed up against the window. I knew I should have gone back into the house and called the police, but something possessed me, almost as if I was obsessing about this car. I grabbed the door handle and quickly opened the door, expecting to do—I don't know what—if I found myself facing a gun.

Irv Caputo's body fell out into the street. It was him leaning up against the door. He was bloody around his neck and blue in the face. I quickly checked for a pulse. He wasn't dead—yet.

I flew back to the coach house as quickly as a man weighing 340 pounds can and dialed 911, and followed it with a call directly to the police. Gayna appeared in the hallway from the bedroom.

"Hey, Pizza Man. What's up?"

"Not now, Gayna. Not now. Go back to bed." But it was too late. Jack was out of the box. Rosanne appeared behind her with a concerned look on her face. Within seconds, I heard sirens, and the spinning red bubble lights of emergency vehicles making light patterns on the walls in the gray morning.

I walked out to the street to greet the squad and to identify Irv. Efficiently they rolled him onto a stretcher, hooked him up to oxygen and began going over his vital signs. Irv was not conscious. "Is this how you found him?" one of the med techs asked.

"I opened the car door and he just fell out into the street all bloody like that," I replied.

Feverishly, the ambulance driver meticulously searched Irv's body for evidence of a gunshot or stab wound. He kneaded Irv's neck carefully with his fingers feeling for a knife slash, all the time being careful not to move his head.

"No broken neck," he finally said. "Looks like someone tried to garrote him though—someone who was too weak to finish the job."

"Is he going to live?" I asked.

"Don't know," said the med tech casually. "He's still pretty blue."

Within ten minutes, Deputy LaFarge arrived. "We picked up the name Irving Caputo over the radio in connection with this emergency run," he announced. "Tell me, Mr. Barchrist—why is it you seem to be winding up right in the middle of these things so much?"

"He's been following me around since I left the police station yesterday, and then, I just found him like this about 5 this morning."

"While you were in your pajamas?"

"Yes, as you probably know, I've been staying in the coach house right behind that house over there," I said, pointing.

"Yes, we know."

The deputy then proceeded to search the Toyota. He found a piece of piano wire on the floor behind the front seat. I went back into the house where I was greeted by a phone call from Trudy. "Well, that was quick," I said. "Have you got something for me on my friend, Johnson Horseman already?"

"Matter of fact, I do," she chortled. "Remember that Wikipedia article you mentioned about him?"

"Yes."

"Well, Wikipedia is an encyclopedia open to contributions from the public. So often people will write in with facts about the subject of an article, and others will write in complaining the facts are untrue and should be removed. You can read all about these skirmishes in the footnotes on these pages, until such time as the Wikipedia board determines if the facts are true or not. But while the board is making its decision, the facts are removed from the main body of the article, but references to them will still remain in the footnotes under a special symbol you can click on to read the disputed facts."

"And? C'mon, Trudy, just tell me without all the technical details. Something just happened that's got me pretty upset right now."

"Okay—well, listen to this. Here's some deleted facts on your boy you can find if you comb the footnotes to his Wikipedia article:

'Johnson Horseman distinguished himself as a conservator of Seminole lands in the late 1950s when he was imprisoned for allegedly murdering an official of the Gainesville City Council who sought to convert Micanopy, Florida, into a hotel resort for visitors to the nearby University of Florida—Gainesville campus. The project would have destroyed the town of Micanopy which was built on the site of Indian settlements going back to 1569. There were still ancient Indian mounds in the town cemetery. The conviction of Johnson Horseman was overturned five years later as a part of one of the first cases in which DNA evidence was found admissible. After his conviction was overturned, Horseman moved to Sarasota where he established a Florida wildlife and Indian conservation group for which he is known today. He then built a home in nearby Arcadia, Florida.'"

"So you're saying it's possible he could be dangerous if the sentences deleted from the Wikipedia article are true. Right?"

"No, it's not me saying that, Winston. It's you."

Chapter 20

Irving Caputo lingered on at Sarasota Memorial Hospital fighting for his life. He couldn't talk because the piano wire used to garrote him had severed his vocal chords. Eventually, he regained enough strength between his groggy barbiturate-induced naps to write a few lines now and again before falling back to sleep. That's when the police began questioning him incessantly.

"No." He didn't know "for certain" who had tried to kill him. His garroting with the piano wire had come, "without warning" from behind.

Had he rented the Toyota so he couldn't be readily recognized from the street as he drove by?

"Yes," he wrote.

Where was his Oldsmobile?

No answer.

Why had he left home? "Because of Lexi Weidenfeld's call."

Where did he stay after he left? Again, he wrote no answer.

Was he following me? "Yes."

Why? "DeVertollo told me to."

Why? "DeVertollo forced me to," he wrote bearing down hard on the pencil.

Had he killed DeVertollo? "No." Did he know DeVertollo was dead? "No."

Who did he think had filed criminal charges against him? No answer.

Again, who had charged him with theft in office?
"DeVertollo maybe."

Why DeVertollo? "Not to run again maybe."

Then, slowly he fell into a coma. He couldn't answer anything in writing anymore. He died shortly thereafter. The nurse who found him dead also found a feeble pencil drawing on the floor beside the bed, made with an unsteady hand. He must have come out of his coma during the night long enough to draw it, the doctor said. No one could decipher what it was, but days later, it came to me as I studied the tremulous drawing. It was a dream catcher—an attempted representation of a dream catcher.

The Irving Caputo funeral was well attended by employees of the Manatee County Engineering Department, people from his real estate office and old friends, as well as neighbors. Lexi Weidenfeld and others associated in various ways with the home building and sales industry in the area were also in attendance. Jack positively lost control of himself. I've never seen a tough-looking big man literally blathering in tears. He was a mess. I hadn't known Irv long, and I guess I wasn't as distraught by his death as the rest of the people at the funeral, except for the fact that Irv's death practically happened on my doorstep. Instead, as the service proceeded, I was absorbed in thought about myself and my current situation.

If I was ever going to get out of Sarasota, and back to the relative peace of Columbus, without first going to trial for one or more of these strange deaths, it was time for me to take a reckoning. It no longer seemed coincidental that I happened to be at the scene every time, or shortly before, each of these men died. First it was Josephski, then DeVertollo and now Irv. Who had a motive for doing who in, and what was the motive? The answers might help me get to the bottom of all this and get me off the sheriff's radar. Unless I could be considered somebody's "hit man," I had no such motives.

One piece of the puzzle still remained, but it was so disconnected it did not even resemble any of the other pieces. That was Johnson Horseman. Why did he want to speak with me again, even to the point of calling my office in Columbus, looking for me? It appeared I was going to have to talk to him once more, even though I didn't relish the thought after having met him once, and after hearing Trudy Fishel's latest on him. I couldn't get the dream I had that night I slept over at Lexi's house out of my mind. Could the ghost we had supposedly seen in Micanopy really have been the ghost of John Horse, Horseman's half Seminole, black ancestor, instead of Julius Josephski, as Lexi claimed? Horseman himself showed no signs of being a person of color, although he claimed Seminole heritage quite determinedly. I thought he was just a weird person when we first met, but after hearing what Trudy had found out about him in the Wikipedia article, I had to admit I was afraid of him. That fear was exacerbated when I thought about the description of his arrest record that Kit-Kat had previously mentioned to me when I first asked her about him.

I glanced over at Jack Rainspring who was still sobbing. He was truly a hulk of a fellow, and when he wasn't crying, he looked plenty tough. If he were to go with me to meet Horseman, that would go a long way toward making me feel safer. But what if Horseman found his presence objectionable? What would Horseman do if I showed up at the meeting with a stranger?

Perhaps Jack could come along under cover, so to speak. It might seem odd, and like an awful lot of trouble to go to, but it would make me feel safer in a second meeting with Johnson Horseman. Jack could protect me if he had to by calling 911 or by personally intervening. He would have to hide somewhere nearby within earshot of our conversation, at least with me in his line of sight. But what would Jack think of all this if I asked him for this kind of help? Would he write me off as being paranoid—maybe even a little wacko—or would he just not want to get involved?

I knew Jack Rainspring had a reputation for helping other people out. It could be physically helping elderly couples move into a semi-care facilities; watching someone's home while they away; walking dogs for people; protecting small children on the neighborhood watch; hauling furniture for the Methodist Church flea market sale, or even cooking meals for shut-ins. He was a kind man, but also a big guy who was plenty tough, but who had a hard time saying "no" when someone asked him for something. Irv had told me all this. So, I decided that after the funeral was over, I would wait a few days and then call him to ask for his help. What was the worst he could say, except "no?"

As the funeral ended, Jack invited people over to the house for food and drink and to exchange remembrances. This seemed odd, as he was in no condition to entertain anyone. Alexis Weidenfeld, who was also extending invitations to the home of Jack and Irv, made it quite clear, however, that she had paid to have a small event catered at the house and everyone was invited. I did not realize how close Lexi and Irv had been until I heard this.

Chapter 21

Even though Jack Rainspring had spoken negatively about Johnson Horseman once before in a short conversation, for some reason, I had assumed the two did not know each other. Clearly, however, I must have been wrong. The long silence that ensued when I attempted to enlist Jack's assistance for the second meeting I wanted to have with Horseman was very discomfiting. I did not, at first, explain why I felt I needed Jack's help, but the length of his reticence after my question made it obvious there was something personal between Horseman and him I didn't know about.

Look, Winston," he finally replied, "I think you should just stay away from him."

"Well, I've already met with him once, and he wants to see me again."

"Nonetheless, I'd steer clear of him this time."

"But, Jack, Horseman may hold the key to the riddle of the murders that are keeping me here. I also think he may have been involved in what happened to Irv." I then explained my perception of Irv's last communication that it was a drawing of a dream catcher. I went on to explain what a dream catcher was and that Horseman had introduced me to the concept during our first meeting, seemingly for no apparent reason.

"He told me, Jack, that he had been like a 'dream catcher' for years when it came to protecting Long Bar Harbor, keeping the high rises away, blocking the break-up of the land into condos, and building of shopping malls and unnatural harbors. He told me there's something beautiful about Florida's natural foliage and wildlife that all the developers want to spoil, and that he tries to make sure such nightmares burn up before they can ruin his dreams."

"I don't know," Jack replied, reconsidering. "If it was going to be me meeting with him, I'd take somebody with me I suppose. I'd also make sure the meeting took place in a very public place. Okay, I'll help you, but just remember, I told you this is not the sort of man you want to get mixed up with."

"Jack, I hear you but I'm afraid I don't understand. Tell me. Why are you, in particular, so adamant about staying away from him?"

"Well, you remember, when we were talking at Moore's Restaurant about all the controversy surrounding the development of Long Bar Harbor? We were telling you about all the environmental issues surrounding the project and all the politics involved? At the time all that was going on, Irv was working for the County Engineers office. I didn't see it or hear it, but according to Irv, Johnson Horseman threatened him to not approve the project if he knew what was good for him."

"Did he threaten violence?"

"I don't know, but Irv seemed very scared and I know he took him seriously."

"Hm—very interesting," I said. "So you're saying Irv and Horseman knew each other."

"Yes, they did, and Horseman threatened him."

"And did Irv follow Horseman's demand?"

"Well, I don't know if it was because of Horseman, or because of something else, but the project never got approved while Irv was with the County Engineer's office."

"So, basically, Irv's last drawing, which I think was an attempt to draw a dream catcher, could have been a sign to let people know Horseman was somehow involved in what happened to him. Maybe Horseman killed him," I speculated.

"But why?" Jack blurted. "Irv never okayed the project while he was with the county engineer, and the project never went through. So where's the motive for Horseman to do Irv in?"

"I don't know, Jack," I admitted, "but maybe if you'll help me, we can find out."

Jack shrugged and said we would need a plan. He recommended it involve a meeting in public, outside where there were plenty of people to see us, and that he should be present but not within Horseman's view. The place where we met should be contained so we could be easily watched. It was decided I would tell Horseman to meet me on June 15 in the park across the street from the Selby Public Library in downtown Sarasota. That park was tiny, bordered by Main Street at the south end, North Pineapple on the west side and Central Avenue to the east. The streets formed a small triangle, easily viewed from anywhere on the perimeter, with the library blocking off the north edge. The library had huge pear-shaped modernistic pillars behind which Jack would be hiding, ready to use his cell to call 911, or ready to jump out and help me, if I needed help.

On the appointed meeting day I found a parking space behind the library and walked over to the park to look for a suitable out-of-the way bench to meet with Horseman. But there were no benches in the park, although I swear I'd seen them there before. Then, I remembered reading in the *Herald Gazette* that all the benches had been removed because the City Council had voted the homeless people who used them for sleeping at night, to be a public nuisance. An ordinance prohibiting camping in the park had been underscored by the removal of the benches. It was simply more expeditious to remove them than to pay the police to constantly make the homeless move along. This would be a significant barrier when talking with Horseman, so I began looking around for an outdoor café facing the park where we could meet. There were plenty of them, but I would have to stand in the park and wait until he arrived.

It was high noon on a Saturday, and there were strains of music coming from somewhere nearby. I glanced back at the library toward Jack wondering if he would know to change vantage points when he saw Horseman and me set out for one of the cafes along the perimeter. I didn't know which cafe Horseman would choose and I trusted Jack to remain flexible and follow out of sight. There was a gaggle of people gathered around a rock band at the west end of the park, where I finally determined the music was coming from, but the rest of the park was empty, except for me. I decided to remain standing alone, closer to the east end near the library to make sure Horseman would find me.

A long time passed, but he didn't show up. Just as I was deciding to give him another 15 minutes before leaving, a speeding Chevy Equinox entered the area and raced down North Pineapple Avenue with tires screeching and engine roaring.

Chapter 22

The first bullet ricocheted off the sidewalk along the west end of the park. The second, third and fourth hit the ground sending up little puffs of dust right in front of my feet. When the fifth was fired, I heard a whap, and the right part of my chest near my shoulder felt like somebody stuck a needle in me to draw blood. I didn't notice anything this bullet hit. The sixth bullet struck the trunk of a Royal Palm. There was a seventh which must have hit a woman pushing a baby carriage along the east end of the little park near the Fifth Third Bank entrance, because I saw her fall to the sidewalk. Then the car disappeared. I turned toward the stricken lady to offer my help, but I don't think that ever happened. Funny, except for the ricochet, the flicking noises as the tufts appeared in the dirt, the whap in my chest and a tock-like woodpecker sound, as one of the bullets hit the palm tree, I heard nothing—no explosions, no gun blasts, not even a crack like the sound of a cap gun going off.

In the middle of the mayhem, a black Chevy Equinox following the car also sped down North Pineapple Street to Main Street, so quickly it was guaranteed to attract the attention of any police in the area. Sirens began wailing, and cruisers began converging on the park, but it was too late. The Equinox was gone, and the lady with the baby carriage lay moaning on the sidewalk as two ambulances pulled up with lights flashing. Three cruisers tore out of the center of town after the speeding vehicles.

I remember seeking shelter behind a white modernistic sculpture of a manatee feeding its young, erected, according to the plaque at its base, by the students of the Sarasota School of Art and Design as a gift to the city. There was blood on it, but I didn't know how it had gotten there, or why I found this little plaque so close to my eyes. Amidst the mini-holocaust, I spotted Johnson Horseman walking toward me from the entrance to the library. His hair was blowing in the slight breeze and his eyes were looking down straight at me, actually straight through me.

"There can be no avoidance of the natural consequences of destroying the nature of gifts bestowed upon us by the Great Spirit," he said. "Be warned!" Then he turned and veered off toward the street before the police came.

Suddenly, my chest grew cold, and I noticed an ever-increasing circle of blood on my white shirt. The ground smelled like freshly mowed grass. About a foot in front of my face there was an ant hill beside the little plaque on the sculpture. In my dizziness, I found myself hoping to hell there weren't fire ants. I didn't seem to be able to move.

"Sir, sir, are you all right?" came a voice from above. "Oh my god, he's hit too!" That was the last thing I remember hearing. The ants were the last thing I remember seeing.

I woke up in the emergency room of Sarasota Memorial Hospital with a two-pronged oxygen tube in my nose and a horrendous pain in the right side of my chest. My right arm was immobilized by bandaging and there was an IV in my left wrist through which something red was streaming. I couldn't move my head, but I glanced down at the IV.

"It's a blood transfusion," said a voice from somewhere in my little tented off space. "You certainly lost enough of your own blood, so they're giving you some back." The voice was Jack's. "Just relax and don't try to talk. If your chest hurts, it's because they just took this out of you." He waived a pan over my face with something clattering around in it. "It's a Winchester 9 mm Luger 115 grain full metal jacket bullet," he said.

A nurse appeared. "Here's something to make you sleep, sir," she said. Gently, she poked a syringe into my right arm. The effect was almost immediate. The next time I woke up I was out of Emergency and in my own hospital room. Jack Rainspring was standing in the doorway giving an interview to two policemen. He was explaining how we had gone down to the park for a meeting with Johnson Horseman. He told the cops he had seen the entire incident and watched me crumple over at the statue of the manatee. He also told them he had kept his eyes on me throughout the shooting, and could describe everything that happened, including a detailed description of the speeding Chevrolet Equinox and the car in front of it with three men shooting out of its windows. But he had not seen Horseman anywhere in the vicinity.

One of the policemen was scribbling desperately in a note pad to keep up with him as he talked. The other cop was speaking quietly into the microphone on his shoulder, getting out an "all-points" bulletin on Johnson Horseman. Suddenly, I saw the I.V. stand move slightly, and I strained, looking over to see who was approaching.

"Kit-Kat. How did you—?"

"Listening to the police reports on the radio," she answered. "When things get slow out on The Trail, I start listening to the police calls on its channel. I heard about the shooting in the park and investigated, and here I am."

Her explanation didn't make any sense to me. I doubted that a police call about a shooting at a park would have mentioned my name, and I really didn't believe that any investigation on her part could have led her to me at Sarasota Memorial so quickly. Besides, what about those oh-so-important HIPPA rights I'm supposed to have to protect my medical confidentiality? Her story just didn't make sense, but I was too drowsy to think much further about it.

"Winston, I've notified your friend, Ms. Harmon, and she says she'll be here soon with her daughter."

How did Kit-Kat even know about Rosanne? I'd never said anything to her about Rosanne or Gayna, and how did she know where to get hold of them? Slowly I drifted into a sort of twilight sleep, hearing what was going on around me, but not really being awake. In the background I could hear Kit-Kat talking with the policemen and with Jack. John Horseman's name kept coming up, but I couldn't make out, or maybe I just didn't want to make out, what was being said about him. Alexis Weidenfeld's name was also mentioned a number of times. Then, when I heard the name of Micanopy, I actually tried to raise myself up from my stupor, but just couldn't make it. Finally, everything just went silent, as did my thoughts. They all must have left me so I could sleep. I dreamed of Kit-Kat getting all the information she seemed to know from a crystal ball.

· · ·

"Winston, Winston—it's time to get up, Winston. They say they want you to get up and sit on the side of your bed." The feel of Rosanne's hand was comforting, like I had come home after a long journey. I opened my eyes slowly to what was essentially a dark room. Except for Rosanne, everything in it felt foreign to me.

"What time is it?" I asked.

"About 10:00 p.m."

I was confused, having forgotten that they'd moved me into my own private room. I thought I was still in the emergency room.

"How long have you been here?" I asked her.

"Since around 6:00. You've been asleep almost five hours. You've been moved out of Emergency into your own room." I looked to the side of my bed and saw Gayna sleeping there in a chair. Rosanne bent down and kissed my forehead. I tried to smile and reach up to hold her, but there was a shooting pain in my chest.

"Just take it easy," Rosanne said. "I'm here to do all the moving around for you."

"Have you eaten?" I asked.

"Yes, they brought us dinner. Are you hungry?"

"Is the Pope Catholic?" *That's astonishing! Am I hungry? I'm always hungry,* I thought to myself. I also thought I was smiling at her. Actually, I was still out of it and slurring my words a little.

"That's good," she replied. "Let me see about getting you something to eat."

"What do they have?"

"I don't know, honey, but it's probably not going to be enough to satisfy you. Your insurance company is not going to pay for the kind of double meals you usually eat."

"That's fine. That's fine," I said. "So I'll use this time to take off a little weight."

She left for a few minutes and went out to talk to the nurse about food for me. When she came back, we began talking in low tones about what had happened in the park. I told her I had learned what went on by listening to Jack's description of it to the police, but I couldn't really remember anything for myself except Johnson Horseman coming toward me and talking to me. I very definitely remembered Horseman doing this, but Jack was acting toward the police like it never happened, and that Horseman was never there. I explained Horseman's very definite views about the Long Bar Harbor project to Rosanne, and all about the dream catcher analogy he had used with me to define his role in stopping it.

"Well, maybe he thinks now that Mr. Josephski is dead, you are somehow going to carry the project on," Rosanne offered. "But why would he think that, unless you told him?"

I went on to describe to Rosanne the role of Horseman's ancestors in Micanopy, and how a ghost in the form of Julius Josephski had appeared to Alexis Weidenfeld on the day we were there. "I have always suspected Lexi Weidenfeld of killing Julius Josephski," I said, "and I almost think that somehow Johnson Horseman had a hand in making Josephski's ghost appear to her on that day. It's all very paranormal, I know, but I think I'm beginning to believe in the paranormal. I find it especially compelling that I'm the only one who saw Johnson Horseman on the day I was shot, and I'm the only one who heard him speak to me."

Rosanne let me go on and on about this for a long time, but I could see she was looking at me with a jaundiced eye as I spoke. "You think I'm crazy, don't you?"

"Not crazy, Winston," she assured me, "but maybe a little bit in shock because of all that's happened to you. Even if you're right, love, ask yourself, what does it all mean? How does it get you any closer to who's responsible for all these killings?"

"I don't know, but as soon as I get out of here, I'm going to start getting to the bottom of it. It's time for someone to have a long talk with Alexis Weidenfeld, and if the police won't do it—I will."

Chapter 23

It took five days to get on my feet without any pain, light-headedness or wobbling. Rosanne sent Gayna back to Ohio to stay with her aunt so she could go back to school, but Rosanne stayed with me until I was up and running—so to speak—again. Thanks to her, I felt good enough to go about my business. One morning, as I was on my way out of the coach house the phone rang. It was Jack.

"The police have Horseman at the station," he announced. "Seems like he took himself for a little cruise down the overland locks to Lake Okeechobee when he should have been meeting with you in the park six days ago. That's why nobody could find him."

"I was just on my way out of here to meet Lexi Weidenfeld for lunch at the Columbia on Longboat Key, Jack. What are they going to do with him? Will they be keeping him overnight under the auspices of Sarasota County's fine hospitality, or letting him go?"

"I don't know. They'll probably let him go if they have no reason to hold him, and right now they don't. As you know, I'm not in a position to say I ever saw him in the park on the day we went down there for you to meet him."

"In that case, I'd better call Lexi and postpone so I can go to the police station. Are you going down there?"

"Yeah, they've called me in, knowing I won't be able to confirm your statement he was there when you got shot."

Lexi was annoyed when I canceled. She made no bones about the fact she was very busy and had .made a special place in her schedule for me. Nor could she guarantee another meeting anytime in the near future. Her deep alto voice was not as soothing as I remembered it. Instead she seemed very much like a certain female politician I knew of, who always sounded out of character when she addressed large crowds in public—forceful—raspy—too forceful. I tried twice to explain the necessity for my canceling, that there was an issue that had to be resolved as to whether Johnson Horseman was present when I was shot. All she said was, "Well. If that's what you want to do, we've all got to do what we've got to do." Her response seemed very strange and totally inappropriate. Here was this woman I had once idolized because of her beauty and reputation, and in whose home I had been an overnight guest when she was feeling fragile and afraid after our foray into the paranormal in Micanopy. Now she was sounding totally selfish and put out.

Well, I couldn't worry about it. I was certain Johnson Horseman had been present in the park on the day I was shot. I saw him there, and by gosh that was an important issue for the police to consider. In truth, I had begun to believe that Horseman, with his dream catchers and all of his ominous threats, was the real force behind all of the murders that were keeping me in Sarasota. But I had no proof. I looked forward to a confrontation with him at the station as the first step toward solving these mysteries.

But the meeting did not go as planned. "Is it not true, Mr. Horseman, that you and I had plans to meet at the park by the library downtown approximately two weeks ago?" I interrogated.

"Wha no. That's not true at'all, sah. Ah started mah journey toward the Okeechobee Locks, last May 30. On the date in question I reckon, if Ah understand ya'll's timeline heeyah, I'd have been somewhere near the Ortona Locks, 'bout half way between Fort Myers and Clewiston."

"Was anyone with you?"

"Jess mah dog and Angeltine."

"And who is Angeltine?"

"We, Ah don't see that's any of you'all's business, but she's mah housekeepah in Arcadia."

"Mr. Horseman, isn't it true that two weeks ago Saturday, you were in the park outside the library in downtown Sarasota?"

"No, sah, Ah'm afraid that ain't true."

"And didn't you come up to me after I'd been shot and say, 'Be warned! You can't avoid the consequences of destroying the nature of gifts bestowed upon us by the Great Spirit,' or something like that?"

"No, sah, Ah didn't."

There was dead silence in the room after that, and then he said, "If you was shot at sah, Ah'm veery, veery sorry ta heeya that. Ah hope ya'll are alright." Jack and the sheriff's deputy just stood there looking at me like I was a little crazy.

Then the deputy said, "Mr. Horseman, you can go now I guess. If we need you again, we know where to find you." Then turning to me, he said, "I'm sorry Mr. Barchrist. Sometimes when a person gets shot they get a little delirious, seeing or hearing things that aren't really happening. You can go too."

"But I know I saw . . ."

"Winston, just let it go for now," Jack said.

"...clear as day, as I was lying there on the ground."

"Yes, yes, Mr. Barchrist. We know what your position is," the deputy answered.

I looked at my watch. It was only about 10:30, still plenty of time to make lunch with Lexi if she would go with me. She probably had made other arrangements by now, but it was still worth a try. When I called her, she remained unforgiving, but, yes, she could still make lunch with me. However, it would have to be downtown, somewhere close. I suggested Marina Jack's and she agreed.

Marina Jack's is right on the water in Sarasota's harbor. A strong wind was flapping the flags outside along the water pretty persistently, so we decided to eat inside. It's one of the seminal restaurants in the Sarasota area. To get there, one has to walk past docks where yachts worth three million and up are moored. The actual marina isn't like any other I've ever seen. It's a two-story white brick and glass building with an open eating area that begins almost at the front door and runs through the entire building to the back where you can sit outside next to the water. There's always a cool breeze in the room. Everywhere you look, you see opulence and beautiful people, and there's always entertainment, even at lunch time.

Today, however, Marina Jack's turned out to be a pretty big mistake, at least for my purpose. Every five minutes or so, someone stopped by our table to chat with Lexi. I began our conversation by telling her I felt Johnson Horseman had somehow played a role in the demise of Julius Josephski and Edwin DeVertollo. For some reason she seemed interested in this. I did not, however, bring up Irv Caputo's death.

I explained about how Horseman and I had agreed to meet on the day I was shot at the park, which would have been our second meeting.

"You really think so?" she marveled. "What was the meeting at the police station all about?"

I began describing the mysterious manner in which my first meeting with him had gone and about all the superstitious matters he'd brought up concerning dream catching. She seemed floored, not about the dream catcher statements, but about the fact I'd been shot.

"When did this happen?" she asked. "I didn't know you'd been shot."

"Two weeks ago," I said. I went on to explain how Horseman had asked for the meeting, and that I saw him there at the shooting, but he denied it.

All she said was, "Hm."

"Why? What are you thinking?" I asked.

"Nothing," she said. "I thought he was still cruising Okeechobee then."

It was shocking! *I didn't even know Lexi knew Horseman, let alone that he'd gone down to Lake Okeechobee. And how would she have known when he went? I certainly never told her he went there. Of course, I could understand how she might have known of him, but it never occurred to me that she actually knew him personally.*

"L—Lexi," I stammered, "I didn't know you knew Horseman, and how did..."

"Hey, Lexi! What are you doing here?" A beautiful woman suddenly interrupted, sidling up to our table and plunking her Coach purse down as she temporarily took a seat with us. "Shouldn't you be back there at the salt mines getting a closing ready or something like that?"

"...he'd gone down to Okeechobee?" I continued. But the last part of my question got lost somewhere as the two women greeted each other. They were obviously caught up in their conversation as if I didn't exist.

"Hey, Angelina, look who's here," the woman called to another woman just coming in the door. "It's our beautiful Alexis Weidenfeld," she continued, still ignoring me. "C'mon over and say hello." Then she turned back to Lexi and began telling her about a building contractor she'd met with a big business down on Marco Island. It was like I'd completely disappeared.

"Oh, yeah," Lexi said. "I know him, but take it from me, he's not your type, Margo. Oh, hey, hi Angie."

"What do you mean?" Angelina said. "Who's not Margo's type?"

Lexi didn't bother to introduce me, and neither of the two ladies saw fit to introduce themselves. It was like I was invisible. While they continued to talk, my tuna salad filled tomato came and I busied myself with that. If only I'd ordered the crawfish etouffee. It would have been much more filling and taken a lot longer to eat. I also probably could have secretly gotten away with a double order of that dish, but with the tuna salad—no. It wouldn't have looked right to have two tuna salad filled tomatoes on my plate, or worse yet, two plates of the same dish.

Just as I was realizing I was still hungry, Margo and Angelina hugged Lexi good-bye, leaning over and kissing the air beside her cheek as women do. Lexi responded in kind, and as they left she shook her head. "Just a couple of my cougar friends, Winston," she said sarcastically.

"So, getting back to Johnson Horseman," I continued, "how did you...?"

"There she is!" a voice said from behind me suddenly, "the most beautiful lawyer in town!" I turned around, knowing this voice would belong to someone who was a stranger to me, but this time Lexi was more gracious.

"Rex Haverty, meet Winston Barchrist," she said, smiling warmly, "Winston Barchrist, the third," she emphasized.

"Hello, Winston Barchrist the third," said a strapping blond man looking down at me from behind, as he offered his hand to shake mine.

"Rex is the biggest mortgage broker in town," Lexi added.

"Oh, now, Alexis, you know that's not true," the man demurred self-consciously. "In truth, I'm the biggest mortgage broker in Sarasota and Manatee counties! Hah," he laughed, "and probably, you could throw Pinellas in there, too."

"Still crowing about the size of your hands I see, Rex," Lexi retorted.

"Well, honey, you probably don't remember, but I put them wherever I can."

Suddenly Lexi's tan complexion began changing to beet red and blotches appeared on her long neck. "Well, Rex, I don't think we need TMI here, but truthfully, how's business going for you? Are you still the master of finance out at Lakewood Ranch?"

"Oh, very definitely," he answered. From there, the conversation degenerated into gossip about the various real estate deals for a million and more taking place in the county. For me, it was downright boring as neither of them said another thing to me. I sat there enduring my disinterest and my continued hunger, wishing once again I'd ordered the etouffee. At least then I'd still have something to do as they talked. I'd be eating. As it was, I had to content myself with snatching glances at Lexi's golden brown knees from time to time when I thought nobody was looking.

Finally, Rex left, and I persisted again, "Lexi, how did you know Johnson Horseman was cruising through the locks at Lake Okeechobee?" There was a long moment of silence as she removed the bun from her now cold hamburger. Finally, she responded.

"I didn't know that," she said.

"But you told me you did. You said you thought he was still cruising Okeechobee on the day I got shot."

"Did I say that?"

"Yes."

"Well, I didn't know that. I didn't actually know he was at Lake Okeechobee. I only knew what you told me, and you must have said he was out on Lake Okeechobee. You told me."

"But I never said a word about it from the time I met you here until now."

"No, no, Winston, you told me all about it on the phone when you were trying to get out of going to lunch with me this morning. Don't you remember? By the way, I'm sorry I got so mad at you when you called to cancel. I'm really lousy in the mornings until I've had my coffee." She looked down at the table, and then up at me again, and smiled her winning smile, blinked her eyes and looked very remorseful. She was beautiful.

Who knows, I thought to myself. *Maybe I was a little cloudy on things. After all, at the police station everyone looked at me like I was nuts when I accused Johnson Horseman of being in the park when I got shot. I really couldn't remember what I said to her on the phone this morning. All I could really remember was my consternation when she got angry at me for telling her I was going to have to stand her up and go to the police station instead of having lunch with her.* I cast my eyes down at my hands, staring and remembering how angry she was.

"I don't know why," I said, "but I was under the impression you didn't know Johnson Horseman personally."

"Wrong impression," she said perkily, "I do know him personally. So tell me, what makes you think he had anything to do with the death of Julius?"

"Because he had a motive."

"Well, I really know him only as an acquaintance, because he gave Julius so much trouble about his development at Long Bar Harbor over environmental issues. In fact, I had a couple of meetings with him to try and help Julie iron things out with him."

"Then you know what a strange bird he is, and about his crazy Indian superstitions—dream catchers and things like that."

"No, not really."

"The first time I met him," I continued, "was after Julius Josephski's death. "He was really throwing off some very ominous vibrations then. He told me that even though Julius was dead, he didn't think the fight for Long Bar Harbor was over yet. Said he'd set up dream catchers all over the Long Bar to prevent any more developmental nightmares out there. And, he was downright threatening about it, very threatening. In fact, he portrayed himself as a dream catcher, figuratively speaking, who was going to protect Long Bar Harbor from the nightmare of development."

Lexi gave me a wry look, as if my thinking was really twisted. I could tell she wasn't going to listen much longer. I had to do something to get her attention back.

"Do you know what this guy's all about?" I asked her."

"I know he's an ardent and well-known conservationist."

"Do you remember our trip to Micanopy, when we were all supposed to be looking for the ghost of John Horse, the Seminole Indian leader from the area? Well, Johnson Horseman is the great, great, great grandson of John Horse. Did you know that? He also spent some time in the Florida Penitentiary until his conviction for murder was overturned because of DNA evidence. Did you know that?"

"Winston, I didn't know those things, and I'm not sure I'm going to accept them as being true now, just because you're telling me they're true. I'm afraid I'd need to see some evidence before I could do that."

I could see Lexi was going to be plenty tough to convince of my theory that Johnson Horseman could have killed Julius Josephski. After all, she was a princess of the legal profession in these parts, with a resume much longer than mine, and everybody seemed to like and respect her. I was a nobody.

"Well, I can and I will provide evidence that what I've said is true. But, first, just hear me out. You do remember what happened to you up at Micanopy, with your thinking you saw a spirit up there and that it was the ghost of Julius Josephski, come to haunt you over your breakup with him? And, you do know, you and I are the only two persons of interest suspected by the police in Josephski's murder? You because you were his girlfriend and your prints were all over his penthouse, and me because I'm the one who was there when he was found dead. The more likely candidate as the killer is you. You must realize that too, don't you? But I maintain there should be a third suspect, and that's Johnson Horseman. The only problem right now is proving it."

Lexi's dark eyes flashed at me. I could tell I was making her angry, probably because I said she was a more likely suspect than me. Whatever it was, I didn't want to make her more angry. I needed her help.

"Just hear me out, Lexi. Keep listening. Johnson Horseman's family still has a lot of influence in Micanopy, and I think he still has access to all the historical sites there. I've thought about this a lot. I maintain that through various mechanical means, possibly the use of holographs, videos and things like strobe lights, he set up that house we were in to make it look like the ghost of Julius Josephski was there waiting for you. He did it so you'd react exactly the way you did and cast suspicion on yourself for his murder, thereby diverting any suspicion that might eventually fall on him for the killing."

As I was finishing my statement, I heard the scrape of her chair pulling back from the table abruptly. She stood up quickly, and her eyes were like daggers.

"That's absurd! What makes you think Johnson Horseman would even have known I was coming up there on that day? Also, I can't believe we ever let a skeptic like you into any of the activities of The Sun Ghost Psychic Trackers. Holographic videos—that's bullshit! What I saw there was real. I'm leaving now, and I hope you were planning on picking up the check, because I'm certainly not."

Chapter 24

Lexi's anger was unnerving, even downright scary. Somehow I'd managed to insult the very person I needed to partner with to get to the bottom of Julius Josephski's death. In truth, she probably knew more about Horseman than anybody else, having bargained with him on Josephski's behalf over environmental matters.

There were also other things I needed to know from her. For instance, why had she and Josephski executed wills with pour-over trusts, leaving everything to her in trust for as long as she lived, if he pre-deceased her? And why had she executed a trust that was a mirror image of that, leaving everything to Josephski if she predeceased him? They weren't married and there was no evidence that they co-owned anything. So what was the purpose?

And, what was the meaning of the unsigned affidavit prepared for Irving Caputo's signature? I didn't understand why Edwin DeVertollo had blackmailed him, causing the Manatee County Engineering Department to delay its approval of the Long Bar Harbor project until DeVertollo gave the project a green light. More important, why was Alexis Weidenfeld the drafter of that affidavit, as the bottom of the unsigned document revealed? Was the banker, Rhett Kessler, correct that there was a feud between Josephski and DeVertollo? What was going on? Did Edwin DeVertollo know that Lexi Weidenfeld was trying to do him in with the Caputo affidavit?

Were Josephski and Weidenfeld working together on this before they broke up? What was the true reason Julius Josephski had gotten so angry when Lexi broke things off with him. Was her anxiety over it the reason she thought she saw his ghost in Micanopy? Under duress, the mind can play some very exotic games on somebody suffering from Post-Traumatic Stress Syndrome. Certainly experiencing a murder is a trauma. Without Lexi, I didn't see any way I could learn the answers to these questions. I had been hopeful that over time I could coax (no actually manipulate) the answers out of her, but now it seemed I had blown it with her big time. The only other person from whom I might possibly get answers to some of these questions was Kit-Kat, but that seemed like a long shot.

Kit-Kat nervously paced back and forth inside her double-wide on Route 41, rubbing her hands together, as I told her what had happened with Johnson Horseman and with Lexi. She no longer exuded the flippant, "capable-of-anything," devil-may-care attitude she'd displayed when I'd first met her. There was a look of concern on her face—no actually, it was a look of genuine consternation. "I told you not to mess around with Johnson Horseman," she chided, "but no, you had to go and do it anyway, and look what it got you. You got shot."

"Yes, you did Kit-Kat, and I now believe you were right, but what you're saying presumes Horseman was involved in the shooting."

"Well, according to what you say, he was. It's just that nobody believes you except me.

"And, I should have warned you about Alexis Weidenfeld too, Winston," she carried on. "When you get too close to the Alexis Weidenfelds of the world, you're getting within striking distance of some of the largest powers that be in this city. That's okay—as long as they perceive you as harmless. But Lexi obviously must not perceive you as harmless. Just beware. She'll strike you like the asp struck Cleopatra."

My thoughts went back to that day at Lexi's house when she walked in on me as I was going through her French Provincial desk. *Had she seen more than I thought she'd seen? Did she know I'd seen her will, her trust and the affidavit she'd prepared for Irv Caputos' signature?*

"She can be mean when she wants to be—and I mean really mean!" Kit-Kat continued. "Hell, she is mean. In fact, if I had to take Lexi's personality and lay it out or divide it up on a table, I'd say that seventy percent of the time she is mean, and nice only thirty percent of the time. If there is anything else in her quiver of personality traits, I'd say it's selfishness and self-centeredness."

"But...."

"Oh, I know, Winston, she's a fine, fine looking lady who can really be attractive when she wants to be. And, everybody accepts her and acts like they love her because of that and because she's got so much money. But, truth be known, nobody needs the headaches she can—and will—bring, if she wants to."

"All I can say Kit-Kat, is that if I can't go through Lexi to get to the facts I need, I'm going to have to go somewhere else, and I hate to say it, but the only other place that's left to go is to Johnson Horseman. I don't know for sure if he's even involved, or if so, the extent of his involvement. We're going to have to go out to his place and snoop around and see if we can find something that gives us a lead. I believe he's somehow involved in what's gone on. I just don't know how."

"Well, what are you talking about here Mr. Barchrist? You can't just go barging into Horseman's house you know, and I doubt he's going to be a gracious host who invites you in and answers all your questions. So what are you talking about?"

"I'm talking about a 'little night work' I guess. You know, breaking and entering, hopefully when he's not around. We lawyers refer to it as the doctrine of *'fractione et ingressus'*."

"Winston Barchrist, that's absurd! You're a professional person. What about your law license?"

"I'm not a lawyer in Florida, and if I don't get out of this damn state, I won't be a lawyer anywhere, at least a lawyer with any clients. I want to go back to Columbus, the city I've come to know and love as my inauspicious dwelling place. I want to go back to my dear Ohio State Buckeyes. Only there do I feel at home and far enough away from the 'madding crowds.' Did you know half the people in the United States don't even know what a buckeye is? They think buckeyes are protruding eyes like buck teeth."

"Winston, settle down, "Kit-Kat interrupted. "I think you're becoming a bit hysterical. I know you want to go home but...."

"Believe me Kit-Kat, if you've got a better idea than *fractione et ingressus,* please let me in on it. I'll do whatever it takes."

As it turned out, Kit-Kat did have an idea, although I don't know if it was any better than mine. Her idea was that she would contact Dr. Ben Temple, of The Sun Ghost Psychic Trackers, and accompany him on a visit to see Johnson Horseman. They would try to interest him in determining whether, because he was a Seminole descendant of John Horse of Micanopy, there was any parapsychic link between his home in Arcadia and the historic home of his heritage still standing in Micanopy that had been occupied by the Levys. Establishing the parapsychic link would involve entering Horseman's house in Arcadia to set up certain equipment and computer devices. Winston would not be involved. Alexis Weidenfeld would be involved only if she learned the contact was being made. Otherwise, Horseman probably did not know any of the players who would be involved.

According to Kit-Kat's plan, when the Psychic Trackers got inside Horseman's house, in addition to running all their usual paranormal tests, they would open drawers, search cupboards and scour closets for documents Horseman had, and anything else of interest that might be there. Horseman could even be on the premises unaware of what was going on, perhaps completely occupied by Dr. Temple's girlfriend, Cherry, under the pretense of an interview. So he wouldn't realize his house was being searched. Cherry was compellingly attractive, and she'd be able to keep Horseman's mind off what was going on inside his house with little effort. She knew how to generate static electricity that would make her hair stand up on end as she talked to him, leading him to believe he and his house were full of energy. She could make her pores stand up in goose bumps, and she would wear tight shorts when she talked to him, in order to keep his eyes on her legs. She might even ask him to feel the goose bumps with his hands.

In addition, a radio transmitter would be placed in the Levy house in Micanopy, with a receiver strategically placed in Horseman's house in Arcadia. Familiar noises, such as the refrigerator running and toilets flushing from the house in Micanopy could be broadcast to Arcadia, leading Horseman to believe there actually was a connection between the two houses. While all this was going on, X-ray technology would be used to reveal what was inside Horseman's closets, drawers and cupboards. Dr. Temple had access to some of the best psychics in the state of Florida, and he could employ one of them to occupy Horseman if Cherry couldn't distract him for long enough while the search of his house was underway.

The woman Dr. Temple would hire knew how to create a scenario in which five or six people would get together in a room, be hypnotized and then blindfolded. Among them would be Horseman. It would then be suggested that water was flowing into the room and could not be stopped. The psychic would tell the blindfolded individuals that although each was of a different height, the water was going to flow until it was above every person's head, except for one, who was taller than the rest. That would be Horseman. Under no circumstances were these people, including Horseman, to remove their blindfolds, even though they couldn't remember which of them was the tallest. Various other suggestions would also be made to aid the blindfolded people in their hearing and feeling of the water flowing into the room. They were to experience these sensations for a seemingly endless period of time, the wetness and the fear, while each of them was in a deep hypnotic state. Finally, each person would be asked to point in the direction in which the water was entering the room and hold themselves in that position. Then, the blindfolds would be removed, as would the hypnotic spells into which they had been placed, and the group of people would all find themselves pointing in the exact same direction, regardless of their positioning in the room.

Kit-Kat seemed certain that with proper planning and execution, her little scheme would work. To me, it sounded pretty far fetched when I thought of what a hard-boiled character Horseman seemed to be. "Can't you do something with your plan that involves Indian dream catchers," I asked her. She pondered the question for a long time, and then to my surprise, came up with a positive answer. "Yes," she said. "We'll hang a bunch of them on the porches of both houses and check each for negative vibrations from the other to see if any bad energy gets transferred."

"And just how are we going to check that out?" I asked.

"We'll wire the talisman we hang on Horseman's porch in Arcadia with microscopic electrical wire to make them glow when it comes time to receive energy from Micanopy."

"That's ridiculous," I said.

"Maybe so, but after watching Cherry's hair stand on end and seeing her goose bumps, plus undergoing the psychic's flowing water caper and hearing the sounds coming from the Micanopy house, I betcha he'll buy it," Kit-Kat opined. "Besides, what have we got to lose? Horseman will either say no to the whole deal from the very beginning, or if he comes to his senses while we're midway through it, he'll throw us out. Either way, you've always got *fractione et ingressus* to fall back on. I just hate to see you risk your law license before you try something else. To say nothing of the fact if you're caught breaking and entering into Horseman's house, the cops' interest in you as a murder suspect will greatly deepen."

I thought I was just standing there looking at her as she talked, and thinking about her plan, but apparently I was unwittingly doing more.

"What?" she said.

"Nothing," I said.

"No, I mean it," she re-emphasized. "What is it? Tell me!"

"No, no."

"I really mean it, Winston. What is it? Why do you have that coy smile on your lips? Now it's spreading all over your face like you swallowed a goldfish or something. What's it all about?"

Against my better judgment, I told her. "Well, I guess it's just you're confirming what I've always really thought. That is that you don't actually believe in all this paranormal stuff, and that really, it's all made up. It's perpetrated by a bunch of contraptions or machines used by humans from behind some sort of a screen, like the Wizard of Oz did from behind a curtain in Emerald City. You remember that movie?"

"Winston Barchrist, you get out of here right now! It really makes me angry you would think that. I put my reputation on the line with the Sun Ghost Psychic Trackers, vouching for you as a true believer so you could come up to Micanopy with us. Now you tell me you were just playing us—playing me—along. G'wan, get out! Don't call me. I'll call you."

Well that's just great, I thought to myself. *Now I've alienated not only Lexi, but Kit-Kat too. And, I did it over the same issue, ghosts and non-belief in the paranormal.* I really needed help, and now it seemed there was no one to help me.

Chapter 25

I was wrong. Jack Rainspring believed that Johnson Horseman had something to do with the death of Irv Caputo, so he was eager to help. Admittedly, I may have planted the seed in his brain by reminding him of his story about Horseman threatening Caputo into delaying the approval of the Manatee County Engineer's office on the Long Bar Harbor project. But I was getting desperate to discover the role Horseman had played in the predicament that was keeping me captive in Sarasota. I was sure Horseman had some sort of hand in the events that were unfolding. I just couldn't put my finger on where he fit in. Three days passed with no word from Kit-Kat, whom I presumed was still mad at me. So I decided to rely on the doctrine of *fractione et ingressus,* and called Jack. I needed his help to break into Horseman's house.

"Yeah, I'm in," he said. "Just tell me when we're gonna do it and I'll be there with my tools."

"Tools? What tools, Jack?"

"Well, we'll need a tension wrench for the keyhole in his lock, a pick to lift the tumblers as we scrub it, and a stethoscope to listen for the tumblers as they fall. We're also gonna need a small step ladder, a crowbar, a screwdriver, flashlights and my .38."

"You sound like you've been on capers like this before, Jack." Nothing but silence. "Well, whatever," I continued. "Just don't tell Alexis Weidenfeld what we plan to do."

"What? Why would I do that? Hell, she's a lawyer. She'd probably be bound by the canons of ethics to report me."

"Well, just don't do it, Jack. Remember, I'm a lawyer too, and right now Lexi hates me."

Jack drove us to Arcadia in the black Lincoln he'd rented to me. The dark road was two-lane all the way, straight east across some of the scrubbiest land in Florida, bisected by canals awash in alligators, and who knew what other kinds of wildlife. Once we got outside Sarasota, the night sounds were positively creepy. We barely missed a steer standing in the road by a broken fence. When we finally came upon a huge grove of palmettos hemming in the road, there was a large swath of blown over rubbish (mostly Australian Pines) cutting through the palms, attesting to the power of Hurricane Charlie that had passed east of Sarasota years ago. The town of Arcadia itself still showed signs of the disaster with blue plastic tarps doubling as roofs in some cases. Johnson Horseman's house was just outside of town, and it was, without a doubt, the biggest house in the area.

It was a low sprawling ranch made of sandstone surrounded by a high stucco wall with an electrically operated gate, that made it impossible for us to drive up very close. So we left my Lincoln in a palmetto grove outside the gate and scaled the wall, which was no mean feat for a man of my girth and heft. Jack set up the ladder and held it steady for me while I clambered over the wall, giving notice from my grunts that we were there to everything that could hear. Luckily, no guards or other passers-by appeared. We then crept forward toward the house, with Jack carrying the ladder and his holstered .38, and me carrying his tool kit.

Inside the wall, to my amazement, there was a black Porsche Targa, very much like the one Lexi drove, parked in the driveway under the well-lit faux Mexican portico setting off the front door. The license plate said "RE-LEST 8." I grabbed Jack's arm and pulled him to a stop. "It looks like he's got company. We need to proceed slowly from here," I whispered. "First let's check all the windows."

Slowly, we began circling the entire house checking to see what rooms were lit. To the left of the front door there was a small high window looking into what seemed to be a dining room, off of which ran a long hallway toward a kitchen or pantry at the back of the house. The dining room was dark, but there was a light shining from the kitchen that reflected a woman standing with her back to the hallway. She wore a sleek black dress and stiletto heels that made her muscular calves stand out. On the other side of the front door was a large floor-to-ceiling window, with a totally dark room behind it. From inside came the ringing sound of a clock striking the hour or the half hour. It was difficult to tell which. Further down from the front door there was another floor-to-ceiling window that looked in on a room that was dark except for a green shaded desk-lamp on a large roll-top desk, with what looked like blueprint scrolls in the cubbies. Next to the desk was the entrance to another long hall that seemed like it also ran toward the kitchen, where there was a light on.

We turned the corner and moved toward the back of the house, past five or six windows, all dark, probably bedroom windows, along an L-shaped wing that seemed to stretch forever. The end of this wing smelled like a stable, with horse hay and straw, and indeed, that's where we found ourselves, in a stable with half-doors, gates and paddocks occupied by horses.

"We don't dare try to enter the house until his visitor leaves and there's been enough time for him to fall asleep," I whispered. "Right here looks like as good a place as any to hang out until that happens."

"No," Jack said. "I think we should first move around to the back of that kitchen and see if we can find out who's in there and how many of them there are. Then we ought to go back to the car and conduct surveillance from there until that Porsche leaves. What do you think about that?"

I agreed, and we started to walk across the barn area back of the house toward the light we could see coming from a large sliding door, the door to the kitchen. It was very dark, and I couldn't see very well. Suddenly my shoes began filling with water and I was sinking. I lost my footing, staggered and fell on my knees into what felt like about a foot of water. The ground had turned from sand and weeds to swamp, and with each step the water got deeper. Jack turned on his flashlight and began moving it around us in ever widening concentric circles.

"Jack, what are you doing?" I whispered loudly. "You're going to give us away. They can see us."

"I'm looking for water moccasins," he whispered back. "If one of them babies gets you, it won't matter whether I've given us away or not. Believe me!"

Suddenly, there was another voice. "Psst-over here," it whispered. "Get over here closer to the house and you won't be stuck in that swamp anymore." Jack flashed his light in the direction of the voice. "Turn that out," the voice said. "Are you trying to get us killed or something?"

It was Kit-Kat! I took a step toward her and then I belly slammed straight into the swamp, nose down, splashing to get hold of something, anything, and thrashing and coughing to recover my breath. "Kit-Kat, what are you doing here?" I gurgled spitting out water as I spoke.

"Shhh," she replied, putting her forefinger up to her mouth to silence me. "You've got to be more quiet."

"How did you know we would be here?" I whispered loudly.

"I told her about it," Jack said.

That made me angry. "I thought I told you not to say anything about what we were planning to do, Jack, and you went ahead anyway and told her."

"You told me not to say anything to Alexis Weidenfeld but you didn't say not to tell Kit-Kat. So when she called to let me know about the little fight you two had, I told her what we were planning to do."

"And, I decided even though you're an atheist when it comes to the paranormal, you could still use my help," Kit-Kat added. "Of course, once again, I was right. In case you didn't realize it, counselor, that's Lexi Weidenfeld in the kitchen right now with Horseman. I recognized the license plate on her Porsche out front— RE-LEST 8. So dig yourself out of that swamp and let's get going. We've got a lot of work to do. Right there, the optics of the situation put Lexi and Horseman in one another's company. Ask yourself why? Are they conspiring about something? What?"

Just then there was a scraping noise as the glass kitchen door pulled back, and a loud blast emanated. It was a shotgun report, echoing into the dark night. Then another blast was fired. Buckshot splashed all round us in the swamp. I dove under the water, as best I could. Kit-Kat ran toward the house and pressed herself up against its wall in the shadows as best she could. But Jack stood his ground. Determinedly, he took the .38 from his holster, held it up with two hands, one steadying the other and fired four shots—pop, pop, pop, pop.

There was a woman's scream from the area of the kitchen door, and the shotgun shooter went down. The shooter disappeared. Eventually, I heard the distinctive growl of a Porsche as it sprang to life, filling the silence of the night. There was a long drawn out acceleration as the car labored through first gear; a slight interruption for the shift to second; then a pop and the relaxed sound of a car speeding comfortably in third gear. If there were further shifts up the gears, I could not hear them. I strained my eyes to see into the kitchen. It looked like the woman was gone.

Chapter 26

The three of us stayed frozen in our positions for what seemed an eon, trying to decide what to do next. Finally, while looking at me, Jack tapped himself on the chest with his forefinger. Then he held two fingers up to his eyes in a "V," looked at the fallen body ahead of us and pointed to it, as if to say, "I'll go look."

Slowly and silently, gun still drawn, he crept toward the body. Kit-Kat fell in behind him but kept her distance. "It's Horseman," she whispered when she got close enough to see. "He's still alive."

Jack leveled his .38 at Horseman's head, bent down and yanked the shotgun from Horseman's grasp, throwing it as far away as he could.

"Y'all 'er trespassin' on mah land," Horseman said feebly. He was hit on the left side of his torso, and the blood was flowing freely.

"You got that right," Jack answered.

"Whah—whah 'er y'all heeya?"

"To look for evidence," Jack retorted.

Horseman coughed. "Evidence of what?"

"The role you played in Irv Caputo's death," said Jack.

"Evidence of why you wanted to meet with me again," I yelled. "To find evidence you shot me in downtown Sarasota."

"Ah didn't shoot y'all downtown, aw anywheya else," he said. "I wasn't theya when y'all was shot. Remembah? We've been all through that already at the poeleece station. Besides, if ah I wanted you dead,

I'd've gone at ya with a knife." With that, he launched into a violent coughing spell.

"Oh, is that so," Kit-Kat remarked. "Like you did with Julius Josephski and Edwin DeVertollo?"

Horseman scoffed.

"Who was the woman in your kitchen with you?" Jack demanded.

Horseman scoffed again. "Get off mah land," he commanded, "or I'll have you'all sued."

"It was Lexi Weidenfeld, wasn't it?" Kit-Kat asserted. "I'd know that car of hers anywhere."

"Okay," Horseman growled. "Q and A period's over. "You'all can rest assured," he continued, "whoevah it was is gonna get the poeleece an bring 'em back heeyah—right soon."

"He's got a point," I said. "Maybe we should...."

"No, he doesn't," Kit-Kat fired back. "If it was Alexis Weidenfeld, and I'm sure it was because of the plate on her car, she's not going to want to get mixed up in this in any way, shape or form. The police tend to ask too many questions for Lexi's liking. She's long gone back to Sarasota by now—you know, to protect her reputation and all that."

"An' what if it weren't Ms. Weidenfeld?" Horseman coughed.

"Well if it weren't, it weren't!" Jack said sarcastically. "Now let's get into your house and have a look around."

"Hey, I'm bleedin' heeyah," protested Horseman.

"Well, ain't that the truth," said Jack. "All the more reason to hurry inside then, right?"

We carried Horseman into the house and laid him out on a bed in one of the bedrooms. Then I hurried into the other room where I'd seen the desk with the blueprints.

"Angeltine! Angeltine!" Horseman suddenly began yelling. "Angeltine, call the poeleece!"

Was Horseman's housekeeper in the house? I wondered. I remembered him referring to her in the police station. *Had she seen what had happened? What would she tell the police if they showed up? No matter what she said, we'd have a hard time explaining our presence on Horseman's property.*

"Jack!" I yelled. "Angeltine's his housekeeper. Search the house. We've got to find her."

"Never mind," came Kit-Kat's voice from the utility room. "I've got her right here with me." Suddenly Kit-Kat appeared holding a sunburned brown-skinned woman with long black braided hair by her arm. The woman looked to be about fifty, had sun-induced craggy wrinkles around kind-looking eyes and was wearing the colorful dress of an Indian from one of the Seminole reservations in the area. She was very big, as women go, almost six feet tall and was very stout, almost like a female wrestler. Unfortunately, she also exhibited attributes of Down syndrome, including mild retardation.

"Don' worry, I not callin' anybody," the Indian woman offered. "Whoever you be, I glad you here. Jess promise me. When you leave, you take me. I don wanna be trapped here anymoe." Her voice was very distinctive, practically baritone, very low, almost like that of a man. Her speech was completely devoid of transitive words like "is" and "am," articles such as "a" and "the," and tenses, other than the present tense.

"Trapped? What do you mean? Who are you?" Jack asked. "And, tell me, is there anyone else in the house?"

"Nobody else here now that Ms. Weidenfeld gone," the Indian replied.

"Well, tell us what's going on. You seem very scared. What are you so afraid of?" Kit-Kat asked.

The woman began to cry. "He like Satan—he like Satan," she said through her tears. "Mr. John like Satan of real world. I Angeltine. I housekeeper. I been here thirty years, ever since my father gave me to Mr. John, and Mr. John won't let me go. He refuse teaching me to drive car. He refuse teaching me to ride a horse. He watch me on cameras." She gestured as she spoke upward toward the ceiling at a small glass half globe resembling a casino eye-in-the-sky. "If people in town see me, they tell him. He say, 'follow her.' I cook for him, I clean for him. I do other things for him, what he wants. Like living in Hell. Nobody ever come to this house—hardly nobody, except Ms. Weidenfeld. His companion me, only me. And what do I do when I'm not doing these things for him? I make dream catchers all day for him."

"What does Alexis Weidenfeld do when she comes here?" I asked.

"Always they talk together low, discussing things I not supposed to hear."

"What things? What things do they discuss?"

"They discuss things like what will happen after...."

"After what?"

"That, I don't know. It something to do with a place called the At-Tah-Thi-Ki in Bradenton by Bay of Sarasota, south of village named Cortez by Spanish people."

"Cortez, that must be Cortez Village," Jack suddenly piped up, "and just south of it along the bay is Long Bar Harbor. At-Tah-Thi-Ki must be the Indian name for Long Bar Harbor."

"At-Tah-Thi-Ki mean 'place of learning' in our language," Angeltine said. "Mr. John and Ms. Weidenfeld say things to each other about preservation of At-Tah-Thi-Ki by combining ownership and myth. What meaning of this? He drive away those who try to destroy it. He do that by using old Indian symbols I make for him, dream catchers what have powers of great spirit and politics. She preserve At-Tah-Thi-Ki from evil forces by owning it herself. She never permit it to be destroyed by white man's new buildings. They have what they call 'symbiotic' relationship to help each other accomplish goals. I don' know what 'symbiotic' means."

"In other words, a mutually beneficial relationship," I suggested.

"I don' know" said Angeltine. "I don' know this word they use—whatever."

"Well," said Jack. "As long as we're here, we ought to take the opportunity to look around the house. Maybe we ought to start with that desk in the den."

"Angeltine," Horseman moaned from the other room. "The poeleece! Call the poeleece." A thin smile creased Angeltine's lips.

"Yah, right, Mr. John. I call police." Then she looked at us and said, "No!"

Instead, we decided an ambulance should be called for Horseman, but not until we were ready to leave. Indeed, he might even have to be life-flighted to Sarasota Memorial Hospital. Angeltine would be the only one there when they came for him.

Chapter 27

Our search of the house produced a treasure trove of documents—site elevation maps of Long Bar Harbor; a written history of At-Tah-Thi-Ki; various surveys of the land on the Harbor; deeds of the land to Julius Josephski; a partnership agreement between Josephski and DeVertollo; newspaper articles concerning developers' plans for Long Bar Harbor; telephone lists of employees in the Manatee County Engineering Department; copies of various letters to Irving Caputo urging him not to release the tract for development; copies of various petitions by environmental groups urging against the development of Long Bar Harbor; address cards with the address of Julius Josephski on them; and a strange report and video on the surveillance of Julius Josephski that had been prepared by a company called Subtle Surveillance Inc. The surveillance report appeared to be an almost minute-by-minute report on what Julius Josephski did inside his rooms at the Ritz from the time he awoke in the morning until he went to bed. Apparently the camera shut off when left the apartment and turned back on when he re-entered. There was no address or phone number for Subtle Surveillance anywhere on the film or video box.

The report showed that Josephski, if home, sat at his piano and played every day from about 3 to 4 p.m., as if he was practicing. First, he would open his sliding glass doors to let air in from the outside. Then he would turn on music on his stereo, and accompany the music with his playing. In this way he played things like the Rachmaninoff Concerto No. II accompanied by an orchestra in the background. He was a very accomplished pianist. There were hours of recording him around his apartment, but the piano playing sessions were the most interesting part of the surveillance. Numeric timing numbers along the bottom of the video in minutes and seconds appeared throughout the surveillance sessions.

"Mr. Horseman," Jack asked, "we found some videos in your house indicating you or someone else had Mr. Josephski under surveillance in his home. What's that all about?"

"Ah told her not ta do it!" Horseman protested.

"Told who not to do it?" I asked.

"Alexis Weidenfeld, that jealous bitch," he uttered.

"Are you saying Alexis Weidenfeld had her own lover watched by a detective agency?"

"That's right—and she kept the films heeyah so he'd nevah find them."

Angeltine sat quietly by Horseman's side as he explained the videos, her eyes downcast and her face ashen. It seemed as if there was something she wanted to add but she remained silent. I queried her. "Angeltine is there something you want to say about this?" Silence. "Have you ever seen these videos before?" She remained silent.

"Alexis Weidenfeld guarded her relationship with Julius Josephski like a mothah lioness guards her young," Horseman volunteered. "Ah think she even paid the security detail at the Ritz to stake out his rooms theyah, to see who visited him. She once told me that as a businessman he was totally trustwuthy, but as just a man, he wadn't."

"So it sounds like you and Lexi had a fairly close relationship if she revealed things of such a personal nature to you," I said.

"Not really," Horseman responded, trying to walk back his previous statements.

"Not really? Then tell us," Kit-Kat interrogated, "What was she doing here his evening?"

"That weren't Alexis Weidenfeld who was heeyah," he lied. Angeltine cast her eyes toward the floor.

"Oh yes it was," Kit-Kat protested. "I'd know that license plate and that car anywhere."

"Besides," I added, "Angeltine here seemed to think that was Alexis Weidenfeld." Horseman shot Angeltine a glance that would have killed her, if he'd had darts attached to his eyes. Then, there was complete silence. "Well," I began again, "what was she doing here?"

Horseman gave up lying. "She, she came heeyah," he stumbled, "ta tell me y'all thought Ah had a hand in Josephski's death."

"And why would she do a thing like that?" I asked.

"She wanted ta know if it were true cuz that's what you told her she said. She was plenty mad when she walked in—plenty accusatory—and such, claimin she wuz gonna bring the poeleece in on the matter."

"Had she been here before?"

"Oh yes, many a time—ta negotiate on Josephski's behalf ovah the Long Bar project. It was like she and Ah had been over all the details of it many a time. But we nevah got anywheyah. She was a hard negotiator, and Ah was jess too stubborn Ah guess," Horseman admitted.

"So the nature of your relationship was purely business, right?" I asked.

He scoffed. "Yep, Ah guess you could say that was it, purely business." He tried smiling faintly, but his lips merely creased without turning up on either side of his mouth. Then he grimaced in pain.

"Angeltine," he ordered, "get me a cold compact awh somethin." The Indian woman got up and left the room. "She's supposed to be mah caretaker," he complained, "but she don't know the fust thing about takin care of anything. All she can do is clean and cook. At least, though, she always does what Ah tell her to do."

Jack, who'd been completely quiet during my interrogation, suddenly piped up. "So tell me Mr. Horseman, is it true you threatened Irving Caputo that if he signed off for the developers on the Long Bar Harbor project you'd take action against him that he'd regret?"

"Caputo? Wha, Ah don't believe Ah know anybody by that name. Who is he?"

"Irving Caputo, one of the administrative people at the Manatee County Engineering Department. Are you saying you don't remember who he is? You don't remember threatening him to not approve the project if he knew what was good for him? We've found letters among your papers here in your house asking him not to approve that project." Horseman was obviously lying. What else had he lied about so far?

"Suh," Horseman protested, "Ah would nevah threaten anybody. A'hm acquainted with quite a few of the Manatee County engineers, but Ah don't know yaw Mistah Caputo personallay, an if Ah did, Ah would nevah have threatened him. Thas just not me. Ah mighta talked to various people about this project or that project, but Ah nevah would've threatened anybody. And fowah the life of me, Ah have no recollection of evah meeting yaw Mistah Caputo."

Jack's questions to Horseman reminded me that I also had a few more questions for him related to the day

I got shot. "So, Mr. Horseman," I began, "why did you want to have a second meeting with me? It seemed as though you had made yourself quite clear regarding the Long Bar Harbor project during our first meeting. Julius Josephski was dead, and it was quite evident you wanted the development of that land to stop with his death. You seemed to be concerned that somehow I might play a role in continuing to develop the Harbor, and you were quite definite in asking me whether the development was going to stop now that Josephski had been murdered. So what was the point of the second meeting?"

"Ah arranged that second meeting with ya'll because Ah wanted ya'll ta have certain information you could carry back to yaw client in Ohio explaining how he could get some of his money back. Ah was afraid he'd try to carry on the project in ordah to recovah his investment in Mistah Josephski's deal. Mah plan involved Mistah DeVertollo's organization buying out Mistah Josephski's partnership with DeVertollo and payin' off your client fowah his interest. Ah decided not to show fowah the meeting Ah planned to have with you about this when the DeVertollo organization backed away from this idea after Mr. DeVertollo's death. So Ah jess went fishin' instead, so to speak, out on the Okeechobee lock system."

"Who presented this idea to the DeVertollo people?" I asked. "You?'"

"Naw. Alexis Weidenfeld."

"Why would she come up with an idea like that?"

"Don't ask. It's too complicated—somethin' to do with huh not having ta contest Josephski's will, awr somethin' like that."

"So I suppose that's how she knew you were out on the Okeechobee locks when you were supposed to be meeting with me. Right?"

"Ah don't know. Ah suppose so." Horseman then turned white and lost consciousness. We had Angeltine call for an ambulance, and we left before the squad got there. No doubt the place would soon be crawling with police. Angeltine wanted to leave with us, but we refused, telling her that we'd be back for her if she didn't say anything about our being there. We told her to just tell the police she had found Horseman shot in the side, but she didn't see how it happened. "Tell them all you know is what you found. Mr. Horseman was lying outside the back door, shot in his side. You picked him up and brought him into the house and put him in the bed," instructed Jack.

Chapter 28

When Kit-Kat and I told the Sarasota sheriff's office
about the videos we'd found at Horseman's house, it
took the necessary steps to have a search warrant issued
immediately. As it turned out, they'd found the cameras
in Julius Josephski's rooms atop the Ritz very early in
the game, but there were no videos inside them. They'd
also found out something else. The hotel doorman had
informed them Uber cars pulled up to the hotel entrance
from time to time and disgorged a man who fit Johnson
Horseman's description. Uber had records revealing a
number of trips between Arcadia and the Ritz. Each
time, the Uber client was Johnson Horseman, and each
time he had used the same Uber driver. On one
occasion a foreign woman accompanied him, according
to the driver. Both had gotten out of the car together at
the Ritz, and the Uber driver was instructed to wait for
them. Curiously, the Uber driver's description of the
foreign woman fit Angeltine—extremely large, tall,
braided black hair and dressed in a colorful Indian-like
or Caribbean dress.

The explanation we gave the sheriff's office for why
we happened to be at Horseman's house when the video
tapes were found was that he had invited me there to
discuss the accusation I was making that he had shot
me. I explained I had asked Kit-Kat and Jack
Rainspring to come along to guard me. While we were
there, Horseman tried to shoot me again, but Rainspring
shot him instead, putting him in the hospital in
Sarasota, ostensibly in a coma. After Jack shot

Horseman, we searched his house for evidence of his role in shooting me, and we came across the video tapes. The sheriff's detectives began investigating our story immediately. With Horseman now in the hospital and unable to communicate, no charges had yet been brought against Jack for shooting him, but he was taken into custody.

Kit-Kat and I went back to Horseman's house with the deputies to serve the search warrant. Horseman wasn't there, of course, and Angeltine didn't know what to do when she answered the door. Totally flustered and very nervous, she could not understand what the police wanted.

"Is this the home of Johnson Horseman?" a deputy inquired.

"Mr. John not here," Angeltine answered. "He still in hospital."

"That doesn't matter," said the deputy. When the Sheriff's deputy attempted to step by her into the house, she shoved him back, barring the door. "Ma'am, I have a search warrant issued by a judge of the Twelfth Circuit Court of Sarasota, Manatee and DeSoto counties. Mr. Horseman need not be present in order for us to serve and execute this writ. Please step aside." He took the search warrant out of his shirt pocket and handed it to her.

Angeltine continued to block the man's entrance, as she shouted, "This matter belong to Big Cypress Indian Reservation, not you. No jurisdiction! Get out! Mr. John always tell me government police have no business here. This house in Big Cypress Indian Reservation jurisdiction." She was quite daunting because of her size. The deputy motioned to his sidekick in the cruiser, and he came up to the door and grabbed her. The first deputy then handcuffed her. "Mister Horse always tell me if police come to door to tell them only Big Cypress Reservation have jurisdiction here," she shouted again.

"Well, I'm afraid that's not true, ma'am," the deputy replied. "Now will you step aside or do we put you in the cruiser?" Angeltine shot a flustered look our way, as if to say, 'Can't you do something?' Then she yielded.

"You not take me," Angeltine warned. "Only Big Cypress Indian Reservation can take."

"We don't want *you,* ma'am. We want something else." The officer turned to Kit-Kat.

"Okay, do you know where these tapes are?" he asked.

"Yes, they're in a drawer in the den. I'll show you."

The police confiscated the tapes, put them in the cruiser and prepared to leave. "Wait a minute. Not so fast," I said. "Don't you want to ask her about her ride in the Uber car with Horseman?"

"She won't know what an Uber car is," said the deputy. "To her a car is a car." Then he turned to Angeltine and asked, "Ever ridden in an Uber car with Mr. Horseman?"

The look on Angeltine's face became vacant. "What be *Uber?*" she asked.

"It's like a taxi, or a private limousine," the deputy explained, "usually black or white, and you have a driver."

Still the blank look persisted on Angeltine's face. "There, you see, as I told you, she doesn't know what an Uber car is," said the deputy with a note of satisfaction in his voice.

"Well, wait a minute," I said. "Angeltine, do you know a man named Julius Josephski?" She looked at me, but her stare was no longer blank. "Well, do you?" I repeated. "He lives in Sarasota in a hotel." She remained silent. "Do you know him?" Her look became perplexed, her demeanor nervous again. "Were you ever in the same room with Julius Josephski?" I asked.

Silence.

"Ma'am," came the deputy's voice. "Answer his questions or I'm gonna take you into the Sarasota Police Station."

"He make for me to clean for him," she suddenly blurted out.

"Who made you clean for whom?" I asked.

"John Horse."

"Who?" I asked again. "Johnson Horseman made you clean? For whom—Julius Josephski?"

She nodded her head "yes."

"So you're saying Johnson Horseman made you clean for Julius Josephski? Is that right?"

"Yes, he make contract for me to clean Mr. Joseph's place."

"And did you clean Mr. Josephski's place?"

"Yes"

"How many times?"

"One time."

"I've been over the videos carefully," Kit-Kat interrupted. "There's nothing there showing her cleaning Josephski's penthouse suite."

I held up my hand to silence her for a minute, and I asked Angeltine, "Was Mr. Josephski in his apartment while you were there cleaning?"

"Oh yes," she answered. "Yes, he there." A sheepish look came over her face.

Kit-Kat began to speak again, and again I held up my hand to silence her. "Let's go outside for a minute," I suggested. "The people from the sheriff's office should come too. Angeltine, you wait here."

We left Angeltine in the den, and went out the front door. Kit-Kat was champing at the bit to say something. "Well, that doesn't square with what we know about these videos, does it?" she announced. "We know every time Josephski left his suite, the cameras automatically turned off. So something's very fishy here. If Josephski was in his suite with her, there should be pictures. There's no such picture."

"Unless someone turned the cameras off while the two of them were together," I opined.

"What? You mean turned the cameras off by hand?"

"That's what I guess I mean. Maybe there's a way we can test my theory. Let's go back inside."

We went back in and approached Angeltine again. "Angeltine," I asked, "do you remember what time you cleaned Mr. Josephski's rooms on the day you cleaned them?"

"Yes. Contract call for two and one half hours of cleaning, 2:30 to 5:00."

"Bingo," interjected Kit-Kat. "That's piano practice time according to the other tapes. When he was home, he practiced religiously from 2:00 to 3:00."

"And did Mr. Horseman take you to Mr. Josephski's that day?" I continued.

"I don't remember."

"Did Mr. Horseman visit with Mr. Josephski on that day?"

"Visit? No."

As we rode back to Sarasota, I asked the deputies to see if they couldn't isolate the day from Uber's records that Horseman rode with Angeltine to Josephski's place. I decided in the meantime I would cross examine Lexi about the video tapes, whether she wanted to talk to me or not. The police were going to have to help. They were just going to have to tear down the castle walls they had erected to protect her reputation, and bring her in for questioning.

Chapter 29

The police refused to bring Lexi in.

"On what grounds?" asked the deputy sheriff. "We've already interviewed her about Josephski's death, and there's nothing to indicate she'll have anything more to say. We like to leave our good local citizens alone in this town unless there's some reason to bother them."

"Mr. Horseman told us that Alexis Weidenfeld was the person responsible for bugging Julius Josephski's suite with video cameras because she was a jealous girlfriend who he felt needed to be watched. Don't you wonder if that's true? That should be enough of a reason to call her into the station—to find out if she admits to that or not. It's time to stop favoring your local citizens who are in the Brahmin class, especially when it comes to murder investigations."

"You may have heard Mr. Horseman say Weidenfeld bugged Josephski's place, but we haven't heard Horseman say that, so I'm afraid we have no grounds to act on your suggestion, Mr. Barchrist." I was talking to Deputy LaFarge, who added, "And, we're not playing favorites."

"Well of course, you haven't heard him say anything about this. He's in a coma at Sarasota Memorial. He can't talk."

"All the more reason not to bother Alexis Weidenfeld, sir. If Mr. Horseman comes out of the coma, perhaps we'll speak to him, and depending on what he says, then perhaps we'll speak to Alexis Weidenfeld."

"Perhaps? What do you mean perhaps? You've got to stop running a nursery school here for the well-known and rich of Sarasota County, and get down to treating them like everybody else."

"Well, if you've got a complaint about the way we're handling this case, sir, I can put you in touch with the right people so you can complain. Until then though, I'd suggest you watch your Yankee mouth."

"No, no. You just go ahead and do your thing, and I'll do mine," I replied. "That'll have to be fine, I guess." With that, I walked out of the police station and over to the Edwin DeVertollo Building; took the elevator up three flights, walked into the Law Offices of Alexis Weidenfeld & Assoc. and announced myself.

"Do you have an appointment?" the person manning the front desk asked. He was tall and thin, almost like he had Marfan's Syndrome, flamboyantly dressed, and groomed like a model in *Esquire Magazine*.

"No," I stated resolutely. "But I can wait. Is she in right now?" I looked around the spectacularly appointed waiting room, which was decorated in a colorful style with mauve colored walls, works of glass by Chiluli sitting around on pedestals, art deco statuesque ashtrays with no ashes in them, Mies van der Rohe chair knock-offs, and an acrylic see-through baby grand piano at one end of the room.

"Sir, I can make you an appointment, but she can't see you today. I'm afraid she's booked very heavily all day ."

"That's not what I asked. I asked, is she in. From what you say, obviously she's in. So I'll wait. Is there a back way out of here, a fire exit or something? If so, I need to call someone in to watch it. She's definitely going to talk to me before she leaves."

"Are you a client. sir? What did you say your name was again?"

"Winston Barchrist III."

"I'll tell her you're here, sir. Excuse me for a moment please." He could have called back to Lexi or her assistant on the intercom to announce me, but instead he rose and walked back beyond a huge floor-to-ceiling aquarium dividing the waiting room from the rest of the office. I could see him through the tank talking to a woman, and then the woman went into an office, presumably Lexi's. In a minute, Lexi emerged from the office and walked determinedly toward the aquarium and into the waiting room.

"Well, Winston, I certainly never thought I would hear from you again." Lexi's eyes were piercing and fixed on me, with no hint of warmth, as she stood up to the full extent of her 5 foot-six-and-a-half inch frame. "Chester here says you want to see me," she said, glancing toward the Marfan man.

"You've got a beautiful office here," I said, trying to deflect her anger.

"Not anything like in Ohio, huh?" There was scorn in her voice, and her eyes were shifting from side to side looking to see if there was anyone else in the waiting room watching us, as if she wanted to avoid a scene.

"Listen, Winston. I'm very busy right now. I wonder if we could meet somewhere after work to discuss whatever it is you've got on your mind. I can have my assistant, Mildred, make us a reservation somewhere."

"I don't think so," I responded. "It's best discussed right here and now, before the police contact you." I was lying about the police, of course.

"The police! Okay," she said, and then sarcastically added, "Boy you really know how to get a girl's attention, don't you? I guess you'd better come back into my office right now. Sounds like this is a situation that calls for privacy." We walked back past the impressive aquarium into the inner sanctum of her office. When I entered, she closed the door but remained with her back up against it, looking very dangerous, but also very seductive. Her demeanor suddenly became extremely gruff. "Okay, what is it? What's this all about, that you had to come busting in here today?" she demanded.

I immediately began feeling self-conscious. I don't know if it was because of my weight and my presence alone with Lexi and her sleek female figure, or because of the image of an easily victimized person I was sure I was exuding. I tried my best to hide my feelings by coming straight to the point.

"It's about the video cams that were found in Julius' suite at the Ritz, and about the tapes from them you hid at Johnson Horseman's." I heard the lock on her office door click behind her before she moved away from the door. Then she began to move past me toward her desk.

She picked up the phone and stated, "Chester, I don't want to be disturbed by anyone while I'm in here. Please tell Mildred—Oh. Yes, and tell all the associates too." Then she looked up at me and said casually, "Take a seat." A heavy silence ensued as she put the papers she had been working on into her desk. As I watched her putting things away, and as I began to sit down, I could see a gun in her desk drawer. Then she went over to a small cupboard on the wall that opened into a little stand-up vanity table with a mirror, and surprisingly, she began applying lipstick and combing her hair. When she was finished, she turned around quickly and said, "So, it appears you've been in touch with Johnson Horseman. Tell me about it. Where were you when he discussed these tapes with you? Did you actually see the tapes you're referring to?"

"Yes."

"Where did you see them?"

"At his house."

"You were at his home?"

"Why are you so surprised, Alexis? Apparently you've been a guest of his quite a lot. As a matter of fact, you were at his house on the same night I was there a few nights ago. You'd just left before me. That's all. Remember the ruckus outside the kitchen door?"

"That was you that night? Hm! Who was with you? It seemed like there were others with you."

"There were," I said. "But they shall remain anonymous. So tell me, what was going on between you and Horseman that night?"

"No," said Lexi, "you tell me what you were doing there that night."

This woman was plenty tough, but suddenly, I felt I was in control, even though this was her office. It seemed like I now had the upper hand. I noticed she kept casting glances toward the vanity on her wall from time to time. I couldn't tell for certain but it looked to me like she had a small pistol stashed, maybe a 9 mil Ruger .380 LCP. I slowly got out of my chair and moved over to the wall pocket vanity, stationing myself in front of it so she'd have to get by me first before getting to any gun in there. Her eyes remained steely, showing no look of alarm. That convinced me that what I'd thought I'd seen in her desk drawer was, in fact a gun, against which I was defenseless. Nonetheless, I persevered, revealing my real reason for being there.

"So tell me, Lexi. What's been going on between you and Mr. Horseman?"

The woman stood up behind her desk, almost scaring my insides out, making feel I was a goner. But instead of reaching for a gun in her desk, she put her fists firmly on the desk and leaned over them, arms straight up and down above her fists. She then delivered her next sentence with alarming confidence.

"Absolutely nothing," she squawked. "Absolutely nothing, and if you knew otherwise from those video tapes you claim you've seen, you wouldn't be here asking about them. Tell me, am I in any of them? What did you see in them? Nothing at all, I'll bet."

"Correct Lexi. But how is it you know that? Why did you have the cameras planted in Josephski's apartment?"

"Wait a minute. Wait just a damn minute! Who says I'm the one who had video cameras planted at Julius' place?"

"That's what Johnson Horseman said. He said you did it because you were jealous and because you didn't trust Josephski as far as other women were concerned."

"That son of a bitch! He's a real son of a bitch, Winston! As you've probably noticed, there are quite a few people around this town trying to ruin my reputation. Now I know Horseman's just another one of those people. He must be trying to ruin me because he wasn't able to get anywhere with me in his negotiations to stop Julius' development of Long Bar Harbor. My guess is that Horseman himself had those video cams planted to try to get a leg up on Julius, either with tapes of discussions Julius had with various people concerning the environmental aspects of the Long Bar Harbor project. Or he wanted to record discussions concerning the manipulation of the County Engineer's Office that everybody knew was going on at the time."

"Well," I asked, "what could Horseman possibly get out of ruining your reputation, either as Julius Josephski's significant other, or with the banks as a real estate investor as reported in the *Herald Tribune*?"

"He was trying to create leverage to use against me so I would betray Julius while negotiating for him."

Her explanation seemed unlikely. As she went on, I remembered various things I'd discovered that were inconsistent with the tale she was now spinning. *She had let it slip earlier that she knew Horseman had gone to the Okeechobee Locks, and she thought he was still there on the day I was shot. How could she have known that? She had admitted she had spent time previously with Horseman, but she never accounted for that time, except that ostensibly she was negotiating with him on Josephski's behalf. But to actually go to his home seemed a cut above meeting for negotiations. Then there were the papers I'd found in the desk at her house, including the affidavit she had prepared for Irv Caputo's signature in which he blamed DeVertollo for threatening him. Why was that done? Caputo had told Jack Rainspring that Horseman was the person who'd made the threat, not DeVertollo. And, why had Lexi tried to arrange to have DeVertollo's people buy out Josephski's interest in his deal with my client?*

Finally, there was the strange ownership relationship of Long Bar Harbor set up in the wills and trusts of Lexi Weidenfeld and Julius Josephski, leaving everything to her if Josephski predeceased her. What was the purpose of that? And, what about the strange claim from the police that my fingerprints appeared on the mortgages Lexi signed in which purportedly, according to the papers, she had fraudulently stated she planned to live in the condos she was actually purchasing for investment. Too many situations to try to resolve here in Lexi's office with her, I thought to myself.

There was also the delicate matter of how I was going to go about extracting myself from her office. Kit-Kat had told me not to trust her and I didn't. When I turned to leave, she could easily go for the lovely little pistol in her wall vanity and fill me full of holes from behind. There would be no problem. It was obvious to everyone in the office I had forced my way in to see her. It could be made quite clear that I had a lot to say to her whether she wanted to hear it or not. She could make up some cock and bull story about how I had assaulted her, maybe even with one of her own guns— easy enough to wipe any prints off it and install mine on it. She could say she found it necessary to shoot me with her pistol in self-defense, and give the police any one of many possible permutations for the scene of her crime. If there was one thing I'd learned about how things worked in Sarasota, it was that the police would move Heaven and earth to keep the Lexi Weidenfelds of the town from being prosecuted.

Finally, I decided the best way to extract myself form this situation was the straightforward way. "Well, Lexi, you've answered all my questions satisfactorily I guess, so I think I'll just leave."

"Yes. Please. Just leave and don't come back—and don't ever bother me again. I can assure you that if you do, I'll take legal measures to have you stopped. Just because you're having trouble clearing yourself of Julius' murder doesn't mean you can try to trample over my good name, and don't try to conflate me with the likes of Johnson Horseman. That's just not going to work for you. You've got nothing there. You hear me? There's nothing there."

I doubted it, but maybe she was right, not that she couldn't be conflated with Johnson Horseman, but that I had no way of proving it. She certainly would deny everything. The video tapes seemed to tell us nothing, and Horseman certainly wasn't going to admit to anything because he was at Sarasota Memorial Hospital in a comatose state.

It looked like I was out of leads. There was, however, one more loose end I needed to run down.

That was how was it my fingerprints could have appeared on the loan documents Lexi had signed for the condos she bought, stating untruthfully that she planned to live in them. Since the police were being completely unhelpful as to that issue, I had only one other place to turn, and that's where I decided to go next.

Chapter 30

To say that Rhett Kessler was surprised to see me is an understatement. At first he acted like he was unsure he remembered me, but when I brought up the Josephski loans, his memory became keener, and he began exhibiting an air of nonchalance. Something was very wrong. It was unlikely a banker would forget a lawyer who had come into his bank to look over loan documents the banker had drafted for a transaction affecting a customer who was not the lawyer's client. Kessler's attitude reminded me of Stanley Schwartzencaup's attitude when he fired me as his assistant in the Irving Caputo case before hiring me. Very curious. The only difference was I wouldn't let Kessler out of acknowledging my needs. I persisted until he had to respond.

"Oh, yeah, the loans I worked on for Julius Josephski while I was still at the Anchors Away Bank. Do you want to see those again? That'll take a little doing since they're all neatly packed away in our archives now. I thought you'd gone back to Ohio, Mr. Barchrist. Tell me, is that pretty little assistant of yours, what was her name, Rosanne? Is she still here with you?"

"Rosanne's a CPA, and, yes, she's still here in Sarasota."

"That's good. There's nothing like working with a pretty woman." He slapped my shoulder and let out a robust guffaw.

"I don't want to see the loan documents again, Mr. Kessler. I just came over here to ask you a few questions."

"Like what?"

"Like tell me, did your bank, I mean Anchors Away, that is, make certain loans on condominiums or other residential properties to Alexis Weidenfeld?"

"Now you know, Mr. Barchrist, being a lawyer, even if we did make such loans to Ms. Weidenfeld, I couldn't tell you a thing like that without violating the federal privacy laws."

"Then you did make such loans to her!"

"No, I'm not saying that. What I'm saying is that I'm not going to tell you."

"Look, Mr. Kessler, the police have told me my fingerprints were on those residential loan documents. How do you suppose that happened?"

"Mr. Barchrist, what are you talking about?"

"The police—the Sarasota Sheriff's Office—that's what I'm talking about. Now what do you know about it?"

"Mr. Barchrist, I can assure you I don't know a thing about whatever it is you're talking about."

"Oh come now, Mr. Kessler. You know the police were here asking questions about me. You don't deny that do you? And, you must have shown them Alexis Weidenfeld's loan documents, and they must have dusted them for prints. Otherwise, why would they have told me my fingerprints were on them?"

Kessler was beginning to look peaked. "I don't know," he said. "I really don't know."

"Tell me something, Mr. Kessler. That day Rosanne and I were here to look at the Josephski loan documents, you excused yourself and went out into the banking area to make a phone call. Who did you call?"

"I don't remember doing that," he said.

"Well, I do. Now who was it you called?"

"I, I really don't remember every call I place, and I don't remember making the phone call you're talking about."

"C'mon, Mr. Kessler. Am I going to have to have the police get a court order to see all of the bank's phone records for that day? Was it Alexis Weidenfeld you called? Did you call Alexis Weidenfeld? Tell me!"

"Why would I call her?"

"I think it was her! And I think you called her when we showed up that day, because I think she had previously contacted you and told you to call her if I showed up wanting to see Julius Josephski's loan documents. She knew that's why I was in town—to look over those loan papers. And you and she are buddies, aren't you?"

"No, we're not buddies. Why would you say a thing like that?"

"Oh, I don't know. Maybe because she's a beautiful woman, and you like beautiful women. Maybe because she's a well-known real estate attorney, and you deal a lot with well-known real estate attorneys in your business. Maybe because she's quite a real estate investor in her own right, and as a banker, you network a lot with investors, especially pretty ones, even doing them favors on occasions."

I looked at Kessler's face. It was sagging now, and it seemed all of his sassiness and boyish looks had disappeared, perhaps because of my withering cross examination. "You know, Rhett," I continued, "now that I think of it, maybe you could really get in trouble here. You've read in the newspapers all about Ms. Weidenfeld's current banking scandal. You know, about her so-called fraudulent statements concerning whether she was intending to live in certain residences she was purchasing, or whether she was buying them as investments, all just so the banks would offer her lower mortgage interest rates on her purchases. Well, what if it got out that you were the one who leaked that information to the press? Or even better yet, what if you were the one who made those loans to her?"

"Wait a minute, I never leak information to the press."

"But you knew about it, didn't you? Because you were her banker, weren't you?"

"Are you trying to threaten me?" Kessler shouted. Some of the tellers looked up from their windows.

I answered him with silence, just complete silence. I had no idea whether anything I was accusing him of was true or not, no proof. I had made it all up. It was pure supposition on my part.

"Let's go into my office," he said.

When we closed his office door, I pursued him even further based on pure speculation. "We don't have to tell the police everything. Just tell me how my fingerprints got on the mortgage documentation Alexis Weidenfeld signed."

He confessed! To my great surprise, he confessed! "On the day you were here," he explained, "I folded some of Lexi Weidenfeld's documents in with the Josephski documents I gave you to look at, and after you touched them, I took them away."

"Why did you do that?"

"Because Lexi told me to, and she told me to show them to the police if they ever came here checking why you were here. You're right. It was Lexi who I called that day while you and your assistant were sitting in my office."

"Why did she tell you to do that?"

"I don't know. I don't know. I was just doing her a favor because she had done so many favors for me. I didn't ask her why, or what was going on."

"Okay, look," I said. "If the police ask you about this again, all you have to say is that you accidentally got some of her documents mixed in there that day, with Josephski's documents. You don't have to tell them she told you to do it. Don't worry, I won't say anything about the two of you conspiring to do it." I remembered Lexi had told me on the way to Micanopy that Julius Josephski said she could fib to the bank about whether she was buying certain properties for investment or personal use in order to get a lower interest rate. *I speculated she had pulled off this little exercise of mixing her mortgages in with Josephski's mortgages for me to see, so I would get my fingerprints on them with Kessler's help. Then she could accuse me of trying to divert publicity and attention from myself as a murder suspect in Josephski's murder by turning her in to the newspapers for alleged mortgage fraud in order to create a diversion. She would later defend herself against the fraud charge by saying she didn't know it was fraud and it was Josephski's idea to fill out the loan papers the way she had, with no intent on her part.*

After all, for fraud, intent to defraud must be proven on the person charged. Josephski's death would keep him from contradicting her and as one of the city's Brahmans, her testimony that there was no intent on her part would be believed.

I was pretty proud of myself as I walked out of the New Band Bank, leaving a crumpled Rhett Kessler behind. I had solved at least one of the mysteries plaguing me, albeit, the least important one. Now I knew how my fingerprints got on Alexis Weidenfeld's note and mortgage documents. But how was I going to prove that I didn't kill Julius Josephski or Edwin DeVertello?

Chapter 31

The next day I went back to the police station to ask if I could watch the videos again. Anton LaFarge came out to the front desk to greet me. "I owe you an apology," he said, "for being a little brusque yesterday. I realize how this case must be fraying your nerves, what with your having to stay in town because of it and all. Believe me, my calling you 'Yankee' is just an expression of speech. I didn't mean anything by it. If you want to come back to the conference room and watch those videos again, please be my guest. We can't make heads nor tails of them. Oh, and by the way, we had Uber check its records at your suggestion. The day the Uber driver transported both Johnson Horseman and a lady into Sarasota from Arcadia to the Ritz was May 15. He arrived at the Ritz a little after 1:30. The driver said he thought the lady was more likely than not an Indian lady."

"May 15? That was the day I was supposed to meet with Josephski. It was the day he was murdered. Well, now you've got another suspect besides Alexis Weidenfeld and me. This information from Uber was a real lead. Horseman could have done it. He could have been up in Josephski's suite while I was downstairs in the Ritz bar waiting for him."

"Or, the Indian woman could have done it," LaFarge surmised.

"I doubt that," I answered.

"Well, we can't interview Horseman unless and until he throws off that coma he's in, but we could interview the Indian lady again who works for him to find out if that was her in the Uber car with him, even though we've failed at that once already."

"First, let's check out something else," I said. "Let's go in and run the tapes for May 15."

When we ran the tapes for May 15 again, they showed the video recorder had been switched off at 1:38 p.m. But if the past history indicated by the tapes was correct, the tapes should have been on and running because Josephski was in his suite, presumably getting ready to come down to the bar to meet me. On the right side of the last frame, just before the camera switched off at 1:38, there was a small white caricature of a hand. "What's that?" I asked, pointing to the hand.

"Oh that's an icon designating whether the video camera was turned off by hand or automatically. If it had turned off automatically, the icon would be of a broken wire with sparks," said LaFarge.

"Well, if you can't interview Horseman yet, I think you'd better go out and interview his Indian house help. She may have some of the answers you're looking for. If you do, can I come with you? I think she'll be a lot more forthcoming if I'm with you. When we were at Horseman's home before, she seemed to open up to me a little. She's completely afraid of Horseman, and he's got her believing that nobody can make her leave his place except officials of the local Indian Reservation."

LaFarge and I drove out to Arcadia. When we got there, a surprise was waiting for us. Alexis Weidenfeld's Porsche Targa was parked in the driveway.

"What's Lexi doing here?" I asked when Angeltine opened the door.

Angeltine looked very disturbed. "Did you hear me, Angeltine? Why is Alexis Weidenfeld in the house when Mr. Horseman's not here?"

"Mr. Horse, he in the hospital, and she here to get his things—things for his work."

"No, Angeltine, Mr. Horseman can't work right now. He's in a coma. You know that. So what is Lexi doing here?"

Angeltine was being hassled, and clearly I wasn't the only one hassling her. Very nervously, she held her hand out waist high but close in to the middle of her waist, thumb up, with her forefinger straight out like the barrel of a gun, and she cast her eyes downward at the symbol she was forming without moving her head. I tried to look into the house beyond her, but she was blocking my view because of her size, and the room behind her was too dark to see anything. Deputy LaFarge appeared behind me in his deputy sheriff's uniform, but Angeltine did not go into her usual tirade against the Sarasota County authorities as opposed to the authority of the local Indian Reservation. LaFarge let me take the lead.

"Angeltine," I said, "when we were talking last time I was here, you told me Ms. Weidenfeld and Mr. Horseman had secret discussions you overheard about 'what will happen after . . .,' but you didn't know what they meant about 'after.' You didn't know 'after' what. You said Mr. John and Ms. Weidenfeld would say things to each other about the preservation of At-Tah-Thi-Ki by combining ownership with myth. He said he would drive away those who sought to destroy it, and he would do that by using the dream catchers, those old Indian symbols you made for him, and through the powers of the spirit and politics. You also said Ms. Weidenfeld would say in these conversations that she would preserve the land from such evil forces 'by owning it herself and never permitting it to be destroyed by the white man's development.' Please tell Deputy LaFarge here, if you can, what this was all about. What were they talking about? You also said they called their relationship a 'symbiotic relationship.' What did you think this all meant?"

Angeltine's eyes grew larger as I spoke. It was obvious she was trying to say something with her eyes but without using her voice. Suddenly, Lexi poked her head around Angeltine's shoulder and said, "You don't have to say anything, Angeltine. Legally you don't have to answer. You don't have to say anything, especially if these men have come to take you away."

"We didn't come here to take Angeltine in," LaFarge said. "We just came to ask her a few questions. But while we're here, let me ask this, what are *you* doing here?"

"What am I doing here? Oh I just came out to ask Angeltine a few questions myself based on what Mr. Barchrist told me when he barged into my office the other day."

"Like what?" LaFarge asked.

"What do you mean 'like what'?"

"I mean like what did Mr. Barchrist tell you when he was in your office?"

"I told her I'd seen the video tapes from Josephski's penthouse while I was here at Horseman's place," I interrupted. "That must be why she's out here now. Either to get those tapes, or to find out whether someone showed them to me."

"Watch out!" Angeltine warned. "She have gun!"

"Is that so?" LaFarge asked.

"Yes, and I have a permit for it," Lexi retorted.

"And did you take it out in front of Angeltine?"

"She point it at me!" Angeltine cried out.

"Ms. Weidenfeld, give me the gun," LaFarge demanded. "You're under arrest."

Lexi revealed the gun, handing it to Deputy LaFarge. He then proceeded to frisk her. "I think you're going to wind up being very unhappy you did this," she warned LaFarge.

"Maybe so," LaFarge answered. "But you can't go waving a gun in someone's face just because you've got a permit for it. That's assault."

"That's what she says," complained Lexi, "but I say I didn't wave any gun in this woman's face. So who are they going to believe down at the station?"

"Ms. Weidenfeld, sit down," LaFarge commanded. "Don't make me have to use my cuffs or I will. We came out here to talk to Angeltine, not you. Now sit down before I charge you with resisting arrest in addition to assault. Mr. Barchrist here is going to ask Angeltine some questions, and I want you to just sit quietly and listen."

Lexi sat down, and I proceeded with my questions. "Angeltine, do you remember telling me that day I was here, the day Mr. Horseman got shot, that the contract he arranged for you to clean Mr. Josephski's apartment was for two-and-a-half hours, from 2:30 to 5:00 p.m?"

"Yes."

"And did Mr. Horseman take you to Mr. Josephski's to clean?" I continued. "Think hard."

"Yes, that is so. He want to introduce me to Mr. Joseph, he said."

"Now before, when I asked you this question you said you couldn't remember. What caused you to remember now?"

"I can't say."

"You can't say, or you don't know?"

"I can't say."

"Does Ms. Weidenfeld's being here have anything to do with the reason you can't say?"

Angeltine was silent. Her face seemed to freeze up and she looked down at the floor. Then she cast a glance at Lexi who was staring at her. When she looked back at me, she had a frightful look in her eyes. "Can we go outside?" she asked.

Outside, she began crying. "I remember now that Mr. Horse take me to Mr. Josephski's," she sobbed. "I remember this because Ms. Weidenfeld here now."

"What does that mean, Angeltine? What's Alexis Weidenfeld's being here got to do with why you now remember Mr. Horseman taking you to Mr. Josephski's?"

"Because they argue about it."

"Who argued about it?"

"Mr. Horse and Missus Weidenfeld. He wanted her to take me there in her car and pick me up after. She refuse, because she said Mr. Joseph and she were no longer together. Mr. Horse didn't want to take me because he has no car and he need to call taxi to do it. He also say, 'he not want to be involved in any way.' She say someone must to introduce me to Mr. Joseph, and she not want to see him again, ever. They argue very loudly. I hear it all."

"Why would Mr. Horseman not want to be involved if he was the one who arranged the contract for you to clean Josephski's place?"

"I don't know."

"Why were you afraid to tell me this in front of Alexis Weidenfeld?"

"I always afraid of her. I think she witch. She does bad things. She wish for Mr. Josephski's death. I know this."

"How do you know?"

"I know. I know because of hateful things she say to Mr. Horse. She remind him that when Mr. Joseph dead, *At-Tah-Thi-Ki* then belong to her."

We all went back inside and LaFarge told Angeltine that if she had some work to do to go about her business. Then I started cross-examining Lexi about why Horseman, who had gotten Angeltine a job cleaning Josephski's place, didn't want to be involved when it came to taking her to Josephski's suite at the Ritz to introduce her to him.

"Am I being charged with something other than assault now?" Lexi demanded to know.

"Well, apparently, the two of you had an argument over that issue, and it was Horseman who arranged the work for Angeltine, so why was there any argument over who would introduce her to Josephski? You didn't have anything to do with this so-called cleaning contract, did you? So why would there even have been such an argument?"

"Mr. Barchrist, I like neither your tone nor your accusatory manner. So I'm not going to say another word to you without my lawyer being present. It seems to me that Deputy LaFarge wants to arrest me and run me in for assault. So why don't we just let him do that and see how that goes for him. And if he wants to ask me any more questions, my lawyer will have to be present. Bear in mind, sir, I have a right to silence, and a right to know with what crime I'm being charged."

LaFarge and I stepped into the other room for a moment, and he whispered, "You know, I really don't think I should be arresting her. As you can see, it's her word against that Injun lady's, but it's going to be my butt if the prosecutor won't prosecute, and I think he won't."

"Okay," I said, "but just remember if the 'Injun' lady gets shot after you don't arrest Lexi, that could be your butt, too."

"Hm," said LaFarge. "I think I'd rather take my chances with the Injun than with Alexis Weidenfeld."

Chapter 32

A few days later, I received a call from Deputy LaFarge. Johnson Horseman had come out of his coma, and was answering questions for the police at the hospital. He had admitted taking Angeltine with him in the Uber car to the Ritz to introduce her to Josephski, but said he never went up to Josephski's suite that day. Instead Josephski came down to meet them, and was waiting for them under the portico over the driveway at the Ritz Carlton's front entrance. Horseman and Angeltine got out of the car and Horseman introduced Angeltine right there. He then he left to meet a friend at the Moose Lodge out on Anna Maria Island. LaFarge further related that Horseman claimed that after Angeltine finished cleaning, he came back to pick her up in the Uber car which he said he had rented for the whole afternoon. He then took her back to Arcadia. At the end of the police interview, according to LaFarge, Alexis Weidenfeld walked into Horseman's room to visit him as the police were leaving. LaFarge found it quite surprising that Lexi could have known so fast that Horseman had come out of his coma.

"But that's not the end of the story," LaFarge told me. "The next day Angeltine was found dead in Horseman's home in Arcadia. I guess you were right," he added regretfully, assuming it was Lexi who had killed Angeltine. "Maybe I should have booked Alexis Weidenfeld for assault the day we were at Horseman's house."

"Why was Angeltine murdered? You suspect Alexis Weidenfeld of murdering her? Have you got anything linking Lexi to Angeltine's death?"

"Nothing."

"What was the cause of death?"

"Looks like she was garroted, so the cause of death is murder. We'll have to wait for the coroner to answer that one definitively."

"Hm," I opined. "That's the same thing someone tried to do to Irv Caputo—with a piece of piano wire. He died in the hospital a few days later, you know. Irv's case is still open, isn't it?"

"Yeah, the investigation on that one's gone cold, at least for the moment. The only thing we have on it are some crazy drawings Caputo made while he was in the hospital before he died. He was unable to talk, so we got nothing else from him. He was too weak to write anything."

"I remember those pictures he drew," I said. "I thought they looked like pictures of an Indian dream catcher. Did anyone ever have my guess confirmed by an expert?"

"I don't think so," LaFarge answered. "Anyways, what is a dream catcher?"

"It's an Indian charm made of a willow hoop with feathers hanging down from it and netting like a spider web inside the hoop. They were used by the Miccosukee to protect people from nightmares while they were asleep."

"Oh, so that's what those things were. A number of them were found on a table next to Angeltine's body. Guess they didn't protect her too well."

"Angeltine told me that Horseman would have her occupy her time making dream catchers for him," I said, "and Horseman told me he hung them all over

Long Bar Harbor to protect the place from the nightmare of development by the big developers."

"Well, you don't think Horseman could have had anything to do with Angeltine's death, do you?" LaFarge asked.

"I really don't see how that's possible, being as he's still in the hospital."

"And you're not supposing Horseman had anything to do with Caputo's death are you? That's one angle I don't think anyone's considered."

"I do think Horseman may have killed Irv Caputo. As for Angeltine's death," I replied, "I couldn't say, although she died of the same thing Caputo ultimately died of—garroting. As for Caputo, yes, I believe it could have been Horseman who killed him. There are many signs that point to him. My friend Jack Rainspring believes Horseman garroted Caputo because he once threatened Irv in no uncertain terms, when Irv worked for the engineer's office, not to allow the county to okay the Long Bar Harbor development, if he knew what was good for him. Horseman's motive for attacking Irv was to keep him quiet about the threat because he feared Irv would expose him while attempting to defend himself against the theft-in-office charges. What better way to silence him than to garrote him so he couldn't speak?

"Furthermore, everyone knows that Horseman was sort of crazy about leaving those Indian dream catchers around to keep the bad spirits away from Long Bar Harbor, which, as you may or may not know, used to be sacred Indian ground called *At-Tah-Thi-Ki*. I know all this about the dream catchers because Horseman himself told me about them when I met with him out at Linger Lodge for lunch. Irv Caputo must have known that people associated the dream catchers with Horseman. That's why he drew a picture of a dream catcher when he was on his death bed in the hospital. He couldn't talk, but he was trying to reveal—to tell someone, anyone—that it was Horseman who had garroted him. The reason he didn't tell the police Horseman had garroted him while they were questioning him in the hospital was because he was afraid Horseman would find out and come to the hospital to finish his work.

LaFarge clucked his tongue. "Sounds pretty much like 'pie-in-the-sky' supposition on your part to me," he said. "A little far-fetched, isn't it?"

"Oh, and there's one more thing I know you may not know," I continued, "Horseman's a dangerous man, capable of killing. He was once convicted of murder in his youth, but his conviction was overturned while he was in jail because it wasn't borne out by what was later found to be a new kind of evidence called DNA. I can show you this if you don't already know about it. It's in a footnote to a Wikipedia article about why the reference to Horseman's conviction ought to be, and ultimately was, removed from the article."

"How do you know that?" asked LaFarge.

"An assistant of mine up north discovered it and reported it to me."

"Well. I'll have to check that one out, but you know if Horseman was later acquitted because of DNA evidence, that doesn't necessarily make him dangerous. In fact, it would seem to show that he's not dangerous."

"No, I think he's been involved in plenty of rough stuff in his distant past," I said. "Otherwise, he would never even have been accused of murdering someone. We just don't know with whom we're really dealing sometimes, or the kind of person he or she really is even when the person is a person of note."

When he heard me say that, LaFarge brought up Alexis Weidenfeld again, chastising himself once more for failing to book her for pulling a gun on Angeltine. "How could I have just let that go?" he asked. Again, I pointed out to him that he had no evidence she was involved in Angeltine's death.

Suddenly, I had an idea. "Tell me, Deputy LaFarge," I asked, "has anyone told Horseman that Angeltine is dead?"

"No, not to my knowledge. Certainly nobody from the station has communicated that to him."

"Has he had any visitors since your people were last out to see him in the hospital?"

"We can easily check that with the nurses on his floor at the hospital, but I think Alexis Weidenfeld was his only other visitor."

"Well, why don't you check that out and call me back with whatever you find out. Oh, yes, and does the hospital have any way of checking whether any phone calls have come in for Horseman? If so, I'd like to know that too. And I'd like also to know if he's made any outgoing calls."

"Why?" asked LaFarge. "What have you got up your sleeve?"

"I'll tell you as soon as you let me know the answers to my questions. Is that okay?"

I had a plan but didn't want to give the police any opportunity to get in its way, accidentally or otherwise. It had been my experience that the police never liked to do anything unconventional. If I revealed my plan, they'd probably have to get it approved from some higher-up officer, and that might waste too much time and also raise the likelihood the plan would get leaked.

"Just check these things out today and call me back with what you find out, will you?" It occurred to me that for better or worse, I was now taking over investigation of this case from the police. I had a willing partner in LaFarge, who was worried he might have left his rear end exposed by not booking Lexi for assault when he had the chance.

It took LaFarge a little over an hour to get back to me. "No visitors so far, other than the police and Weidenfeld," he reported, "and no outgoing calls from Horseman's room phone. He's had only one incoming call since we last talked to him in person, and that was about two hours ago."

"I think I can guess who called him," I said.

Chapter 33

I told LaFarge I was going to the New Band Bank to see Rhett Kessler about straightening out how my fingerprints got on Lexi Weidenfeld's mortgage documents. But that was a lie. I had already done that. Instead, I planned to visit Horseman in his hospital room and try to trick him into admitting that he and Lexi were in league against Josephski. My theory was that Lexi had seduced Josephski into making her heir to all his interests and to the land he owned out at Long Bar Harbor. That was why the wills and reciprocal trusts I found in the desk drawer at her house existed. But in order for her to inherit that property, Josephski had to be dead. So, I continued to theorize, she had conspired with Johnson Horseman to kill him.

DeVertollo may have also wanted Josephski dead, but probably not actually killed. According to Kessler, DeVertollo certainly needed Josephski to be financially dead. He had tried to cause his financial ruin by throwing whatever political monkey wrenches he could into the approval processes needed from Manatee County for the Long Bar Harbor project in order to delay it. That would drive Josephski into financial ruin by costing him as much in interest and carrying fees as possible. He planned to delay the project, according to Kessler, until Josephski agreed to lower the profile of his portion of the Long Bar Harbor project by making it smaller so the main attraction would be DeVertollo's shopping mall, not Josephski's hotel and club. Lexi knew DeVertollo was squeezing Josephski and so did

Josephski. She hated DeVertollo for what he was doing to Josephski's fortune, and thus to the value of her inheritance. Therefore, she had a motive for wanting to see DeVertollo dead, but whether she had a hand in his death, I didn't know. Clearly she had tried to pin it on both Irv Caputo and me in her discussions with the police on the day of DeVertollo's murder.

She also had another scheme cooked up for disposing of DeVertollo's interference with her future fortune. She had prepared the affidavit I found in the desk drawer at her house which Irv Caputo was supposed to sign. That affidavit, which never was signed due to Irv's untimely death, alleged that DeVertollo had threatened Irv as a county engineer not to issue any of the permits that would allow the Long Bar Harbor project to proceed. The affidavit, possibly prepared at Josephski's urging, stated that DeVertollo had threatened to expose Caputo's homosexual proclivities if he would not do DeVertollo the political favor of delaying the Long Bar Harbor approvals. If made public, the affidavit would have seriously hurt DeVertollo's reputation with the public and with the banks. Therefore, it could be used as good leverage to give up his plans for harming Josephski financially.

The process was probably moving too slowly, however, to save Josephski financially, and this was where Johnson Horseman came in. Horseman was actually the one who threatened Caputo, not Edwin DeVertollo. Horseman knew Caputo could expose him, but he didn't know about the affidavit Lexi had prepared, laying the blame for threatening Caputo at DeVertollo's feet. So Horseman decided to silence Caputo before he disclosed that the well-respected Indian conservationist had threatened him. Thus, he followed Caputo and garroted him in his car outside my place on Westmoreland to insure that he could never accuse Horseman of threatening him.

Of course Horseman also had a motive for wanting Josephski dead. It was the best way, so to speak, of saving the ancient Indian spiritual site, *At-Tah-Thi-Ki*, from extinction. What better way of preventing Long Bar Harbor from being developed, after Lexi's negotiations on Josephski's behalf fell apart than to terminate Josephski's life?

This is where my theory got shaky because there was no evidence to support that theory that Horseman was responsible for Josephski's murder, not even circumstantial evidence. It was pure conjecture on my part, based on the fact that Horseman had a motive.

I surmised the negotiations over Long Bar Harbor had thrown Alexis Weidenfeld and Johnson Horseman together on a number of occasions. Gradually, the two of them realized although Horseman's interests and Josephski's interests could never be reconciled, Lexi's interests and Horseman's interests in seeing Josephski dead coincided completely. She wanted Josephski dead so she could inherit the land on Long Bar Harbor, and he didn't care who owned the land as long as it was never developed.

If Lexi inherited Long Bar Harbor and promised not to carry out the development, that would stop all development of that area. The problem was she would be the obvious suspect in Josephski's murder because her fingerprints were everywhere in his apartment, she had an inheritance coming from him, and the two of them were headed for a break-up. It was due to the ill-fated advice he'd given her on the condos she'd purchased, and the controversy it led to with the banks, as reported in the papers. Sooner or later, it would come out how bumpy that break-up really was, and suspicion that she killed Josephski would fall on her. To the Lexi

Weidenfelds of the world, reputation was more important than almost anything, even Julius Josephski.

So someone else had to do Josephski in, because she would be the logical suspect. The best candidate to kill him was Horseman, who wasn't really associated with Josephski in any public way. All Lexi had to do to breathe life into her scheme was promise Horseman she would never develop the land she inherited from Josephski for commercial or residential use. That was easy enough to do. Of course, she was only in her late thirties at the time, and Horseman was approaching his late eighties. She merely had to outlive him in order to escape her promise and turn Long Bar Harbor back into a multi-million-dollar development. As a result, there was a strong motive for Lexi to conspire with Johnson Horseman to kill Julius Josephski.

Why Horseman arranged for Angeltine to clean Josephski's suite atop the Ritz must have had something to do with the deal between him and Lexi. But I couldn't figure out what that was. It was a question still to be answered.

It was a certainty, however, that the one person who could have overheard them plotting Josephski's death was Angeltine. Of course she had! That's why Lexi showed up at Horseman's carrying a gun while he was in the hospital. Indeed, she showed up at Horseman's with her gun within days of my telling her I knew she had hidden the video tapes at Horseman's house and we had listened to them. She knew Angeltine must have heard enough of their conversations to know what was transpiring between them. So she went out to Arcadia to silence the Indian woman. The only reason she hadn't, was because Anton LaFarge and I showed up while she was there and interrupted her plans.

Lexi and Horseman must have discussed killing Angeltine to silence her after the police left his hospital room during her visit on the day he came out of his coma. Although there was no proof they discussed it, it had to have been clear to both of them at the time that another attempt at shutting Angeltine up had to be made. So Lexi went out to Horseman's home again in Arcadia. This time, she garroted Angeltine, probably choosing that method at Horseman's suggestion, since the police now knew she had a gun that could easily be traced through ballistics and gun registration. My guess was the one telephone call Horseman received at the hospital was from Lexi. I surmised she called him to let him know she had accomplished their plan to silence Angeltine once and for all by killing her.

I knew in order to prove my theory that Horseman killed Josephski, I would have to construct a trap, either for him or for Lexi, or both, that would get them to confess. No easy task, that's for sure. My confrontation with Lexi in her office had proven there was no point in engaging in a frontal assault. In addition to all her other qualities, she was a tough lawyer who dealt only with the facts. If I could show her no evidence, I could get nothing out of her. As for Horseman, he had shown he knew how to lie and was good at making up stories. But once it was proven that he lied, he would tell the truth.

So far the only inconsistency I had been able to catch in the stories of either of them was the issue of whether Lexi knew Horseman was at the Okeechobee Locks or not, when he and I were supposed to be having our second meeting. I was still uncertain of the real reason Josephski's apartment had been bugged, although I knew either Horseman or Weidenfeld had it bugged because the video tapes from the surveillance cameras wound up at Horseman's house. And, finally, I had no idea why I had been victimized by the drive-by shooting in the park, and whether Horseman was involved. The only other things I knew about both these individuals for sure was that Lexi believed very strongly in the paranormal and that Horseman believed very strongly in spiritual Indian things. Hence, Lexi's supposed experience with the supernatural in Micanopy, and Horseman's obsession with dream catchers. Other than that, the only thing I knew about both of them was they could be cruel, threatening and self-serving.

Knowing what I knew for sure, and speculating about what I didn't know, I set about constructing a trap for either Horseman or Weidenfeld, or both. The question was, should I involve anyone else? In thinking about the problem, the answer was "yes." I had to depend on a few others to make my little scheme work.

Chapter 34

So I called the only three people I knew I could rely on: Jack Rainspring, Kit-Kat and Rosanne. Then I went to the nursing desk on Horseman's floor and asked about his condition. The nurse told me he was doing well, and had been taken downstairs for a CAT Scan. Upon hearing he wasn't in his room, I snuck in and disconnected his patient phone. For my plan to work, nobody had to be able to get hold of him until the trap was ready to be sprung.

When I came back out of his room, I asked the nurse to whom I'd spoken what her name was and when her shift changed. She said her name was Kathryn Beall, and she was going off in fifteen minutes. I called Rosanne and asked her to call Lexi Weidenfeld in twenty-five minutes, introduce herself as Nurse Beall and say she had been asked by Johnson Horseman to call her and tell her to come to the hospital at 5 p.m. to see him on a matter of great importance. Then I went back to the visitor's lounge and patiently waited for my cell to ring. When it finally did, it was Rosanne with a report for me.

"Winston, I don't know what you're up to, but I did as you asked. I called Alexis Weidenfeld at her office, told her I was Nurse Beall, and to be in Johnson Horseman's hospital room at 5 p.m. It took almost half an hour to get through to her because I was put on hold. But I insisted I needed to get through to her directly."

"Did she ask you what it was all about?"

"Of course, she did, and I told her I didn't know, and all I knew was Mr. Horseman was insisting, saying it was very important."

"Did she ask why he had failed to call her himself?"

"Yes. And I told her like you said—that he was downstairs getting a CAT scan."

"Is she going to come?"

"She said she would. I also followed your instructions about Detective LaFarge. I called him, gave my name as Nurse Kathryn Beall, and told him Horseman needed to see him at the hospital at 5 p.m. because he wanted to make a statement. LaFarge said he'd come, too."

"Great."

"Winston, what in heaven's name are you up to?"

"I'm not sure I'm up to anything, but if it works out, or even if it doesn't, I'll explain it all to you later. I haven't got the time to do that right now though. Let's just say if it works, we're gonna get to go home. Bye, love."

I stayed in the visitor's lounge until 5 p.m. when I saw Lexi walk into Horseman's room. Two minutes later, LaFarge knocked on Horseman's door. Then I walked in and sprang my trap.

"Winston! What are you doing here?" LaFarge was surprised to see me.

"Well, what are *you* doing here?" Lexi demanded of LaFarge.

Before LaFarge could answer, I said, "Well, I'm here because somebody in this room's going to jail, and it isn't going to be Anton LaFarge or me."

"Is this why you were so insistent on seeing me?" Lexi asked, looking at Horseman.

"Whut da ya'll mean? Ah nevah insisted that ya'll come here to see me."

"You had some nurse call me and tell me it was very important I come over here. That's why I'm here," Lexi replied sternly.

"Ah certainly did not do that, most certainly not."

LaFarge interrupted, speaking to Horseman. "Well, a nurse called me too and said I needed to come over here because you wanted to make some sort of statement to me."

"Well, Ah certainly nevah told any nurse to do a thing lock that! I ain't got nothin' ta say ta ya— specially not ta ya'll, or anyone else down at the sheriff's office. I got rights ya know. I got mah right to silence."

The time had come for me to lay out my theory of who murdered who and why. "Well, Mr. Horseman," I started out slowly, "I think you killed Julius Josephski, and I think I can prove it. I think you stuck a knife in his back and then wiped away your fingerprints. In fact, I think you and Ms. Weidenfeld here colluded to murder Julius Josephski."

"That's absurd," shouted Lexi. "What you think doesn't matter anyway. Where's your proof? I'm getting a little sick of accusations from a hick like you from Ohio. Matter of fact, I think you killed Julius and you're trying to pin it on me. That's why you were at the bank looking over my loan documents." Then she tuned to LaFarge and said, "If you check it out, I'll bet you'll find his fingerprints all over the originals of my loan documents."

LaFarge drew in a deep breath, getting ready to say something, but Horseman interrupted him, "Mistah LaFarge, if this man thinks Ah murdered Julius Josephski, why don't Ah just take a little lie detector test on that there subject. Fat boy here's ridiculous. Ah think he's had too many Po-Boy sandwiches ta eat or somethin." A thin smile creased Horseman's face. Then his lips got thinner, almost disappearing. "Why, Ah nevah heard such crap," he added. "And ta think, he calls himself an attorney."

"I can prove everything I just said," I insisted, but knowing I really couldn't without a confession from Lexi or Horseman. "Mr. Horseman's housemaid, Angeltine, told me all about it. Let's just call her and see what she has to say right now."

LaFarge's eyes grew to twice their normal size when I said this. "But...but...she's...." LaFarge stammered.

"Let's just see what she says," I insisted. "Let's call her right now."

Johnson Horseman and Alexis Weidenfeld looked at each other, both knowing they were in no position to let anyone know they knew Angeltine was dead. No news of her death had yet come out publicly, even though they both knew Lexi had disposed of her. LaFarge looked at me like I was crazy. I raised my hand to stop him from saying anything, and said, "Let's call her right now." Pretending not to know Horseman's phone had been disconnected earlier to prevent Lexi from calling in to him to ask why he wanted her to come to the hospital, I picked up the phone to dial.

"Your phone's dead," I said, as I stumbled around Horseman's bed to reconnect it. Upon making the connection, I asked him for his home number and placed the call.

"Hello?" A voice came from the other end.

"Is this Angeltine?" I asked.

"Yes. I Angeltine," came the almost baritone voice from the other end. Kit-Kat had her imitation of Angeltine finely honed.

"Angeltine, this is Winston Barchrist. I'm here in Mr. Horseman's hospital room with some other people. Mr. Horseman and Ms. Weidenfeld are saying you didn't tell me the two of them colluded to kill Julius

Josephski. Could you set them straight on that please?" There was a pause as the voice at the other end was talking.

Then I responded. "Yes, I believe it was yesterday I was out there speaking with you. No, you won't need to worry about that. Mr. Horseman's still here in the hospital, and he can't even get out of bed yet, and if you repeat what you told me yesterday when I was there, they're going to arrest Ms. Weidenfeld right here on the spot."

Horseman scoffed as I handed him the phone. "Hello, Angeltine? Is that you?" he said.

"Yes," came the baritone voice, loudly enough for everyone to hear, even though only Horseman was holding the receiver up to his ear. Horseman looked at Lexi searchingly, and Lexi looked back in disbelief.

Then Horseman continued, "Tell me if ya'll saw Mr. Barchrist yestaday at the house, and if ya'll did, tell me, whud he say ta you, and whud ya'll say ta him?"

Again the low, almost manly, voice could be heard. "Yes, I see him. He ask what I know about Mr. Joseph's murder. I say I know Mr. Horse and Ms. Weidenfeld make plans together to do it."

"That's impossible!" Lexi screamed.

"She's lying," Horseman said as Lexi glared at him. Both Horseman and Weidenfeld were now in complete disarray. Horseman began insisting there was something very wrong going on here, but he didn't know what. He emphatically denied he killed Josephski, and again offered to take a lie detector on the subject.

"What good do you think that'll do you?" Lexi mocked. "Do you think that's the only question they're going to ask you? Did you murder Julius Josephski?"

"What do you mean by that?" LaFarge asked. "Are you insinuating he didn't murder Josephski, but he had a hand in the murder?"

"I did not kill Julius Josephski," Horseman swore.

"Well, if you didn't, then who did?" I persisted.

"Angeltine," he scowled.

"Johnson, don't go there," Lexi exclaimed.

"Angeltine? Are you saying Angeltine killed Julius Josephski?" I asked skeptically.

"Angeltine killed Julius Josephski with huhr knife when Ah took huhr to his suite at the Ritz to clean it," said Horseman. "She did it becuz he sexually assaulted huhr while she was cleanin' his place, an when I got theyeh to pick huhr up, she was cryin' becuz of what had happened to huhr an becuz of what she done to him in self-defense. Ah wiped the apartment, and Ah mean I wiped everything in the apartment she touched, clean of huhr fingerprints, and then Ah took huhr home. Futhumore, this here's not a matter for the Sarasota police, or for the Sarasota County Sheriff's Office. This here's a matter within the jurisdiction of the Big Cypress Indian Reservation Council." Then looking at Anton LaFarge, he said, "You have no jurisdiction over this, suh."

"Lots of luck with that argument, you buffoon," Lexi admonished. She began pacing, just like she had out in Micanopy when she thought she'd seen the ghost of Julie Josephski. She became flustered and unsettled, almost to the point of getting hysterical. "I believe Angeltine is dead," she said. "That's what I believe. So that couldn't have been her on the phone just now. You probably think I'm getting delusional, but I'm not."

"And why do you believe she's dead?" LaFarge asked.

"Because those are the vibrations I'm receiving right now. I don't know why I'm receiving this message, but

I am. Go out to Horseman's house and you'll find her body."

"We already have, Ms. Weidenfeld, and we found her body. She is dead, but how could you know that? Nobody else knows except the sheriff's office, Mr. Barchrist here, and the local person who found her and reported her death.

Suddenly Lexi collapsed. It was a beautiful example of syncope. First, she complained of light headedness, and then she fainted. It took almost five minutes to revive her, and when she returned, she was hysterical, talking all about the plans she and Horseman had made to do away with Josephski. Maniacally, she insisted that she be allowed to tell us all about it. She went on and on in a great flight of words.

Chapter 35

LaFarge allowed me to come along when he took Lexi to the police station to give her statement, but he wouldn't allow me to sit in while she made it. Finally, he emerged from the interrogation room and asked who it was I had arranged to play the role of Angeltine during the phone call I purportedly made to Angeltine on Horseman's behalf from his hospital room.

"Why that was a woman named Stella Starboard, otherwise known as Kit-Kat," I answered. "I thought she played her role very well, mimicking Angeltine's voice and manner of speech perfectly. She picked up all of Angeltine's voice inflections when she, Jack Rainspring and I were out at Horseman's a week or so ago, where she heard Angeltine talking. Rainspring got Kit-Kat back out to Horseman's house and snuck her by the policeman guarding the scene today in time for her to take my phone call supposedly to Angeltine. Why? Will that affect the usefulness of Lexi's statement in a court of law?"

"I don't know," he said. "You're the lawyer. We read Ms. Weidenfeld's Miranda rights to her before she gave her statement here in the station. After we read her rights, she just began talking freely and openly. But I suppose there's a question of whether she gave the statement of her own free will, since she was tricked into it by making her think that was Angeltine on the phone when Angeltine was actually dead.

"On the other hand, Ms. Weidenfeld declared to our interrogator that she so strongly believed in the paranormal that to her it was actually Angeltine speaking on the phone, and she couldn't be dead. Or if she was, that was her ghost speaking. Of course, it wasn't the Sarasota County Sheriff's Office or the police that tricked her. It was you who tricked her, the way I figure it, not us. We didn't know it was going to happen, or anything about it. Our hands are completely clean, and you weren't associated in any way with our office when you did this. So I have a difficult time seeing how this confession could be excluded from evidence as a coerced confession.

"Well, putting all the legal minutiae aside, can you tell me what Alexis Weidenfeld told you in her statement? Just tell me what transpired in the interrogation room from beginning to end. Can you?"

LaFarge answered, "We brought her in and told her she had a right to silence, that anything she said might, and could be held against her, that she had a right to an attorney and, if necessary one could be appointed for her. After each sentence, I asked her if she understood, and she indicated yes. Then she said that she was so upset and alarmed by hearing Angeltine's voice on the phone that she wanted to talk about it, and she signed a written statement waiving her Miranda rights and began talking. Frankly, after listening to this lady about her experiences with the paranormal, I think she's a little nuts. I don't see how she can believe in all that stuff, but that's what she told us. It was all coming from the paranormal zone of reality."

LaFarge further indicated that Lexi admitted she and Horseman had been planning to kill Josephski for a long time. It began once they realized Josephski was not going to negotiate a settlement of the differences between him and Horseman over the development of Long Bar Harbor. Lexi had convinced Josephski to leave all his interests in Long Bar Harbor to her upon his death. Horseman, however, convinced her that was not enough to insure she would wind up with Long Bar Harbor when Josephski died. The property might be developed by the time he died and sold off to others as developed land. Because the reciprocal trusts Lexi and Julius had executed mentioned only Long Bar Harbor, Josephski's interests in that land and the rental proceeds from it, *but not any proceeds from an actual sale of the property to outsiders,* Lexi could wind up with nothing if the development was sold before Josephski died. In other words, he had tricked her. In any case, because Josephski was refusing to limit his development of Long Bar Harbor in any way, without Josephski dead, Horseman was going to lose his fight to preserve any portion of *At-Tah-Thi-Ki* in its native state. The spirituality of the area would be completely gone."

According to LaFarge, Weidenfeld further admitted she never had any real personal interest in Joseph Josephski. Only his money, his power and his real estate holdings interested her. So, as a part of their plot against him, she and Horseman paid a private investigation company to follow his every move and watch him through surveillance cameras placed in his suite operating only while he was at home. This was done solely so they could determine the most opportune time to strike. According to Lexi, use of the private investigation company and the surveillance cameras had nothing to do with trying to catch Josephski cheating on her with another woman. She simply didn't care about that, but the surveillance cameras paid off in another way. They revealed that at the same time every afternoon he was home, he sat down at his piano to practice. As a result, the hours when he was practicing the piano provided a perfect time to assassinate him.

Neither Weidenfeld nor Horseman, however, wanted to involve themselves in the actual dirty work of killing

Josephski, so they came up with a plan to have someone else do it. According to Lexi, Horseman had complete control over Angeltine. Angeltine was somewhat dull and practically his captive, and she did everything he told her to do. So Horseman spent months filling Angeltine's head full of stories about how Josephski was trying to obliterate all memory of the ancient Indian spiritual site, *At-Tah-Thi-Ki,* by turning Long Bar Harbor into a white man's big development. This, he kept telling her, would be another nail in the coffin containing the remnants of the Miccosukee tribe from which her ancestors had come. But she could help to prevent this, and insure the long proud Miccosukee history in this part of Florida by using her knife to stab Josephski while she was in his suite, ostensibly to clean for him. Then Horseman arranged for her to become Josephski's cleaning lady, and on May 15, he took her to Josephski's penthouse atop the Ritz at about 1:30 p.m. and introduced her to Josephski. Horseman carefully instructed her to wait until Josephski was deep into practicing whatever piece he was playing for the afternoon and then to strike him from behind with the knife she would be carrying under her apron. He told her to twist it, twist it again and strike once more. This, he told her, would make her a hero among the Miccosukee forever in the tribe's glorious history.

On his way out of Josephski's suite, after making the necessary introductions, Horseman turned off the video cameras. He returned at 4 p.m. to collect Angeltine and to wipe the entire suite clean of any fingerprints he or Angeltine might have left behind.

"My gosh, Lexi's story is gory—almost satanic," I said.

LaFarge went on. "The one thing Weidenfeld and Horseman had not banked on was you showing up to meet with Josephski. That was a surprise, and later forced them to make adaptations to their plans."

"But she told me on our way up to Micanopy at the end of May that Josephski had told her who I was and that I was coming to visit him," I said.

"That was a lie, Winston. We asked her if she'd ever heard of you before Josephski died and she said 'no.' Apparently, she learned of your existence and purpose in coming to Sarasota on May 15 at the time we informed her of Josephski's death. The surveillance company had no way of knowing you were coming, either. While they tracked Josephski around the city, they were not privy to any of his conversations in the various meetings to which he went. His phones weren't bugged and there was no mention of you on any of the video tapes that were made while he was at home."

"You mentioned adaptations in their plans that were made because of me. What were those adaptations?" I asked.

"With Josephski out of the way, there were two loose ends left to attend to—DeVertollo and you," LaFarge continued. "Weidenfeld wanted to get rid of DeVertollo by getting her friend, Irving Caputo, to sign an affidavit she had drafted for his signature and then publicizing it around town. The affidavit would have shown DeVertollo's untoward exercise of influence over the workings of county government. Among other things, it accused DeVertollo of threatening to expose Irving Caputo as a homosexual, if he didn't stop approval of the Long Bar Harbor project from occurring until the delay had lasted long enough to destroy Josephski financially. But Horseman didn't think that exposing DeVertollo in this manner would be enough to stop the development from proceeding, especially since you had shown up on the scene representing your client from Ohio. So he took matters into his own hands by putting Angeltine up to another crime, this time stabbing DeVertollo in the parking lot. According to Ms. Weidenfeld, she spread the word to the police that you had been seen in the vicinity of the stabbing shortly before it occurred, casting suspicion on you."

"And what about me?" I asked. "Did she say anything about why Horseman asked for a second meeting with me?"

"Yes," LaFarge answered. "After DeVertollo's death, Weidenfeld and Horseman were still afraid your client would try to carry on the Long Bar Harbor project on his own, together with DeVertollo's successors in his development organization, Cravenstall Ltd. So Weidenfeld went to Cravenstall and tried to convince them to buy out the interest of your Ohio client completely. Which they agreed to do. That is why Horseman set up a second meeting. It was to convey their offer to you. But before that meeting occurred, the people at Cravenstall revoked their offer. That left no alternative to keeping your client out of the deal except to get rid of you. You were his only means of access to what was going on down here with the Long Bar project. That was the reason for the drive-by shooting in the park instead of a second meeting between you and Horseman."

"Was Horseman involved in that shooting?" I asked. "Was he there?" LaFarge's answer to that question was that Weidenfeld told the interrogator that Horseman was definitely involved, but she didn't know if he was actually there. He had made plans to meet you in the park, but when the deal fell through, she thinks he might have arranged for the shooting, but avoided being there personally by taking off for Lake Okeechobee.

"Horseman was also afraid that you, or your Columbus client, would simply step into Josephski's shoes, pay off his debts and continue with the Long Bar

Harbor project. Weidenfeld was worried if that happened it would tie up Josephski's estate for so long that before, or by the time, everything was cleared up, your client, as one of Josephski's creditors, would wind up owning everything Josephski owned before his death. Then she would be cut out of her inheritance from Josephski. Of course, this would only occur after your client had paid off all Josephski's other creditors, and perhaps after a long hard-fought lawsuit. So, after DeVertollo's death, Weidenfeld also felt you and your client should somehow be eliminated from the scene."

"So Weidenfeld ended up like Horseman, wanting to take DeVertollo and me out, as well. Did she say anything about who was responsible for killing Caputo?" I asked.

LaFarge responded he thought it was Horseman, although he had no evidence yet. Apparently, Weidenfeld did not know who killed Caputo, except to say that Caputo was a good friend of hers.

"Did Weidenfeld admit to killing Angeltine?" I asked.

"Yep, although she claimed that the killing was in self-defense," said LaFarge, "although she certainly had a motive for knocking her off. Both she and Horseman certainly knew that Angeltine was in a position to screw them royally just by talking to the police department about what had gone on and everything she had overheard. Nobody knew what Angeltine might say or do. Certainly, if Angeltine was in her right mind, she had no interest in admitting she had killed Josephski or DeVertollo. The only question was whether Angeltine was in her right mind. In my opinion, both Weidenfeld and Horseman didn't think she was, and they had a strong interest in getting her out of the way, just to make certain she never talked. Horseman wasn't in any position to do that, but Weidenfeld was.

"Well, what's going to happen next?" I asked LaFarge..

He didn't know the answer. He was sure there would be a Grand Jury investigation concerning whether Weidenfeld and Horseman conspired to bring about Josephski's murder. He also thought there would probably be a Grand Jury inquiry as to whether Horseman conspired to have DeVertollo killed, but he wasn't sure about that. Further investigation of that case was probably required, he thought, before Horseman would be brought up before the Grand Jury.

But there was one thing upon which he was very clear. "There's no need for you or any of the people here with you to hang around Sarasota any longer, unless you really want to do that," he advised.

"Nope," I told him. "Summer's on its way here now with all the rain, the heat, the bugs and the hurricanes. I think it's time for this Yankee to go home. Soon we'll be heading into football season up north. So, I think my girlfriend and I will just go."

"What a shame," said LaFarge. "As long as you're already here in paradise, why not stay at least a few more days and just enjoy yourselves."

Chapter 36

Three days later, on July 9, as our Delta MD-88 roared upward from Sarasota International Airport toward the southeast and began making its huge arc back around to the northwest toward Columbus, Rosanne snuggled into me—I loved it when she did that—and said, "Winston, you know someday maybe we ought to think about coming back here to live. Gayna would like the idea. She could get herself a yellow bikini."

"No way!" I said. "Not unless somewhere along the way I inherit a couple of million bucks first, which I don't think is ever going to happen. Besides, I don't want to miss the changing seasons. Fall is so pretty and winter is always a nice change, with its pretty white snow, so long as it doesn't last too long."

"Oh you just don't want to live too far away from your beloved Ohio State Buckeyes," Rosanne complained. "Wouldn't you like to have a nice little boat and be able to go to the beach whenever you wanted? We could get a cute little place on the water somewhere."

"Sounds like a million bucks, right there to me," I said.

"Don't be so sarcastic," Rosanne complained. "You could probably make a lot of money down here."

"Oh, and how would I do that? I haven't even got a license to practice law in Florida. How would I make money? Steal it? Rip off seniors for life insurance policies they don't need, or sell them work on their driveways that deteriorates in one season? Oh, I know—I could become a bagger in a supermarket or a Wal-Mart greeter. I see an awfully lot of men doing that sort of work in Florida, although to be a Wal-Mart greeter, I think you need to know Spanish. I know there's also a lot of work available as a Home Depot sales specialist too, if you're a retired plumber, carpenter or electrician, or something like that. And while I'm amassing my fortune, we could live in a trailer park, maybe even in a double-wide."

"Okay, Winston. I get it. You've had a horrible stay here in paradise and you don't ever want to see the place again. I can understand that, but eventually your opinion will change. I know that, too. Look at it this way. You've met a lot of people and you've learned an awful lot while you were down here."

"Yeah, I've learned an awful lot about the paranormal. That and a dime will get you a...." Suddenly, I stopped because I decided it was time to put the "kibosh" on this whole conversation. So I leaned over and whispered in Rosanne's ear, "Besides, we're not even married." That did it. She pulled away from me and refused to say another word until we landed in Columbus, which wasn't until 12:37 p.m.

At Columbus International Airport, nobody hugged me good-bye, which I would have liked very much. Instead, Rosanne was busy giving me one of her frosty stares. All she said was, "Call me sometime." That left me with no alternative other than to go down to my office, which I did, by cab because Rosanne would not offer me a ride. There was nobody at the office when I arrived. Marinda was probably taking a long lunch in my absence. So I sat down at my computer and began writing a long memorandum to my client, Charles Venable, summarizing my trip. Marinda would have to clean up the report, with proper punctuation and spelling, and then email it to Mr. Venable.

In the memo, I described how Julius Josephski had died and how Lexi Weidenfeld had admitted conspiring with Johnson Horseman to have him murdered at the hands of Angeltine. I offered my opinion that, based on her confession, Weidenfeld would be indicted for these things, at a minimum, on charges of conspiracy to commit murder, and on being an accessory to the murder of Josephski. She would also be indicted under a murder 1 count for killing Angeltine. I further indicated my opinion, knowing Lexi, that she would not find any plea bargain offered by the prosecutor acceptable, and that her criminal case would therefore go to trial and she would lose. A fight on appeal would develop over the issue of whether her confession should have been excluded from evidence at her trial, on the grounds that it was not a voluntary confession (I omitted my role in tricking her) and I added I didn't know what the answer to that question would be. In the interim, I explained, if nobody paid the mortgages on the properties Josephski was holding at Long Bar Harbor, the banks would successfully foreclose on all of them.

As for Johnson Horseman's role in the entire affair, I predicted no case against him would be sent to the Grand Jury until more evidence could be obtained, because of "weaknesses" in Weidenfeld's confession concerning him. Again I made no reference to my trickery. The lack of any evidence that Horseman believed in the paranormal to the point he could have accepted Kit-Kat's voice on the phone as being Angeltine's, invalidated anything Weidenfeld said against him that was drawn from the phone conversation between her and Angeltine.

Weidenfeld was simply incompetent to testify to such matters about what Horseman could have known, seen, believed or not believed that were discussed in the phone conversation.

In other words, he could simply deny it all, and claim Alexis Weidenfeld was nothing but a delusional kook. I also emphasized that Horseman did not believe Josephski's death meant the end of the Long Bar Harbor development because he was certain Mr. Venable would try to carry on the project in Josephski's absence.

As a result, there were only three options open to Mr. Venable to recover the money he had invested with Josephski. These were: (1) to pay off Josephski's debts, and bring a will contest action to try to stop Alexis Weidenfeld from inheriting Josephski's Long Bar Harbor property under the mutual estate plans she and Josephski had set up, (2) to wait until the bank foreclosed, and then buy the properties from the bank and try to interest Cravenstall Ltd., as successor to DeVertollo's interest in the Long Bar Harbor development, in going into business with him in order to finish the project; or (3) to go to Cravenstall Ltd. and try to convince them to buy out the interest in the limited partnership agreement Mr. Venable had with Josephski. I further mentioned that the latter two of these plans assumed that Cravenstall, Ltd, was successor to Mr. DeVertollo's interest in the Long Bar Harbor project, which might or might not be the case. All of these options were clumsy, time consuming and had no clear outcomes.

I also indicated that the question of who killed Mr. DeVertollo, or had a hand in his murder, was unimportant in determining how Mr. Venable should proceed, and that the same was true of the question of who killed Irving Caputo. I left the draft email on

Marinda's desk with a note asking her to please clean it up, so I could come in tomorrow and read it before sending it out to Mr. Venable. Then I called a cab and had the driver take me home.

Chapter 37

It seemed like it happened right after I got home and lay down for my nap, but actually the phone didn't ring until about 4:30 p.m. When I picked up, it was Marinda. She was exercising the usual business-like directness that had slowly become the hallmark of her personality after I had promoted her two years earlier from a Molly-Maid who cleaned my office to being my personal and secretarial assistant. Only the high-pitched squeakiness of her voice belied her former less professional status.

"Mr. Barchrist, first of all, welcome home. Secondly, I've finished your email for Mr. Venable. Thirdly, I'm sorry to have to tell you this, but Mr. Venable was found dead in his office the day before yesterday."

The last part of her message hit like a ton of bricks. "Did you just say Charles Venable is dead?" I asked.

"Yes, sir."

"What in the world happened? I think he was only 61 or 62." Still struggling to wake up from my nap, I found it hard to comprehend what Marinda was saying, let alone the ramifications of what she was saying. Charles Venable was my largest client. How long would it take his estate to pay the sizable bill I had racked up working on his behalf in Sarasota? Where would my legal fees come from now?

"It was in yesterday's *Dispatch*," she replied. "He was found slumped over his desk with a knife in his back. No fingerprints around, other than his."

"Oh my gosh. Oh my gosh!" I said under my breath. A horrible feeling of déjà vu crept over me.

"Probably murder," Marinda squeaked.

"Probably," I replied sarcastically. "Were there any more details in the newspaper?"

"I don't remember."

"Do me a favor, Marinda, will you? Get Officer Jerry Shapiro at the Police Department on the phone if they can find him, and patch him through to me here at my apartment." Jerry was neither a desk cop nor a detective. He was a motorcycle cop who had a beat, and my office over the Dairy Mart in German Village, was on his beat. So we knew each other well, because he stopped in at the Dairy Mart for his donuts every day.

"Okay, boss, and do you want me just to send off your email to Mr. Venable now, or did you want to check it over first?"

"Marinda, the man's dead. I don't see any reason to––never mind. I'll check it over first." *No point in showing impatience with her intellect*, I thought to myself. She always did the best she could, even if she was a little slow in the thinking department.

Marinda was able to get the police to find Officer Shapiro, and to have him call me. As we spoke, I could imagine him talking into the microphone on his shoulder, parked out in the city somewhere on his motorcycle, with his revolver, mace, taser and billy club hanging from his black leather belt.

"Jerry, could you please check to see what the department has on file so far about the death of Charles Venable, and let me know?" Silence greeted my request.

Then came the answer. "You know I can't do that, even for you, counselor. That's a police matter, and I could lose my job talking out of turn about an open case." I let my own complete silence greet his response.

Then he said, "Okay, pal. I'm on it....anything for one of our city's biggest lawyers."

That was Jerry Shapiro—a real wise guy. He never missed an opportunity to rub a person's nose in it. It was his way of saying I was not only overweight, but I was struggling with my career and I had just lost my one big client, Charles Venable, who Shapiro felt was out of my league anyway. Jerry also never missed an opportunity to let you know he was doing you a favor. Other than that, he was a worthwhile acquaintance to have. He knew Charles Venable's death was a tragedy for me business-wise, and for my law practice.

"Thanks, Jerry."

I hurried back to my office where Marinda was working over her normal eight hours. "You sounded so concerned on the phone," she said, "I thought I'd better just stay an extra hour to see if you needed anything from me, boss. I know Mr. Venable is—*was*—our biggest client. What's going on?"

"Something really fishy," I told her. "Please try to get hold of Anton LaFarge at the Sarasota Sheriff's Office, and thanks for staying here for me." Remembering how I had narrowly stopped myself from hurting her feelings in our earlier conversation, I added, "I like it that you're always watching out for me."

Marinda tried, but without success, to get hold of LaFarge. Nobody at the Sarasota Sheriff's Office seemed to know where he was, just that he had taken a few days off after 'cracking' the Julius Josephski murder case. I asked her to give me the phone.

"Was Alexis Weidenfeld indicted for the Josephski murder?" I asked the deputy sheriff at the other end of the line.

After about ten minutes of explaining who I was, the deputy had an "ahah!" moment. "Oh, you're Winston Barchrist—*the Winston Barchrist*, who helped Officer

LaFarge solve the Josephski case. Everybody around here knows of you. Yes, there was a true bill issued in that case."

"Was a man named Johnson Horseman also indicted?" I asked.

"No, there has been no indictment of Mr. Horseman yet," said the Deputy.

"What's a true bill?" Marinda asked. I has asked her to listen in on the other phone and take notes during my conversation to Sarasota.

"It's a written decision of a Grand Jury," I explained, "signed by the Grand Jury foreperson that the Grand Jury has heard sufficient evidence from the prosecution to believe the accused person probably committed a crime, in this case, conspiracy to commit murder, and should be indicted for it. Thus, the indictment is sent to the court, and a trial takes place."

"Well, I read your email to Mr. Venable. Why wasn't Mr. Horseman also indicted?" she asked.

"We'll have to wait until we can get hold of Anton LaFarge to find out the answer to that one," I said. Then I asked the deputy, "Where is Mr. Johnson Horseman now?"

"Uh, I'm afraid we don't know exactly, sir."

"How could you not know that?"

"He was released from the hospital almost a week ago, sir, but not taken into custody because of—I don't know—something about his case being under the jurisdiction of the Miccosukee Indian Reservation, or something like that."

"That Indian reservation jurisdictional thing again, as if the Seminole Indian Reservations of Florida were a sovereign nation—that's utter bullshit," I remarked.

"Mr. Barchrist!" cried Marinda. "Your dignity, what about your dignity?"

Taken aback by my swearing, the deputy said meekly, "I don't really know, sir. I could connect you with Commander Harcourt in the front office if you like. Perhaps he could better explain to you what happened."

"No, that's alright. I'll just wait until Anton LaFarge gets back from wherever he is and talk to him about it. Thanks anyways." When I hung up, I felt like I was back in Sarasota, not up north in Columbus, Ohio. The only person I knew who had an interest in getting rid of Charles Venable was Johnson Horseman, because he was afraid Venable would carry on with the Long Bar Harbor development. That had become obvious to me from my first encounter with him. If Horseman had gotten out of the hospital a week ago, could he have had time to get up to Columbus and murder Charles Venable? The murder also fit into Horseman's *modus operandi*—a stabbing in the back with no fingerprints around—or was that Angetine's *modus operandi?* Clearly, I needed to read the Columbus Police Department's report to find out everything they had concerning the matter so far.

Chapter 38

"That's unbelievable," I said when LaFarge finally called me back. He had begun telling me the story of how Lexi Weidenfeld had slipped between the fingers of the law. After she was indicted for conspiracy to murder Julius Josephski, she was released pending trial upon posting a $100,000 bail bond.

Just back from a short vacation at Isle of Mirada in the Florida Keys, LaFarge was greeted by news that the Sarasota County judge to whom her case had been assigned did not particularly consider a person with a reputation like hers to be a flight risk. With the utmost electoral pusillanimity (county judges were graded by members of the Sarasota Bar Association for purposes of re-election), he said he recognized her need for freedom in order to aid her attorneys in the preparation of her defense. (This particular judge had been on the bench for 28 years through 14 elections.) "Her lawyers will need to have her examined by a psychiatrist," he proclaimed, "and with her help, they will have to gather expert testimony about the paranormal and how it might have affected her case. That's a lot of preparation, even without the added inconvenience of jail."

"Personally," LaFarge continued, "I think the judge recognized she was cuckoo right off the bat, and that she needed time at home to recognize and accept her situation and to muster a defense. He also wanted to give Lexi's attorneys whatever they needed in order to prepare arguments for the suppression of her confession. He said it was on the grounds that she was nuts when she gave it and that she was tricked into giving the confession by your phony phone call to a dead Angeltine. Imagine a person like the great Alexis Weidenfeld believing that someone she herself had killed, was still alive and speaking to her in the paranormal over a telephone. Yet that's what she swore she believed as a result of that little scenario you cooked up for her and Horseman in the hospital, Winston. She believed it, and that little scenario may yet be enough to invalidate major parts of her confession, although not the part where she admits she killed Angeltine. The thought is, your trick made her confession involuntary."

"Well, I suppose crazier things can happen," I said, "such as the prosecutor's failure even to attempt to indict Horseman. What can you tell me about that?"

"The prosecutor chose not to take Horseman to the Grand Jury for a number of reasons. First, there was all the bad publicity. The Seminole Indian Nation of Florida put up quite a row over the matter, picketing his office and writing letters to the editor. They even held a demonstration downtown at the corner of the Tamiami Trail and Gulf of Mexico Drive in favor of Horseman. Horseman has quite a good reputation among the Seminoles in Southwest Florida, and is quite well known. Second, there was the question of the weaknesses in Lexi's confession. Was it coerced because of your trickery? Certainly, there was no evidence that Horseman accepted the idea the ghost of Angeltine was talking to *him* too on the phone in the hospital that day. Unlike Lexi, he professed belief in the paranormal was insane. And, more important, wasn't Lexi's statement to the police just hearsay? At least the part about Horseman arranging for Angeltine to be Josephski's cleaning lady, and the part about his filling her head full of reasons to kill Josephski, as well as the part about his turning off the video cameras when he left Angeltine. Lexi didn't see or hear any of that first hand. She just wasn't present when it occurred. So those statements in her confession are hearsay and subject to exclusion from the evidence. Plus, it's an election year, and the prosecutor is running for office. Purely and simply, he was afraid if the Grand Jury wouldn't indict Horseman it might suggest to the voters he was a trigger happy politician who discriminated against the local Indians, all of whom vote in our elections, even though they maintain the law of their reservations pre-empts everything, including county jurisdiction.

"Well, I certainly wish your county prosecutor and your county judges would grow some *cojones,*" I said sardonically. Originally, I thought it would be easy to pin Mr. Venable's murder on Horseman. But now I'm left with two people each of whom had a motive, and were able and willing to kill my client. There was Lexi, who was out on bail, and Horseman, who was just plain out of jail and free. Lexi's motive would have been to preserve her inheritance, and Horseman's motive would have been to stop the development of Long Bar Harbor at any cost. Now, I don't even know how or where to begin to find out 'who dunnit'?"

"Well, my friend," LaFarge said sarcastically, "whatever you do, I wouldn't advise using trickery. The word on the street is that Lexi Weidenfeld's confession is going to be thrown out, excluded from evidence by the trial judge's ruling."

Several days passed before Jerry Shapiro called me back. When he did, he told me there really wasn't much more in the Columbus Police Department file that hadn't already been mentioned in the *Columbus Dispatch.* Charles Venable, age 62, a small man of 5 foot 6 and ½ inches, weighing 145 pounds, was found slumped over the desk in his office in the evening by a member of the cleaning crew who had the contract to do his building. There was a knife in his back that had been thrust into him four times, apparently with a downward motion from above and behind, and twisted in two of the wounds. Nobody else was present when the body was found. The cleaning person halted cleaning the office as soon as he saw the body and called the police. There were no signs of a struggle. Although Mr. Venable's prints were found all over the office, along with those of his assistant, no other prints were found. The knife handle had apparently been wiped clean of any prints. Venable's appointment log, and that of his assistant, indicated he had had no appointments scheduled with anyone in his office on the day in question. The knife had been tagged Exhibit A, and taken to the evidence room. The only other item taken from the office and tagged as Exhibit B for the exhibit room was a curious Indian symbol hanging from the outside door knob to his office. The symbol was taken and tagged as an exhibit because it didn't seem to fit with the meticulous décor of Venable's office, which was *American Heritage* in nature. The interrogation of Mr. Venable's assistant was proceeding.

"What did this Indian sign look like, I asked?"

"I don' know," Shapiro said. "You've seen them around, I'm sure. They've got feathers and beads. I don't know what they're used for—some sort of talisman, or something like that, maybe just for decoration. They're very flimsy looking."

"Do you think you could get me into the evidence room to see it, Jerry?"

"No, counselor, I don't think so. That's asking a little much, seeing as you don't really have anything to do with this case."

"But Charles Venable was my biggest client, Jerry."

"Whah! So what? He may also have been Graeter's Ice Cream's biggest customer, but that doesn't get them into a police evidence room to see all the confidential stuff we've got in there. Right now, that thing is the sole property of the Police Department. I don't want to risk my job."

"You won't lose your job over something like showing me that one item."

"Sorry, but I'm afraid you'll need a court order to get what you want here, counselor."

"I can't believe you're going to be like this, Jerry. Apparently you've forgotten all the big cases I've helped you guys solve in the past. You remember the Karen Sverenson case, don't you? Where she disappeared, and we caught her husband Leo stealing from her trust to pay his gambling debts. And what about the Robert Steinglass murder and the shooting of the new Columbus Symphony director, Igor Bashenko? Didn't I help you guys solve those cases?

"Alright, alright, Counselor, would a photograph of this Indian charm or whatever it is be enough to satisfy you? I guess I can do that without risking my job by escorting a lawyer into our evidence room for no explainable reason."

"Yes, Jerry. That would be good enough at least for now."

Chapter 39

Two days passed. Then, as I stepped into my office, Marinda announced, "Officer Shapiro stopped by this morning and dropped this photograph off for you. He says you owe him now."

"Yep. That sounds like Jerry," I answered, casually looking down at the photograph. My mind was a million miles away, but suddenly I was startled.

"What is that thing anyways?" Marinda asked, referring to the photograph.

"It's called a dream catcher," I said, barely able to believe my eyes. "It's an Indian amulet that's supposed to keep nightmares away from Indians as they sleep." What was so startling about it to me was that it was a dream catcher exactly like the ones I had seen Angeltine manufacturing for Horseman when I was at his house in Arcadia. It was just like the dream catchers Horseman was known to have placed around *At-Tah-Thi-Ki* to ward off the nightmare of the development of Long Bar Harbor. It told me Horseman might have come to Ohio after getting out of the hospital to finish the work he had started in Florida, which was to end the Long Bar Harbor development by getting rid of the key movers behind it. Horseman as much as told me at Linger Lodge on the day we met that he was concerned Mr. Venable might try to carry on where Josephski had left off.

My initial instinct was to call LaFarge in Florida, and alert him and the Sarasota Sheriff's office to this new information in my hands. But did it prove

Horseman had been to Ohio? He was not a stupid man. Surely, he had enough sense not to leave a sign of his commitment to stop the Long Bar Harbor development at the murder scene of one of the larger investors like Venable who was behind that development. Why would he call down suspicion on himself for Venable's murder, when he was already suspected of committing two other murders of key players in the Long Bar Harbor project? The connection, of course, between Horseman and Venable and the development would not be obvious to anyone in Ohio except me. But it would certainly be obvious to anyone in the law enforcement hierarchy in Sarasota or Manatee counties.

On the other hand, Venable himself could have hung the dream catcher in his office. He could have gone out to a craft store and gotten a dream catcher. It was to remind himself of what was going on with his investment down in Florida, after I had earlier explained everything I knew about Horseman to him. That was doubtful, however, especially since the particular dream catcher involved here perfectly replicated the kind Angeltine had been making for Horseman.

I decided to call LaFarge to find out whether he knew anything about what Horseman had been doing since being released from the hospital. Had he left the area or taken any trips? "No," said LaFarge after checking. Horseman had been very cooperative with the police after he got out of the hospital, and the police had shadowed him for a time to watch what he did. "He's been right here in Sarasota or Arcadia ever since he left Sarasota Memorial."

"Just in case your guys are wrong," I said, "could you also determine whether he's bought any airline tickets to or from Columbus recently?"

"Yes, I'll do that. Meanwhile, you should check Columbus hotels to see whether he's used a credit card at any of them. Do you think we should also call him in and question him about the Venable case?" asked LaFarge.

"I think you should hold up on questioning him," I replied, "until I see whether I can collect any more evidence on what's happened to Venable. Meanwhile, what date is Lexi's trial set for?"

"No trial date yet," said LaFarge. "You knew the judge ruled her confession was inadmissible, didn't you?"

"What? No! All you told me was that her attorneys were working on that. What grounds did he use to invalidate it?"

"That she was tricked into confessing to being a part of a conspiracy to murder Josephski by making facts appear to exist that didn't exist, namely that Angeltine was alive when she was actually dead. The judge ruled she was coerced into confessing she was part of a conspiracy to kill Josephski. It was by you driving her temporarily insane because she knew Angeltine was dead but believed she was speaking to her anyway by virtue of her professed belief in the paranormal. The part of her confession pertaining to the murder of Angeltine was allowed to stand, however, because she knew she had killed Angeltine when she confessed to her murder. But the part of the confession pertaining to a conspiracy to kill Josephski was ruled inadmissible because she was under the false perception created by somebody else that Angeltine was still alive."

"Well, where will that leave her in terms of a trial?"

"It probably leaves her only with one count against her, Murder One for Angeltine's homicide. The prosecutor also thinks he's got evidence, other than her confession, that Lexi killed Angeltine. He's got her fingerprints on the dream catcher she twisted around Angeltine's neck and the testimony of some locals from Arcadia who saw her speeding out of Horseman's driveway on the day of the murder. Don't forget, the judge's order also didn't declare Lexi temporarily insane at the time of Angeltine's murder, only at the time of her confession to it.

She won't be tried for conspiring to have Josephski killed, at least not without new evidence, say for instance evidence from Horseman that the two of them conspired to kill Josephski. Right now, she remains under arrest for Angeltine's murder, and she's still out of jail, based on the bond she previously posted."

"So assuming the prosecutor's got the evidence he says he has that she murdered Angeltine, she'll still be tried for Angeltine's murder. What is her defense going to be?"

"I hear that her defense in going to be that she did it in self-defense, because Angeltine attacked her first with a knife."

"Is there any truth to that?"

"I have no idea. I'm off the case now. All I know is that Ms. Weidenfeld is claiming she went out to Horseman's home again, the day after you and I were there to speak to Angeltine. You know that time Weidenfeld turned out to be there too, when Angeltine accused her of waving a gun around. Weidenfeld claims that the second time she went out there, Angeltine tried to attack her."

"Why did Lexi go out there again?"

"According to her, to finish their discussion about the papers of Johnson Horseman which Weidenfeld had come out to retrieve when we were out there the first time. In any event, Angeltine purportedly attacked Weidenfeld the second time, and Weidenfeld strangled her with one of the dream catchers Angeltine was making, by smashing the ring of the dream catcher over her head and twisting it over and over again until Angeltine lost consciousness."

"Well," I said, "I suppose that's plausible, but there are a lot of other facts we know about Alexis Weidenfeld now that cast serious doubt on her story that it was self-defense."

"Yeah, but so what?" LaFarge mocked. "In this town Alexis Weidenfeld wears the armor of *la noblesse*. That makes her impervious to any real harm unless she's being attacked by a *noble* who's much higher up the social ladder than she is."

"Well, if Lexi's going to be able to wriggle out of all these close calls with the aid of the local judiciary down there, which I seriously doubt will ultimately happen, that makes it much more imperative that Johnson Horseman be prosecuted for his role in these Long Bar Harbor-associated murder cases. Do what you can, Anton, to find out if Horseman has purchased any airline tickets to Columbus, and what he's been doing with his credit cards. Oh, and also send me one of the dream catchers Angeltine made. I want to show it around to the police up here."

Chapter 40

After I hung up, I started thinking, *what if Johnson Horseman didn't kill Charles Venable, and someone else was trying to implicate him in Venable's murder by leaving a dream catcher hanging from his door? Who else would have any interest in seeing Charles Venable dead? Who else would perceive a dream catcher as a sign showing that Johnson Horseman had been present with Charles Venable in his office?*

The only possibility I could think of was Alexis Weidenfeld. Maybe Lexi had come to Columbus herself to dispose of Venable, and was trying to frame Horseman for it by leaving one of the dream catchers Angeltine made for him in Venable's office. Weidenfeld may have wanted to prevent Mr. Venable from stepping into Josephski's shoes, which he could have done by contesting Josephski's will, stopping the foreclosures, paying Josephski's debts and purchasing the property for himself. Then, Mr. Venable could have continued the Long Bar Harbor project himself without regard to Lexi's inheritance rights, and sold it off for a profit.

But would she have taken the risk of jumping bail, leaving Florida and coming to Columbus to take out Venable? Then going straight back to Sarasota before her next court hearing? Only if she could be assured no hearings would be set in her case while she was gone and nobody would come around to check on her and find her missing. No, Lexi was too careful a person for that. Jumping bail was a crime in itself.

But the idea was worth checking out, so I called LaFarge back and asked him to check airline records on Alexis Weidenfeld to determine whether she had purchased any tickets to Columbus. "You might also check out at Rectrix Aviation," I told him, "to see if she just might have chartered an executive jet from them to come up here. This lady's rich enough to do it, and she would have been in a hurry to get here and back."

Another possibility was that Cravenstall Ltd. wanted Mr. Venable out of the way and desired to pin his murder on Johnson Horseman. Clearly Cravenstall didn't want Venable as its partner in Josephski's stead in the Long Bar Harbor development. That was why it had originally put Horseman up to telling me they wanted to buy Venable out. But withdrawing that offer before Horseman could make it at our meeting in the park, left the possibility open that Mr. Venable would become a partner, and the thought of that was still unacceptable to them. So they paid a hitman to get rid of Venable and tried to cast the blame on Horseman. Farfetched as it was, if this latter scenario had taken place, obviously it would have left absolutely no leads that could have implicated Cravenstall. The only thing I could think of to do to check the theory out would be to have Trudy Fischel hack Cravenstall's computers and look for clues that would implicate it. One call to Trudy quickly disabused me of that idea.

"Getting into their computers would be no problem," she said. "But the job of reading through all the stuff pulled out of them would be monumental. It would cost tens, maybe hundreds, of thousands of dollars, with very little probability of any return. First of all, nobody would have any idea what they were looking for, and second, the old 'needle in a hay stack' analogy applies. It hardly seems worth it," she argued.

Besides, there were rumors in Sarasota before I left that Cravenstall was teetering on the brink of bankruptcy. Due to DeVertollo's untimely death, it was likely to be a Chapter 7 bankruptcy, which would put the company out of business. So why spend all the time and money to raid Cravenstall's computer? Neither of these alternatives to Horseman actually having carried off the crime himself really seemed viable. Still, why would a dream catcher have been left laying around in Mr. Venable's office?

A few days later, LaFarge called me back with, as he put it, "some good, and some bad, news."

"So give me the bad news first," I said.

"I checked to see if there were any airline tickets involving trips by either Horseman or Weidenfeld departing Sarasota, Tampa or St.Pete's and landing in Columbus, Ohio, over the past three weeks. There were none."

"So that's the bad news," I said. "What's the good news?"

"Then I went out to Rectrix Aviation, as you suggested, to see if, on an outside chance, Alexis Weidenfeld had chartered a jet to Columbus."

"And she had?" I said excitedly.

"No she hadn't."

"So you're killing me with suspense here. What did you find out? What's the good news?"

"Well. Do you know who Jesus Agronez is?"

The question gave me pause. I had heard the name, but I couldn't place it right off the bat. I had met so many people during my stay in Sarasota, assuming this man was even from Sarasota. With a name like Jesus Agronez how could I have forgotten who he was?

"Jesus Agronez is a home builder in Sarasota and Manatee counties," LaFarge prompted me. "He's actually the largest home builder in the two counties, due to his work on Lakewood Ranch, which spans the two."

Now I remembered. Rhett Kessler had told Rosanne and me that Jesus Agronez was the third main developer involved in the Long Bar Harbor project, the one who was going to build all the homes that would make the development into another Lakewood Ranch. It was he who would add the element of a residential community to the project, while Josephski made it a high dollar tourist's attraction with its own golf course, hotel, club and harbor. DeVertollo would develop it as a retail shopper's haven. Argonez' name had slipped my mind because during the six weeks I'd spent in Sarasota, he never once surfaced in association with any of the four murders that occupied my attention. He was never a suspect, and I never saw or talked to him.

"Well, what about Jesus Agronez?" I asked.

"While I was over at Rectrix checking to see if Alexis Weidenfeld had chartered a jet to fly up there, I noticed that although her name didn't show up on its records, Agronez' name did, for three different round trips. The three trips occurred on May 30, June 15 and July 6. It looks like on the first and second trips, he stayed for two nights each. Curiously, on the third trip, he flew in and out the same day."

"That's very interesting," I said. "His first trip to Columbus was about two weeks after Josephski died, and right around the time DeVertollo was murdered. His second trip occurred on the day Horseman stood me up for my second meeting with him. That was the day I was shot in the park. Just prior to that, Cravenstall had backed out of its plan to have Horseman present an offer to buy my client out of his deal with the newly deceased Josephski. The third time Agronez was here was two days before I arrived home from Sarasota."

"So what does that all add up to?" asked LaFarge.

"Nothing," I said, "unless we can somehow show that Agronez and Mr. Venable were together during the first two trips Agronez took. They may have been together because Agronez, like some of the others in the Long Bar project, was attempting to negotiate to buy out Venable's interest in Josephski's property. Why Agronez did not stay over the third night can only mean one thing. He did not succeed in convincing Venable to sell. Can you send me a few photographs of Agronez? I'll check them out with the people who work with Venable to see if any of them have ever seen the guy."

"Will do. Also here's another fact that might throw some light on the issue," said LaFarge. "Yesterday, a tax lien auction was held on all the properties upon which Josephski has defaulted under his mortgage obligations. Agronez bought the tax lien certificates for all of them. What does that tell you?"

"It tells me Agronez wants that land so badly he is willing to buy the tax lien certificates on it, hoping to foreclose on them at a later time, risky as that is. With Josephski, Venable, DeVertollo dead and Cravenstall bankrupt and out of his way, he's got a clear path to grabbing the property. No bank is going to be willing to pay the millions in back tax debts that need to be paid just to own the property after foreclosure. That leaves the way open, wide and clear for him."

"Do you think Agronez killed Venable because Venable wouldn't agree to sell him the land?" Lafarge asked.

"At this point, Anton, I'm willing to believe any of these people would do anything if it served their financial purposes. Send me those pictures of Agronez, okay?" I'm going to start asking some questions around Venable's office to find out if Jesus Agronez was ever there. After all, what else do we have on this? Nothing, the way I see it."

Chapter 41

I received five different computer scans of Jesus Agronez from LaFarge the next day. I took them over to Mr. Venable's office, where I methodically went through them with everyone I could find who had worked for Mr. Venable. I talked to secretaries, people who worked in the mail room and janitors. I also questioned members of the building's management, the office's accountant, and even Mr. Venable's real estate closing agents and rental property managers.

Surprisingly, three of these people had seen the person in the photographs before, but they couldn't remember exactly when. One, a rental agent, saw the man sometime in May he thought, sitting with Mr. Venable in his office and talking with a site map spread out before them. He remembered the man in the photograph because he was wearing some sort of Aztec or Southwestern Indian symbol as a necklace instead of a tie. The second person, a closing agent, who saw him, remembered him because he came through the office door with Mr. Venable from lunch sometime in June. Venable introduced the man to him, and he remembered that the man's first name should have been his last name, or vice versa—"Johnson or something like that." The third person to identify him was a secretary who worked in the copy room. She remembered seeing him as he stood outside the door of the copy room in June, waiting for her to finish making copies of an agreement he wanted, but she had no idea what the agreement was about. She remembered him because he seemed particularly fidgety and impatient with her, and because a huge paper cut opened in his hand when she finally gave him the document she was Xeroxing. It was so bad that she ran to the medicine cabinet for some tincture of Mercurochrome with which to treat him and she bandaged his hand. As she remembered the incident, "it took forever for the bleeding to stop." As for the date of July 7, which was two days before I arrived back in Columbus, and the date Agronez apparently made his round trip to and from Columbus in one day, nobody had seen him.

"Do you remember anything Mr. Agronez said to you at the time he cut himself?" I asked the secretary who had tended to the paper cut.

"Who?" asked the secretary.

"Mr. Agronez. This man's name was Jesus Agronez."

"Oh no, no, no! It wasn't! I certainly would have remembered a name like that. His name was Johnson, or something like that, not Jesus Agronez. Look I'm a Southern Baptist, and I certainly would have remembered if his name was Jesus. That's a name you don't hear too much anymore."

"But look at this picture," I said. "Doesn't he look Hispanic to you? Hispanics still use that name."

"Maybe so," she answered, "but I don't care. This man called himself Johnson, Johnson Horseman it was, not Jesus. How could you forget a name like Johnson Horseman?"

"Do me a favor," I said. "Do you still have the Mercurochrome bottle you used to fix up this guy's cut?"

"Yes, I think so."

"Those bottles have a little glass dropper inside them used to apply the Mercurochrome. Don't they."

"That's right."

Could you let me borrow your mercurochrome bottle for a few weeks or so? I'll buy you another one."

"Yes. I suppose so."

I took the Mercurochrome bottle and immediately went to FedEx, where I mailed it, two-day-express, to LaFarge with a letter telling him everything I'd discovered while flashing the pictures he had sent me of Jesus Agronez around Venable's office. After explaining that there were three witnesses who had seen Agronez in Venable's office, according to their recollections based on his picture, I continued with my new theory that Agronez had been passing himself off as Johnson Horseman to everybody. Analysis of Agronez' DNA and anything matching it that could be taken off the Mercurochrome dropper would prove this. We would then be able to show Agronez had come to Columbus at least twice to visit Mr. Venable, and that while he was here, he was attempting to pass himself off as Johnson Horseman by wearing a dream catcher around his neck, and by telling everyone he was Johnson Horseman. "Oh yes," I added, "and you might attempt to determine if Jesus Agronez was on any type of blood thinner, such as Coumadin or Warfarin, because it took so long for his blood to clot after the paper cut he received."

LaFarge could see where my theory was headed, and he accepted the immediacy of carrying out my analysis. If I was right, the only thing left to do was to call Jesus Agronez in and see if he could be worn down into confessing to the murder of Charles Venable. The motive for the murder was Agronez' efforts to get Venable to agree to give up his claim to Josephski's portion of the Long Bar Harbor project had been unsuccessful. Getting rid of Venable had become the only other option Agronez had to assure himself a path to the land by buying up the tax liens on it without any competition. His purchase of all the tax lien certificates showed how interested he was in obtaining the land.

If I was right, we would have the evidence showing the two men were together in Columbus. We would have the evidence that no agreement was ever reached between them. We would have the evidence that after the attempt to make an agreement failed, Agronez came and went from Columbus in one day, which was just enough time to stab Venable. And we would have the evidence that Agronez was parading around, wearing a dream catcher and trying to pass himself off as Johnson Horseman. All we would really need was his confession he killed Venable because he couldn't get him to agree to sell his interests in Josephski's land at Long Bar Harbor to Agronez.

Chapter 42

"Give me three days to get some affidavits," I said, "and I'll come to Sarasota with a few items that'll enable you to arrest Agronez on suspicion for the murder of Charles Venable, although it would be better if you could get him to come into your office voluntarily." It was Monday of the following week, and I was talking to LaFarge on the phone. "In the meantime, if you haven't done so already, please get whatever paper evidence you can from Rectrix Aviation proving that Agronez chartered a plane three different times to fly roundtrip from Sarasota to Columbus, and the dates of the flights. You've got the Mercurochrome bottle, don't you?"

"Oh yes. It's nicely locked away."

I then went back to Mr. Venable's office and took affidavits from the secretary who attended Agronez' paper cut, the rental agent who saw Agronez wearing the Indian symbol around his neck, and the closing agent to whom Mr. Venable had introduced Agronez to as "Mr. Johnson," as they were walking in the door from lunch. The rental agent later identified the Indian symbol he saw hanging around Agronez' neck as the dream catcher the police had found hanging from Venable's office door. Then I gathered up the pictures of Agronez I had used in examining all of these people, and headed for the airport. I also packed the photograph of the dream catcher Officer Shapiro had supplied me from the door to Mr. Venable's office.

When I arrived in Sarasota, I went straight to the Sheriff's office and laid out all of the evidence in front of LaFarge. He would do all the questioning of Agronez when they brought him in, and seek a confession from him. I was to watch the whole thing from behind the one-way mirrored glass window to the interrogation room, and from time to time offer suggestions as to the direction in which the questioning ought to go.

The next day Agronez voluntarily came into the Sheriff's office purportedly for some routine questions about his relationships with Julius Josephski and Edward DeVertollo. Jesus Agronez was a very rich man, but he was essentially a thug. A short stocky Hispanic with a face pitted by a severe case of smallpox years ago, he wore a gold ring on every finger of one hand and an outsized crucifix on a chain around his neck along with a St. Christopher's Medal. This was a man who never traveled without his bodyguards, whom he did not hesitate to order around in Spanish, no matter what the situation, or who was present. He also could speak flawless English and was cool as a cucumber in situations requiring him to deal with Anglos. He wore a black suit with a yellow sport shirt open at the neck which emphasized the ample cross on his dark chest.

After being told the meeting could result in his arrest for the murder of Charles Venable of Columbus, Ohio, he scoffed and asked, "Who's Charles Venable?" LaFarge and I just looked at each other.

"Let's go in here, sit down and talk," LaFarge said, leading Agronez toward the interrogation room. At the same time, he invited Agronez' bodyguards to sit down outside the room, offering them Coke and coffee.

LaFarge started out by placing the picture of the dream catcher I'd brought from Columbus on the table in front of Agronez. "Mr. Agronez," he said, "can you tell me what this is?"

"Yes, it's an Indian symbol of some sort?"

"Do you know what it's called?"

"A dream catcher or something close to that I believe," Agronez said.

"And do you know who Mr. Johnson Horseman is?"

"Yes. He's the founder and the leader of the Florida Wildlife Association. He's also one of the more important Seminole Indian politicians or leaders in this area."

"Mr. Agronez, is there any way you know of that one might associate this Indian symbol"—he put his hand on the dream catcher picture—"with Mr. Johnson Horseman?"

Agronez looked up, almost with a twinkle in his eye and laughed. "Well, you see, heh, three developers in this area, Julius Josephski, Edwin DeVertollo and me have been trying to develop a site called Long Bar Harbor along the northeast edge of Sarasota Bay near the town of Cortez for more than two years now. Mr. Horseman bitterly opposes that, and Josephski and Devertollo are dead now. But Mr. Horseman bitterly fought against that development's going forward when they were alive, and he did all sorts of things to try and stop it, including trying to influence the county commissioners against it, maybe even bribing them. Being a fourth or fifth generation Seminole Indian, or something like that, he also believed in the old Indian black magic. He thought these dream catchers had the power of the spirits behind them, and they would keep the developers with their tractors and diggers and things away from the Long Bar Harbor development site. So he used to go out there with some of his people and hang these things all around the site. Pretty crazy, huh?"

"So, then," continued LaFarge, "you would associate Johnson Horseman with these things called dream catchers. Correct?"

"Everybody who knows anything about the Long Bar Harbor site would."

LaFarge then went on to ask Agronez if he'd ever been to Columbus, Ohio, and Agronez answered "No." Then LaFarge whipped out documents from Rectrix Aviation showing that Agronez had chartered a jet and flown to Columbus three times in the last three months. But Agronez never lost his cool. "Oh, that was for my wife," he explained casually, "well, actually for our daughter." She started summer school up there at Ohio State this summer, and Lydia flew up there with her to get her situated for the summer term." A long silence, electric with anticipation followed.

Then LaFarge, as if he had suddenly made a decision, leaned across the table toward Agronez and said, "Well, what would you say if we could show you affidavits from people in Columbus who say they saw you there. They say they saw you in the offices of Charles Venable whom you claim not to know. What would you say to that?" He then spread out the affidavits I had brought to Sarasota on the table in front of Agronez. He also spread out the photographs of Agronez that had been shown to these people. Agronez asked for a glass of water. Watching him through the one-way window looking into the interrogation room, as he drank the water, it seemed to me like he never lost a beat. He just reached over toward the affidavits, put on his glasses and started reading, as an aide came in to take away the glass. From time to time, he stopped and matched up the dates on the affidavits with the dates on the Rectrix flight documents. He looked at the photographs again and again. For half an hour, the room was silent as he studied everything. Then he looked up.

He swore in Spanish under his breath. Then he said, "There is not a word in any of these affidavits about me. If these are the photographs you were showing these people, all of the people are referring to the person in the pictures as Johnson, Mr. Johnson, or Johnson Horseman. I think we should terminate this interview now. You have insulted me by calling me a liar."

"Before you go, Mr. Agronez, I have one more question for you. As you can see, one of the people who gave an affidavit said she applied tincture of Mercurochrome to your hand because of a paper cut you received when she handed you a document she was Xeroxing for you. We have that bottle here, complete with the dropper inside that it comes with. Will you give us a DNA sample?"

Now Jesus Agronez was no longer the calm *cabellero* he had been when he walked in.

"No. I am going," he said in a raised voice. "I have my rights and you know it. I want an attorney. You can't hold me here," and he got up and left with his regalia of bodyguards in tow.

About four hours later that day, LaFarge reported to me that the lab had found Agronez' DNA on the Mercurochrome dropper. He'd left his DNA on the glass of water he was given during his investigation, and it matched with what was found on the stylus of the Mercurochrome bottle.

"Perfect," I said.

LaFarge was jubilant. "We shall now invite Jesus Agronez to come down here and visit us again," he crowed, "but this time he'll be placed under arrest."

Chapter 43

The next time Agronez entered the Sarasota County Sheriff's office, the only guards with him were deputy sheriffs and his attorney. LaFarge was there. I was there, and the Franklin County prosecutor from Columbus was there. Agronez' retinue of bodyguards was absent.

"Jesus Agronez, I am hereby placing you under arrest on suspicion of murdering Charles Venable of Columbus, Ohio, and I am consigning you into the hands of the County Prosecutor from Franklin County Ohio." Handcuffs were then clamped around Agronez' wrists, and LaFarge proceeded to Mirandize him. He then asked, "Is there anything you would like to say?"

Agronez' attorney jumped in. "What do you mean, 'on suspicion of the murder of Charles Venable?' What have you got to show his involvement?"

I then came forward, clearing my throat. "He has lied repeatedly here. He says he was never in Columbus, but his DNA on a Mercurochrome dropper from the office of Charles Venable in Columbus, Ohio, proves he was there. Not only that, but he has attempted to divert the blame for Mr. Venable's murder to a Mr. Johnson Horseman. Thus, during three sightings of him in Mr. Venable's office, according to the affidavits we have, he passed himself off as Johnson Horseman, once even to the extent of wearing a dream catcher, which is a favorite object of Indian symbolism to Mr. Horseman. After the murder, he even left a dream catcher mysteriously hanging from the doorknob of Mr.

Venable's office. He also made Mr. Venable's murder appear like it had been done by the same person suspected of the murders of Julius Josephski and Edwin DeVertollo, with knife wounds in the back and no evidence of the killer's fingerprints anywhere. That suspect was Johnson Horseman, although later it was determined that Mr. Horseman's maid had committed the murders. Mr. Agronez had certainly read enough in the newspaper accounts here in Sarasota of the murders of Julius Josephski and Edwin DeVertollo, of which Mr. Horseman was suspected, to know how those two other murders scenes appeared to the police.

"As for his motive to kill Mr. Venable," I continued, "the fact Mr. Agronez has purchased every one of the tax liens auctioned off on the Long Bar Harbor properties that were formerly under the control of Julius Josephski, shows Mr. Agronez' purpose in doing away with Mr. Venable. We believe that after Mr. Josephski's death, these properties ultimately had the potential of coming under the control of Mr. Josephski's chief investor, Charles Venable, if he was able to arrange financing to clean up all Josephski's bank debts on them. That would have made Mr. Venable a partner with Mr. Agronez in the Long Bar project. But Mr. Agronez wanted all of the project for himself. So he came to Columbus on two different occasions to negotiate the purchase of Mr. Venable's interests in Mr. Josephski's holdings. Ultimately the negotiations were unsuccessful, because Mr. Venable would not sell. Here we don't know what the roadblock was. When Mr. Agronez failed after two attempts to buy the Venable's interests in the land, however, there was no avenue left to him for getting rid of Mr. Venable as a partner. So he came to Columbus for a third time on July 7. Mr. Venable's murder did not require an overnight stay in Columbus, and Mr. Agronez had a rented plane at his disposal. There was time enough to accomplish the murder within a twenty-four-hour period, and that's exactly what he did. He flew into Columbus, murdered Mr. Venable, and left on the same day. We have the records from Rectrix Aviation, showing he was here for less than 24 hours."

"Mr. Agronez, have you got anything to say about all this?" LaFarge piped up.

The Franklin County Prosecutor, who had been assiduously listening to everything then came to life. "Mr. Agronez, you know, in Ohio you could receive the death penalty for this. If you wish to confess, however, I'll see to it that my office does not seek the death penalty in your case."

There was a long silence in the room. Agronez drew in a long breath and let it out slowly. Fumbling with the crucifix around his neck, he then turned to his attorney and they conversed in Spanish.

Agronez then turned back to LaFarge and began....

"No," yelled his attorney. "Don't say a word. It's all circumstantial evidence! Wait. Think! They have nothing concrete."

EPILOGUE

Eight months later, the Estate of Charles Venable paid my legal fees. It was enough to put my law practice on easy street for the next year. At his death, the interests of his heirs all went into a testamentary trust, of which I was the trustee. The trust wound up arranging to pay off all of the debt Julius Josephski had incurred in connection with the Long Bar Harbor development. Accordingly, the testamentary trust succeeded to Josephski's interests in the Long Bar Harbor project. Thereafter, the trust, at greatly discounted prices, proceeded to pick up the Long Bar Harbor real estate Cravenstall, Ltd. released through its trustee in its Chapter 7 bankruptcy. Edwin DeVertollo's entire interest in Long Bar Harbor had been held by Cravenstall.

After his extradition to Columbus, and his plea of guilty to the murder of Charles Venable, Jesus Agronez was sentenced to life in prison at the Ohio State Penitentiary in Youngstown. Thereafter, his wife sold all his real estate at Long Bar Harbor to meet living expenses for herself and the 11 Agronez children in their mansion on Bird Key. The Charles Venable testamentary trust was the purchaser.

Alexis Weidenfeld was convicted of manslaughter in the death of Angeltine Ardontique. Her Murder 1 trial for killing Angeltine had ended in a hung jury. Thereafter, she pled guilty to manslaughter under a plea bargain agreement worked out by her attorneys and the prosecutor. In return for her plea and her acceptance of a reduced sentence, the Sarasota County Prosecutor opted against retrying her case. Alexis Weidenfeld then received a sentence of fifteen years without parole, to be served at the Florida Correctional Institute in Central Florida, a women's prison. She was stripped of her license to practice law, and her home and all her property were sold to pay her legal fees. She steadily refused, however, to give any evidence regarding Johnson Horseman's involvement with Julius Josephski. Horseman visited her every week in prison, bringing her dream catchers from time to time, which were consistently removed from her cell by correctional facility officers. Kit-Kat, along with Dr. Ben Temple and his girlfriend Cherry, of the Sun Ghost Psychic Trackers, also visited her. Three years after entering the Florida Correctional Institute, she disappeared without a trace. There was no evidence of any breakout attempt. The only object found in her cell after she disappeared was a dream catcher similar to the one's made by Angeltine Ardontique for Johnson Horseman.

Johnson Horseman was never arrested for, or convicted of, any crime related to Long Bar Harbor or any of the principals involved in its development. In 2016, he participated in the opening of a huge vacation preserve called *At-Tah-Thi-Ki* located just south of the town of Cortez in the area formerly known as Long Bar Harbor. The project was developed by the Charles Venable Testamentary Trust and its beneficiaries. Horseman was known to have a 15% interest in the vacation preserve, which enabled him to participate in all of the profits of the marina, golf course and hotel there, rents from the *At-Tah-Thi-Ki* shopping center, all entrance fees to the park, and proceeds from the numerous sale of homes in the area. How he obtained his interest is not a matter of public record. Nor is it a matter of public record whether the local Miccosukee Indian tribe was a beneficiary of his interest in any way.

The murder of Irving Caputo remains unsolved to this day. Jack Rainspring never completely recovered from the loss of Irv. Eventually, he moved back to his home in Iowa.

Rosanne and I returned to Sarasota and bought a condo on Ana Maria Island, which we still use for vacation purposes. Gayna, who is now about to be 20, goes to the University of South Florida Extension in Sarasota, and she lives in the condo during the school term. Kit-Kat keeps an eye on her for us. We are still not married.

THE END

ABOUT THE AUTHOR

David Selcer graduated from Northwestern University where he attended the Medill School of Journalism. He received a Juris Doctorate from Ohio State University College of Law, after which he practiced labor, employment and civil rights law for 35 years. He received a first place award from the Chanticleer Book Review. He lives in Columbus, Ohio, from where he has authored the Buckeye Barrister Mystery series since 2013. *Dream Catcher Murders* is number four of the series.

www.ingramcontent.com/pod-product-compliance
Lightning Source LLC
Chambersburg PA
CBHW050400260626
47156CB00003B/810

9 781946 063281